Crystalline Connection

Crystalline Connection

Bob Maddux and Mary Carpenter Reid

Huntington House Publishers

Huntington House Publishers
P.O. Box 53788
Lafayette, Louisiana 70505

Library of Congress Card Catalog Number
91-72326

ISBN 0-910311-71-4

Printed in the United States of America

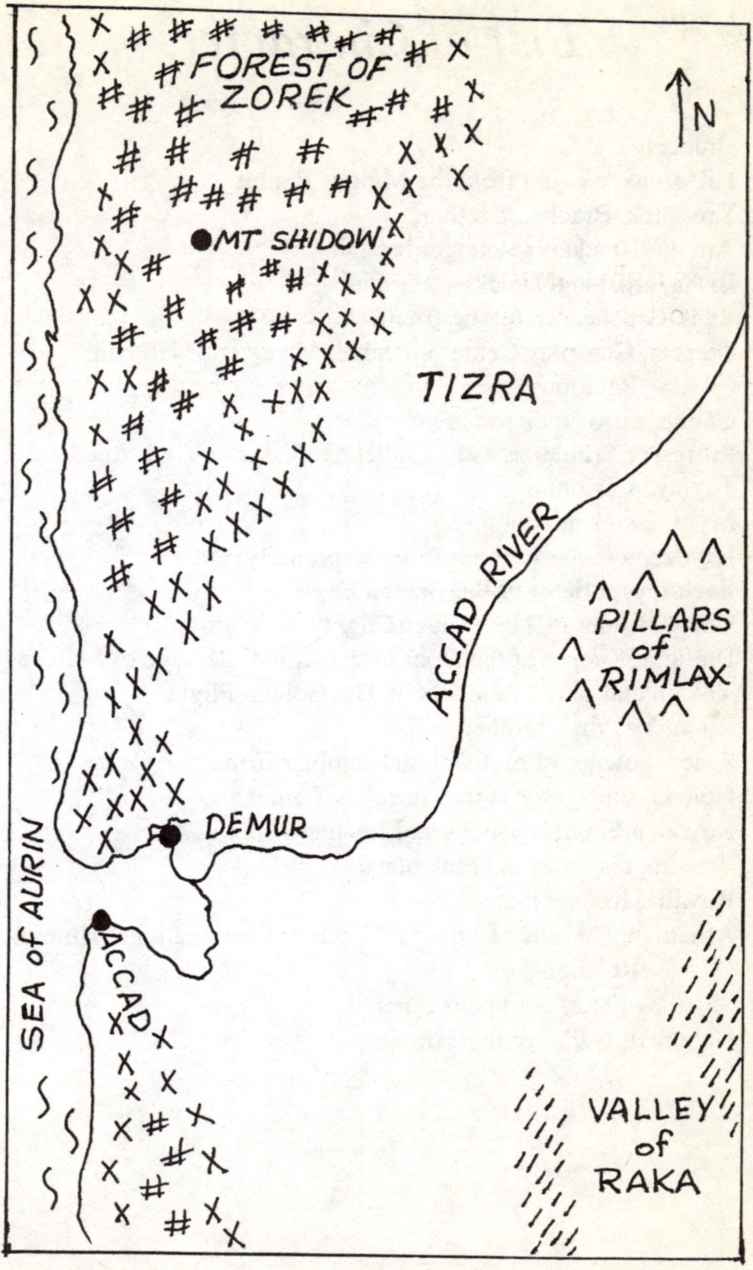

MOUNTAINS
X LOW MOUNTAINS
//// BARREN HILLS
^^ BARREN PILLARS

List of Characters

Bracken
Hiffornak, a being from the Mingus Realm
Kressdek, Bracken's father
Amont, Bracken's younger brother
Lisha, artist and Bracken's friend
Silas, Bracken's lifelong friend
Trasent, Currency Center's Branch Manager of Human Relations
Catine, astro studies student
Professor Frimleter, astro studies professor at Tizra Academics
Taylay, a Trionite
Myra, Bracken's mother
Layozz, a miner living in The Community
Zactor, proprietor of the Brazen Eagle
Chepa, leader of The Golden Flight music group
Dalfang, Keeper of the Door to the Anindi Passage of Malchag
Yaavin and Shor, members of The Golden Flight
Roon, Yaavin's brother
Aleena, owner of motivational seminar firm
Golens, supervisor at the Currency Center
Dayon, a Finlanley living in Malchag
Wissim, leader of the Finlanleys
Rovalla, Roon's mate
Arnaman, Currency Center's Director of International Human Relations
Shad, owner of a gippens ranch
Nebuzarr, leader of the Trionites

Introduction

For the time will come when men shall mold the truth and trust in fables, and they shall seek mentors whose words appease the ear and please the pride.

From the Volume,
as revealed to the people of Ebbern

On a planet far, albeit near,
In a time that no one keeps,
Ever lulls an ancient song,
Biding til the last of Ebbern sleeps.

Still, in shadows of the triple moons,
Truth waits for the heart that aches,
Truth to soar above the dark,
On the day that all of Ebbern wakes.

CHAPTER 1

Bracken hesitated, poised at the opening to another dimension. The enticing oval corridor unfolded before him in a profusion of trailing green vines. Drawn by the lure of things unknown, he followed where it beckoned. The mass of twisting tendrils and fleshy leaves parted before him as if tunneled by a single-minded breeze.

The passage veered and climbed a gentle slope. Bracken's thoughts fluttered like the rivulets of water dancing down the incline. *I was right! There is a realm beyond the visible reality of Ebbern.* The pungent scent of moss filled his lungs with charged air. His senses surged in delight.

For as long as Bracken could remember, he had burned with desire to find that which was not apparent. And now, because he'd stumbled upon a small silver box, he was on the brink of incomprehensible discovery.

He'd sighted the box wedged between the dried roots of a downed tree while walking alone in the familiar forest near Tizra. He lifted the lid, not realizing that the mysterious green stone within could be a link to the elusive, ultimate truth he sought.

In his open palms, the stone glowed with green radiance, casting rays of light with every movement. Then, as if drawn by a powerful force emanating from the gleaming object, Bracken raised the stone to his forehead. He felt the stone's effect at once, carrying his mind beyond the natural plane. Guided by his awakened perception, his body followed until he reached this corridor.

Now, in this strange realm of the green stone, golden light filtering through foliage streamed into the passage. Every particle shone and twinkled. Motes of dust turned to shimmering diamonds. Fueled with anticipation, Bracken rushed to the crest of the slope. Each step brought new light, new promises.

Light flooded the corridor until it thickened into a glistening wall. A small door of an emerald substance appeared in the center of the wall. Compelled to continue his journey, Bracken touched the door. It opened.

Another tunnel, longer than the previous one, stretched before him. Soft ferns grazed his hands. Purple flowers fluttered in softly-moving air. Bracken stroked a flesh-like blossom, his fingertips relishing the touch.

Then, out of the unknown, an indefinable warning pricked him, as quickly and sharply as the point of a pin. Pleasure melted into fear.

Every sense alerted, Bracken searched for a clue to this panic. The green plants and twisting vines stilled and lay placid. He heard a clicking sound, like the noise of insects chirping. The sound haunted him. He felt someone secretly observing him, playing with his mind as with a pawn. His ear strained to listen. *Laughter* . . . he concentrated . . *chirping* . . . *more laughter*.

But again, the warm effect of the mysterious green stone filled his body. Bracken's fear subsided. Everything became golden.

Light radiated from light. Bracken walked on light. It condensed, rolling into a bright cylinder through which Bracken passed to another room, a room with no ceiling. Abruptly, all light swirled and solidified into a marbleized platform beneath his feet.

Out of the surrounding darkness, a pulsating glow appeared, drifting toward Bracken, carrying within itself an embryo-like being. As it neared, shadowy images in the apparition revealed a large head and bloated torso bearing tiny arms and legs. The creature stopped, hovering a little higher than Bracken's head.

Gentle tones of communication sounded. "Welcome, Bracken."

"Who—what? How do you know my name?" The words floated without origin or destination, tossed by waves of confusion, as if they had not originated with Bracken.

"My name is Hiffornak." A soft hum of energy vibrated as the creature spoke.

"Where am I?" Bracken implored.

"Few of your kind have penetrated this far. We are pleased to see one so diligent in his search for knowledge." Hiffornak's head seemed to nod approval. "I have been sent to tell you that your hunger will be rewarded."

The luminous being's words rippled across Bracken's thought patterns like the soothing strokes of a masseur's hands. They kneaded away anxiety, tempting him to cast aside resolve and bask in their comfort.

But, Bracken seized his opportunity. "Yes! I want knowledge, more than can be found on Ebbern. I have questions. Lots of questions. Is there a force in the universe greater than Ebbern? Is there a center of power that can overcome our chaos? What happens after death? Are we destined to spend eternity as mere particles of dirt? There's so much I want to know. . . ." Bracken's determination failed, and his monologue faded on a note of sadness.

"Do not despair. There is knowledge to be gained. Our kind know far more than can be found on any planet." The being shrouded in brightness moved closer. "Our simple dominion is one of happiness. We have a timeless and peaceful history, interrupted only when others like yourself join us, seeking a higher existence."

The being began a slow, small orbit. Bracken tried to see beyond the creature, but a curtain of darkness blocked his view.

Hiffornak continued, "We are from another plane which is linked to yours by this passage."

"Linked? Then, why haven't we on Ebbern seen you before? Why haven't we—why haven't I—traveled to your plane?"

"Such is not easy for you. We creatures of light can move freely through progressive spheres of energy. It is a simple thing for us to pass into this region." The speaker's luminous form wafted about, as if demonstrating its mobility. "Many of your kind do venture from your planet in search of our domain. However, most are as children playing games."

"I'm not a child!" Bracken snapped, irritated that a man entering his third decade must state the obvious.

"Ah, yes. As I was saying, some seek this plane for purposes of diversion." A sort of lofty diplomatic grace cloaked Hiffornak, reducing Bracken's defense to prattling. "Some even arrive by *accident.*"

Embarrassment crept over Bracken. He did feel like a child, playing out some unfamiliar game. He wished the game would end.

Bits of recent reality intruded into his exalted state. A siren wailing through his forest, the colored lights atop a Pirax vehicle . . . the search . . . for him? No . . . they searched for another quarry. But Bracken had found the silver box.

"However," Hiffornak drew Bracken back to the domain of the stone, "we know that you honestly seek truth and not simply pleasure. That is why you are here. You are the one who is to be entrusted with knowledge and awareness."

Now, pride in being chosen for some great purpose bolstered Bracken's confidence. "Show me how you are capable of seeing events happening in my world."

"Your world is soon to be destroyed."

"Ebbern destroyed? How can you say that?" Bracken did not want to hear this kind of truth. "You must be wrong!" What was happening to the lovely realm of the green stone? Where were its soothing, stroking sensations?

Hiffornak continued, "Exploring new horizons of discovery is not without sadness. But, there is one hope for Ebbern. Because you have a searching spirit, Bracken, you will learn much. You will learn how to save your planet from destruction."

"What will happen? It's the terminus bomb, isn't it? Tell me what I can do! I must know!"

"Many levels, some more elusive than others, hold answers to untold mysteries."

"Answer me! What can I do?"

"Bring your friends here to meet me. Others must be educated, although they will not reach your level. Only you will save your planet."

"How? Tell me how." Bracken heard himself babbling. "I want to save Ebbern, but I don't know how."

The creature ignored Bracken's pleas. "We are aware that certain inhabitants of Ebbern discourage, even forbid, you who seek to rise above a paltry existence. The hunt for true freedom is oppressed by selfish leaders who insist on upholding old traditions and outdated teachings." Hiffornak's hypnotic tones reached out with gentle touches. "You are weary, but soon you will be refreshed."

A euphoria flowed over Bracken, washing away his frustration, bringing a feeling of renewal. Peace spun a protective cocoon around him.

The glowing creature drifted upward to an ethereal station and communicated with a philosophic inflection. "Life is a cycle."

Bracken sighed, as if reluctantly awakening from a dream.

"Some will make the ultimate sacrifice," Hiffornak predicted, "but those who die will come again. Noble ventures will repeat themselves, finding success eventually. We are all like the passing rays of the sun, vanishing only to beckon the coming of another day. It will be through you, Bracken, that Ebbern will see another day."

The sounds of Hiffornak became less distinct, as though the creature were leaving. "Now, it is time that you returned."

"Not yet! There is so much I need to know."

"Bring your friends here. Then I will instruct you further. Time is short. Your planet's at a critical point."

Bracken reached out, engulfed in an urgent sense of loss. "Don't go!" The threatened deadline brought a new urgency to his searching. But the glowing being seemed to ignore his plea, its words now a fading monologue.

"Bring them soon . . . bring them soon." The cloud of light dimmed, its bidding growing distant. "Follow the surge from the stone. It will lead you to me. . . ."

Bracken found himself alone, staring toward where he had last seen the creature. Fearful reality nipped at him. He became aware of his surroundings. He felt chilled, uncertain. The power of the mysterious stone that had brought him here was fading.

A purple glow formed around Bracken. He turned and quickly retraced his steps, the purple glow clinging like a layer of lustrous clothing.

Ahead, murky fog unfolded as petals of a blossom, revealing an opening. Apprehensions begged Bracken not to enter. An unknown seemed to lurk there, but it waited for him and drew him close until he pushed his way through.

He emerged on the opposite side in a maze of gloomy tunnels crisscrossing through a darkened chamber. Where was the golden light that first led him along the corridor? Guided by the sensations of the stone, he rushed down an obscure path. But the sensations grew feeble. He strained to follow them. He must hurry before they left him.

Reality tugged again, pulling him toward his own dimension. Confused, his pace quickened. His breathing grew heavy. His heart pounded. If the stone's effects vanished, would he be trapped? Where?

The passageway darkened, forcing Bracken to slow his steps. A familiar sound chirped through the tunnel. The haunting laugh had returned.

Ahead, Bracken glimpsed a bright flash of red. It glimmered like a beacon, then retreated into an intercepting passage.

Abruptly, footsteps padded from behind. Bracken turned to look and saw the curtain of darkness again. Two creatures streaked from it. They were not radiant, as Hiffornak had been, but were covered with serpentine skin and bore hideously contoured heads.

Bracken tried to run. He whirled back, at once met by the sound of a new advancing terror, indistinguishable except that it emitted a low rasp in perfect time with lumbering, heavy footsteps. Bracken pivoted, again facing the serpentine creatures, their jaws swinging open to expose vicious fangs.

Bracken flailed his arms, fighting off an enveloping force that sapped his strength, sucked him downward, plucked at every surface of his body. He pulled free. Dark forms chased him. He sprinted through a passageway, momentarily evading his pursuers until a new rush of motion from behind compelled him to look over his shoulder. An army of unidentifiable forms scurried through the dusky light toward him. He raced blindly on.

Without warning, the tunnel ended. Bracken's body slammed into a rock-hard surface. He screamed in pain and grabbed his shoulder, as if to corral shattered bones. He felt himself slipping away. He slid down the cold, jagged wall, its rough edges sending splinters of anguish tearing into his skin.

With his last trace of consciousness, Bracken sighted a new form, one that appeared and stood between him and his pursuers. It seemed to hold forth a shield of white light, edged in red, which repelled the evil madly rushing to consume him. But how could this being, so graceful and delicate, save him?

Bracken cried a soundless plea for help.

The scene vanished, leaving only a trace of red seared across Bracken's memory. Then, it too, disappeared.

CHAPTER 2

Bracken lay face down, his confused mind working to sort a maze of fragmented images. He opened one eye and saw a crosshatched pattern of vegetation. A prickly pillow beneath his head pressed into the hollow of his cheek. Around him, tall shapes reached toward an afternoon sky. His right shoulder scraped against what he perceived to be the rough bark of a tree.

He was safe, back in his forest. Yet the memory of the terror he had just faced seemed to slither darkly at the back of his consciousness. His look gripped the soil. Slowly his fear began to subside. He breathed deeply and relaxed, reassuring himself.

But a distant sound renewed the sense of danger. He cringed. Someone . . . something had rescued him from unspeakable horror. Now, a new force threatened.

Bracken squirmed into a thick undergrowth. The feeling of danger intensified. Footsteps! The danger couldn't be real. There had never been anything to fear in this forest so close to home.

A masculine voice shattered Bracken's imaginary bubble of safety. "Over there! I was in those trees when the Pirax closed in."

"You're crazy! We've already looked there," a second man growled. "This way. Hurry. We're losing the light."

Bracken tried to think. Was this tiny cosmos of trees and sky real? Or, was that other place real?

Hugging the ground, he held his breath and watched dusty boots—one, two, three, four—stride this way and that, from tree to tree, like adolescent boys learning to dance. One dancing boot executed a sharp turn. Metal glinted. Another turn, and the wicked looking knife retreated beneath a coarse pant leg.

"Tell me again." The man with the knife cursed. "You saw a guy out for a stroll, and you were stupid enough to leave it in plain sight?"

"Not in plain sight. And if I ever see him again. . . ."

This was no dream. Those men wanted something. Maybe they thought Bracken had it.

"Sure! With the Pirax chasing you, you wouldn't remember what your own mother looked like."

The second pair of boots moved closer. "Hey, here's something! I'll. . . ."

"Shut up! Somebody's coming."

"Pirax?"

An arm's length from Bracken's face, a meaty hand stopped in mid-air over a half-hidden object in the undergrowth. In dismay, Bracken recognized a lump of brown leather. It was his own pack, carelessly discarded earlier.

"I'm not waiting to ask. Let's get out of here!" Both men sprinted away.

Bracken staggered to his feet and grabbed his pack with its load of books. How could he explain to a law enforcement official that he'd come here seeking space and solitude, relief from a job and from classes at Tizra Academics? He started on the familiar path home to Tizra. But, it was no use. He eased to the ground and slouched against a tree. When no Pirax officer materialized, Bracken's head dropped to his knees. He felt confused, scared, and elated all at once. Events had moved so quickly since he returned from the Mingus reality. He tried to sort them out. Was Ebbern to be destroyed? Did he really have only a short time?

"Bracken!" someone called. It was his father.

A younger voice, still changing, said gleefully, "Here you are!" It belonged to Bracken's brother. "Mother sent us to find you."

How like her, Bracken's foggy logic reasoned. He'd told her that morning not to expect him home for the evening meal. Who had she worried about all the years that Bracken had spent traveling around Nerkush?

His father and brother stood over him. When they could no longer be ignored, Bracken sat up, yawned, and ran a hand through his light brown hair.

Kressdek settled himself on a fallen log. "Thought Amont and I would find you here." He heaved a sigh, evidence that the extra pounds clinging to his sturdy frame had exerted a toll during the walk from Tizra.

"I had studying to do."

Kressdek shrugged. "You know how mothers are, even when their sons are grown. Besides, she thinks I need exercise." The older man chuckled and patted his stomach. But his eyes, as blue as his son's and almost as clear, lingered with unusual interest on Bracken.

Awkwardly, Bracken hurled a seed pod at his brother. "Catch!" Amont laughed and sent it flying back. Could Kressdek sense anything of what Bracken had experienced that day? Bracken himself wasn't certain what had happened. Images of a chamber filled with warm light spun into his mind. Greenish, crusty scales shuttered the light, grinding this way and that, squeezing and expanding, stealing Bracken's own breath.

"Everything okay, son?"

"Sure," Bracken said quickly and diverted further questions by observing, "you're not working late tonight?"

"Everything's under control. This is a busy season in the moisture business. But, a man can't work night and day," Kressdek uttered the trite phrase self-consciously.

The setting sun's rays sliced through the high trees. The fragrant atmosphere of this spot in the forest triggered happy childhood memories for Bracken. His thoughts finally began to focus. He drummed his fingers on the ground, deriving satisfaction from its solid reality. Not yet ready to attempt the walk home, he tried to make conversation, often a difficult accomplishment with his father. "The new man doing his job?"

"Okay. Of course, it's not like he was family."

Bracken groaned inwardly at his own foolish question. To avoid pursuing the sore subject, he pointed to his brother, who was ripping bare branches from a rotting log. "Soon, Amont will be a real help to you. When he's old enough, you won't be able to keep him away from the office." Suddenly Bracken felt pulled from the familiar moment with his family. His senses surged. The terror of it all came rushing back—the hidden fears, the fangs, the talons pulling him down to his death. He shook the memory and tried to focus on his father's pleasant features.

Kressdek looked fondly at the child of his later years. "A man likes to think that at least one son wants to follow in his footsteps, to take over the family business."

"Father . . ."

"I had hoped . . . I thought that when you came back this time . . ."

"I'm glad . . . grateful . . . to work with you part-time so I can take the rest of the classes I need."

"Of course, moisture supply is dirty work."

"You know that doesn't bother me. This time around, I'm going to finish school. . . ."

"I want you to finish school."

". . . and then, I'm going to build my own career."

The mounting friction peaked. "You don't think running our business is a real career?"

Bracken replied patiently, "I didn't say that." He looked away from his father's furrowed brow and graying temples. He's not old, Bracken told himself. Amont will be ready to take over long before Father is willing to let go.

A night bird rustled overhead branches. Amont threw a rock at it and laughed triumphantly when the bird flew from cover.

Kressdek closed the discussion. "It's getting late." He made no move to leave.

Bracken hated this tension between them. He tried to remember that his father's stringent childhood had molded character traits where work took precedence over almost everything, leaving little room for nurturing relationships.

Bracken tested his legs again. More confident, he moved to the log where his father sat. Among the evening stars, Ebbern's three moons had risen, the translucent crescents reflecting pale light. Trying to salvage some semblance of comradeship with his father, Bracken recalled occasional successful discussions about legends of the past. "That must have been quite a sight the time when the stars fell."

"Indeed," Kressdek willingly followed the lead. "Accounts have passed down of how the heavens seemed to erupt in flames."

Amont wandered near. "Tell about it, Father! Tell about the night the stars fell."

Kressdek protested mildly. "You've heard the story many times."

"Tell it anyway."

Kressdek stood and hitched up his pants, obviously pleased. He found a comfortable position on a flat rock and leaned his elbows on his knees. "It is said that stars collided. Some called it a war in the sky." Kressdek warmed to the subject. "Herdsmen who were high in the mountains said that the stars began to fall. Most vanished, but others reached the ground, bringing fierce fires that burned the plains. The herdsmen told countless tales of mystery that surrounded the descent of the burning stars."

"Like we're sitting around telling stories," observed Amont, straddling Bracken's log.

Bracken ruffled his brother's hair. "Yes," he encouraged, seeking to prolong the still-needed respite.

"Then came one special star." Kressdek's voice picked up new animation. "This star did not burn out like the others. It became brighter as it grew closer, until night was as day. Those brave enough went to Mt. Shidow where that star fell. Its radiance warmed them and brought peaceful feelings."

Amont interrupted, "And then the Night Ruler appeared?"

"I'm getting to that. At first, people named the brilliant star that fell on Mt. Shidow the Shining One. They said he was magnificent. Beauty seemed to spread from him like a mist spreads over the valley. There was magic in his touch. But, after a while, that light dimmed, and in its place, stood the Night Ruler."

"What did he really look like?"

"I don't know, Amont. People only said that he was wise and wonderful, and he promised marvelous things."

"Everybody said that?"

Kressdek shrugged. "A few did not believe in him and were afraid. But they were dismissed as fools. Every place on the planet that the Night Ruler went, he gathered new followers."

"All over Ebbern? Even Accad?" Amont named the bustling city on the seacoast.

"Remember, this took place before Nerkush was established as a country, and I suppose Accad was no more than a fishing village, and

Tizra only a tiny settlement. But, people scattered over the planet believed the Night Ruler's promise of plenty and pleasure."

"Did he deliver?"

"Well, the times of plenty and pleasure have come in cycles, some long and some short, through these many years. Always, just when the promise of the Night Ruler seemed about to come true, troubling changes would take place." Kressdek paused thoughtfully. "Then, somewhere, a leader would rise up and lead some of the disbelievers to a time of contentment and peace, and even some followers of the Night Ruler would lose heart in him."

Amont imitated his father's story-telling mannerisms. "But, contented and peaceful times were short-lived, and soon the promises of the Night Ruler overshadowed them, and people would again seek plenty and pleasure. And again the troubling changes would come."

"You know the story as well as I." Kressdek smiled. "Yes, just when plenty and pleasure seemed within reach, changes would take place. Sometimes the changes were horrendous—great, belching storms in the seas, and a tearing and twisting of the land. Confusion scattered friends and families. Hatred ripped at the people's hearts, and they slaughtered one another without mercy. Men were sold as slaves, and monstrous beasts roamed the land."

Amont sought a seat beside his father, but he took up the story with relish. "Creatures of darkness crept from the sea and devoured men. Even now," he lowered his voice menacingly, "it is said that beasts lurk in dark places, waiting to prey upon those disloyal to the Night Ruler."

In the silence that followed, Bracken suppressed a shiver. No matter that he had heard this tale since childhood and didn't believe it anyway. His recent experience in the dark passage of terror had somehow changed him. Perhaps such myths had some basis and facts. He shrugged and smiled at his father.

"Of course," Kressdek sat up and rolled his shoulders, "many people laugh and call the entire account imaginary."

"What about you, Father?" asked Amont.

"We must respect the stories of our fathers."

Bracken toyed with a slender branch, snapping it into small pieces. "You didn't answer the question. Do you think the stories are true?"

"A pat *yes* or *no* to that is difficult. But, I will say this: the stories of our fathers should be kept alive."

"Including those in the Volume that Mother reads?"

"Including those. Let each person make his own choice as to whether or not he believes them."

"Come on, Father," Bracken persisted, unwilling to acknowledge what he had just barely admitted to himself. "Surely you have already made your choice. If you don't agree, you disagree. Isn't there some kind of deadline?"

Kressdek rose with uncharacteristic nimbleness. "I may not

believe them word for word, but at least I respect the stories of our fathers." He pointed an accusing finger at Bracken. "Aren't you always touting your value of knowledge? Aren't you the person on a perpetual search for," his voice climbed to a sarcastic peak, "the *true gem*? Why, you've hunted for years for some sort of truth that will give you bigger and better answers than the rest of us have."

"Sorry, Father." Bracken sighed. So much for a spirit of comradeship.

Kressdek stalked away on the moonlit trail toward Tizra with Amont on his heels. Bracken followed, seething at his father's outburst.

Sometime later, Kressdek coughed artificially and then remarked to his subdued companions, "A good night for walking."

Bracken ignored the overture. "Seriously, Father, you don't believe that there is a being called the Night Ruler who lurks around every corner, waiting for a chance to cause havoc?"

"Apparently you don't?"

Before Bracken could answer, Amont yelled, "Look!" He grabbed his father's arm and pulled him to a stop. "There, on the other side of the brook, above the hills. What is it?"

Kressdek and Bracken turned to the sky where Amont pointed. Kressdek gasped softly. Bracken stared, transfixed.

An oval disk skittered about, paused, and then swooped close. A low humming noise accompanied the glowing object that soon looped back and disappeared behind the hills.

"What was that?" Amont demanded. When Kressdek failed to reply, he asked again, "You saw it, Father. What was it?"

Kressdek resumed walking toward Tizra. "A sky-flyer."

"It didn't move like a sky-flyer."

"Don't argue," Kressdek snapped. "Could be a new design."

"I don't understand."

"There are many things we don't understand." Kressdek walked faster. "I tell you, it was a sky-flyer."

Bracken tarried. Of course, his father was right. It must have been a sky-flyer. He looked at Ebbern's moons, now nearly hidden by clouds. His experiences that day seemed just as obscure, nearly hidden from memory by clouds of disbelief. Had he really found a mysterious green stone? One fragment of an otherwise unbelievable collage of images haunted Bracken. A flash of red clearly appeared and reappeared in his mind's eye. It continued to do so until late that night when he finally fell asleep.

* * *

Back in the forest, two beams of light scurried through the trees, skating along the ground, exploring fallen logs.

"It's no use. We'll never find it."

"It's got to be here. Keep looking."

One light halted its dizzy pace. "Hey, maybe this is the place. Yes! I've found it."

"Careful how you open it."

The two lights hovered side by side. "The box is empty! Somebody used it! Somebody used our property."

CHAPTER 3

"Breathe slowly," the soft voice urged. "Relax completely. Let tension seep from your body, from your mind. Breathe in only the good. Breathe in only strength. Breathe out negative thoughts."

It might have been easier for Bracken to relax had he been sitting somewhere other than on the bare floor of a Tizra Academics classroom. But he and his friends had wandered into this career day exhibit on reaching one's potential and decided to give it a try.

Lisha seemed comfortable enough. She tossed her golden hair back from her face. As always, she wore little make-up, and Bracken saw the faint sprinkling of freckles that enhanced her natural look. They exchanged glances. She bestowed the special smile that he was beginning to think she reserved for him.

Bracken's closest friend, Silas, leaned his sturdy frame against a wall, dark eyes twinkling, wearing a poorly-disguised grin of amusement on his round face.

Their leader, a meticulously-groomed woman who could have been somebody's grandmother, entreated, "Visualize a light within your heart. Look within yourself to find that light. Your heart holds the warm and radiant center of your being. Seek the center."

Bracken searched dutifully for his center. The Potentials exhibit claimed that its methods enabled the career-minded person to achieve desired goals. And recently, Bracken had become a career-minded person. He listened to the gentle voice of the instructor.

"Continue breathing in self-esteem. Breathe out negative qualities. Picture yourself approaching a conference table. The table is smooth and shiny. The head chair is empty. Take your place at the head of the table. Other people sit along the sides of the table. No one can make you move from your place."

Following instructions, Bracken tried to feel the smooth wood of his chair and smell the leather upholstery.

"You are compassionate toward subordinates. But you sit at the head of the table because you are willing to experiment, to reach within for qualities and energies, which enable you to surmount ever-higher challenges. You are open to change."

Bracken certainly did consider himself open to new ideas, and the quality of being compassionate to people under his command was appealing, almost noble. He listened more intently.

* * *

Later, Bracken walked with Lisha across campus toward the art booth, his arm around her waist. He enjoyed the appreciative glances cast her way, especially ones coming from younger students nearer Lisha's own age. Anyone would be attracted to her sparkling brown eyes and pretty smile, but he was intrigued by her personality that radiated a sort of vulnerable idealism.

She stepped up on a low wall and shaded her eyes. "What happened to Silas?"

"Probably visualized himself right to sleep."

"Don't be silly! He can't help it if his ideas are oriented to tangible objects, like bridges and buildings."

Bracken agreed. "He prefers to create on firm foundations."

"His scale model in the structural engineering display is a stunning piece of art in its own way."

Bracken helped Lisha off the bench and through a grassy area lined with booths representing student organizations. "My favorite artist on campus is not Silas." He gave Lisha an affectionate hug.

She returned it, leaving to take her turn at the art studies booth. "I'm doing pastel portraits. Shall I draw a quick sketch of you? You could give it to your mother."

He chuckled. "How about doing one tomorrow? You promised to spend the day with me."

"Our booth is here to make a profit for art studies." She winked. "But perhaps I could arrange a discount."

"Tomorrow, I wager I can get my art work free."

She planted a kiss on her forefinger and blew it in his direction. "Get out of here."

Bracken wandered back to the recruiters' exhibits. A mockup of an out of atmosphere vehicle drew attention to a firm interviewing technical graduates. Uncertain times faced everyone. It was rumored that the Nerkush War Agency planned further tests of the powerful terminus bomb. Established nations in the far corners of Ebbern already had the weapon. How long before emerging nations also entered the arena? The warning he had heard from the glowing one came again. It haunted him.

Bracken quickened his pace, overcome with a sense of urgency. Sometimes he wondered why he'd bothered returning to school in the face of a threatened holocaust. Was it a waste of time to complete even the few classes he needed? Somewhere lay answers to Ebbern's problems. On the other hand, somewhere, a rewarding career awaited him.

Bracken found Silas in a crowd clustered around a man who invited, "Sign up for a free weekend seminar at Demur."

"It wouldn't be hard to spend a weekend with her." Silas told Bracken, cheerfully pointing to a scantily-clad female posed on the beach at Demur. The model gazed dreamily out over the Sea of Aurin.

Bracken's full lips curved in a grin. "You've got it wrong, Silas. It's supposed to be a *self*-awareness seminar."

"Hey, if I put my mind to it, I could probably do a lot better at this stuff than I did here." Silas wagged his thumb at the Potentials exhibit. "How about you? Did you get all grounded and centered?"

They moved to the Currency Center exhibit. The representative was fit, trim, and wore a suit that undoubtedly cost more than Bracken's entire wardrobe. Trasent was the picture of an image-conscious, successful professional. In fact, except for a small gap between his two front teeth, he looked perfect. Slightly older than Bracken, he displayed more vitality than Bracken would have expected from an employee of the prestigious Currency Center.

Trasent's dark eyes skimmed the printout of Bracken's records."A strong aptitude in statistics."

Bracken found classes in statistics easy. But, he wanted a more socially-conscious career than working with mundane financial records. A job at the Currency Center sounded dangerously similar to keeping the business accounts over which his father labored daily, using an out-dated system. Bracken decided to move on.

Trasent detained him. "Are you familiar with our training program?" Bracken shook his head. "We look for a few select people to participate in a special bridging program. The participants continue studies on a part-time basis here at Tizra Academics while they begin work at the Currency Center."

Silas whistled. "Heavy schedule."

Bracken was thinking the same thing.

Trasent smiled. "Not too heavy. The Currency Center hours are flexible and geared to an individual's class schedule. In fact, many people find that the bridging program allows more free time than a standard entry-level position." He shot an encouraging glance at Bracken. "I'm here to meet with promising individuals who want to explore careers in the financial field."

Silas offered in a half-whisper, "Go on, Bracken. I'll hang around."

Bracken whispered back, "Me? Work at the Currency Center?"

Trasent gave Bracken a look that indicated that only a fool would not pursue this opportunity. Bracken followed him inside.

* * *

Later, Bracken found Silas at the astro studies booth, munching a sphere of white pastry.

"Buy one of these from Catine," Silas told him, grinning at a girl behind the booth. "And get a free ticket to Professor Frimleter's show."

"What kind of show?"

"I don't know." Silas licked sweet, white powder from his lips.

"It's for a worthy cause," a student urged, "our astro studies group. And the show is great."

Inside, the lights dimmed. A spotlight played on Professor Frimleter, accenting the tall, thin man's gaunt features. His skin was nearly as white as the sweet powder that exploded with each bite of the pastries sold outside. Dark shadows filled the hollows of his face. His straight black hair, which was parted sharply in the middle, faded into the background. The effect was a moving colorless portrait.

Discordant music introduced a new set of lights that illuminated a large, three-dimensional display of planets and stars. The spheres began to revolve in orbit. The lighting changed again so that out of the blackness of space came the sole source of light, the sun. Bracken found himself listening intently to the professor's discourse on heavenly bodies surrounding Ebbern.

Professor Frimleter's face remained an unhealthy white even after the house lights came on. In the stark classroom atmosphere, Bracken soon lost interest. He and Silas had exchanged signals to sneak out when a question caught Bracken's attention.

"Professor, will you discuss the possibility of life on other planets?"

Frimleter pursed his lips. "Please define life."

"Life. You know, like you and me?"

"The accepted theory holds that there is no life as you define it on the near planets."

"What about on distant planets?"

"Yes," spoke a girl at the front of the room. It was Catine, who had sold pastries. "What about intelligent creatures anywhere in the universe? We heard a report in class concerning contact with life from outside our planetary complex."

The professor's gray eyes darted over the group. "We have studied such theories in class. That question adds an intriguing aspect to our discussion here. It happens to be one to which I've devoted considerable thought."

At the mention of contact with life from outside the planetary complex, Silas and Bracken both settled back in their seats.

"Some studies," Frimleter said, "conclude that not only is there evidence of intelligent life, but there is growing evidence that such life seeks to make contact with us."

A collective gasp rippled across the classroom.

From deep in Bracken's memory came a scene of undulating green vines beckoning, forming an inviting corridor. He cast away the unwanted recollection. For months, he had fought to bury persistent, sometimes terrifying images. Still the experience with the mysterious green stone returned to haunt him, although less and less often.

A guest asked dubiously, "You mean this space disk stuff that people talk about could be true?"

A snort of disbelief came from the back of the room.

The Professor smoothed his hair down from the center part, on one side and then the other. "There have been reports from extremely reliable sources on *space disk stuff*, as you call it."

Catine urged, "Why don't you tell him, Professor? Tell him what you think." She endorsed her instructor with a look of unabashed pride.

Frimleter, rubbing his bony hands, appraised his audience carefully. "The entire celestial network is too large for us to presume that we are alone. In our own planetary system, there may not be visible signs of life beyond the apparent. But when the huge array of stellar structures is considered, the possibilities are unlimited."

Someone asked, "The possibilities for intelligent life?"

In the silence that followed, came the Professor's answer. "Why not? Can we be so shortsighted and proud as to imagine ourselves to be the only intelligent creatures inhabiting this vast universe? It's naive to suggest that we are alone."

For Bracken, the room suddenly darkened. A single radiant light glided near. *My name is Hiffornak . . . from another plane . . . linked to yours. . . .* Bracken grabbed his chair, suddenly dizzy. He held his breath. Just as his lungs threatened to explode, the radiant light popped, and the Tizra Academics classroom wobbled back into focus.

Professor Frimleter was saying, "Yes, I might even call it foolhardy to suggest that we are alone."

"Why isn't the Nerkush Space Agency investigating this theory?"

Frimleter shook a long finger at his audience. "Yes, why?" he demanded. "There have been a few space probes, a little cautious tinkering at the edge of infinity." Then, gray eyes focused on some point above the audience, he declared, "It remains for those of us who are bold enough. . . ."

He clamped his thin lips together, slicked down his hair again, and continued, "Nerkush needs to expand its efforts in this area. Considering that we are capable, should war occur, of annihilating this planet, it is obvious that any alternatives which surface should be explored with open minds. We must make a step of moral and intellectual evolution, or we will destroy ourselves. If we aren't capable of taking that step, then it's not beyond the realm of possibility that a more intelligent force would desire to intervene and aid us in taking such a step."

Frimleter's own nervous cough shattered the stupor that engulfed his audience. "You people certainly raised an interesting sidelight." He squeezed out a thin laugh. "That's proof that astro studies is not a dull subject." He checked the time with a worried look and abruptly dismissed the group, "Thank you for your attention, ladies and gentlemen." He hurried from the room.

Bracken jumped to his feet. "Let's go, Silas."

"Wait," Silas grumbled. "Did he say life from other planets might be trying to contact me?"

Prodding Silas, Bracken growled, "Come on. I have to talk to you. It's important."

A girl behind them snickered. "So that's the famous astro studies expert?"

Another said, "Yeah, he's an expert on outer space." She laughed. "I can believe that. He's been there!"

Bracken wasn't laughing.

CHAPTER 4

"I tell you, Silas. I saw a creature from another level." Bracken hurled a brown bottle toward a smoldering fire he and Silas had built in the forest clearing. His aim faulted by the sweet, intoxicating krem they were drinking, the bottle glanced off a rock. Glass fragments glittered in the firelight.

"Which level is that?"

"What kind of buddy are you?" Bracken demanded. "A guy spills his guts about the most powerful experience of his life, and he gets sarcasm in return."

"I know that people once used Mingus Stones. But stones were outlawed thirty years ago, about the time we were born."

"I found one. It was almost as big as my hand."

Silas shook his head. "People who fooled around with that size stone without gradually working up to it went crazy. You're not crazy. At least, I don't think you are. Face it, Bracken, you never touched a genuine Mingus Stone, big or little."

"Yeah?" Bracken challenged.

"Tell me," Silas goaded, "why have you kept this fantastic experience secret all these months, unless it was a dream and you just now remembered? Having some creature tell you the planet is whirling to destruction and only you can save it is not what I'd call ordinary chit-chat."

"I didn't want to talk about it. But today, that skinny professor practically guaranteed extraterrestrial life."

Silas yawned. "If you found a mysterious green rock and then passed out, you had guzzled too much krem."

Bracken and Silas sat in the forest outside Tizra, their backs against a fallen log, feet silhouetted against the fire. It had cost Bracken dearly to dredge up strange and fearful memories of the green stone. Now, Silas was discounting it.

Melodious notes sounded as Silas began to strum the stringed instrument that he cradled. Bracken had composed that song as a teenager. His parents had hated it. He reached for his own stam and joined Silas.

How often during childhood had they escaped to this corner of the forest? Why, even as adults, they'd holed up here many nights. He remembered a particular one, a decade ago, the night they'd decided to leave home and strike out across Nerkush.

They played their stams with abandon, singing, or letting the instruments sing beneath their skillful fingers. At times, the music drove the two men in flights of soulful power. The treetops stirred. Music floated on the breeze, almost with a life of its own. It echoed from a distance, like quiet calls from behind the sky. With the calls came a presence, drawing closer, as if blown to the source of the music by the wind of another world.

Finally, satiated with melody, Bracken and Silas placed their instruments aside. They leaned back, their energies spent.

Silas offered, "I'm trying to believe you."

"I wouldn't lie to you, buddy. But, I can't explain what happened." Bracken poked the fire, igniting bright flames and sending sparks swarming upward. "NAFIS wants everyone to believe the stone steals your mind. But, who can believe NAFIS?"

Silas snorted, "The famous Nerkush Agency for Illegal Substances."

"I hear that stones are turning up in Accad."

"In the Community, no doubt." Silas slapped his knee and cackled. "I bet NAFIS is working overtime."

"Yes, and a stone could conceivably find its way from the Community here."

Silas countered, "Even in the old days when stones were plentiful, they say big ones like what you claim to have uncovered in a silver box were hard to come by—and dangerous."

"If stones are getting to the Community, somebody has located the Mingus Mine. How would you like to be the guy who first discovered the mine?"

"Cibbmingus? Nope. He's been dead a long time."

Bracken passed another bottle of krem to Silas and opened one for himself. The golden, foamy liquid slid down his throat. "They say a NAFIS crew is snooping on Mt. Shidow—looking for his mine, no doubt."

Bracken wiped his mouth on his sleeve and traded the krem bottle for his stam. His fingers ran over the strings in a soothing background melody. The night air changed. It settled, damp and clinging, moving only to make room for drifts of fog that glided in through the trees as if on wings.

Perhaps, Bracken admitted, Silas was right, and the encounter with Hiffornak had not been a Mingus Stone experience. Bracken decided not to speak of it to anyone else. Still . . . he picked on his stam thoughtfully, searching out a new tune. "You know, we could hike over that way and find the Mingus Mine ourselves, before the NAFIS team does."

"Huh?" Silas sounded sleepy.

"Most of Mt. Shidow is wilderness, but that wouldn't stop two people who have already explored part of it, like we have."

"Leave it, Bracken. Strange things go on around Mt. Shidow. Mystical stuff. There's supposed to be an ancient gathering ground."

"Rumors."

"Anyway, old Cibbmingus carried the secret of his mine to his grave. Besides, we're changing our lifestyles. Remember? Getting smart."

"I know, but . . ."

"I plan to let people pay me for work I want to do. And it sounds like you're headed for the Currency Center's bridging program."

"I'm considering it," Bracken admitted. "I'd have more freedom there than stuck in a regular job. Pay's not bad. Wonder what kind of rig Trasent drives."

"Whatever, it's certain that he didn't need his father's signature to buy it, like we did."

Bracken snorted. "My first career objective is to get credit that's good around the globe." He picked idly on his stam, his thoughts returning to the Mingus Mine. "How hard can it be to spot a mine when you know the general location? I can get explosives."

"Count me out. If NAFIS is combing Mt. Shidow for the mine, it's because they intend to seal it permanently in order to cut off the source. And those guys mean business!"

Bracken struck a sharp cord, taken aback by Silas' blunt refusal.

"We've been a lot of places together," Silas said with unusual solemnity, "some of them downright unpleasant. I'm finding it harder and harder to share your zest for a good search. This time, you'll have to go it alone."

"You wouldn't let me down. We owe it to ourselves to take a look. Who knows what we'll uncover."

Silas moaned. "You always have to be hunting for something exotic. Obviously, since I never know what it is, I can't be of much help. So don't ask me to go along."

Silas' objections only spurred Bracken on. "Don't you see? Wisdom and truth exist beyond what most people accept . . . and power, too. There's so much that we don't understand."

"I don't have to understand everything."

"But this is a lead. Let's follow it. There are invisible forces, like the stuff Frimleter was talking about, like . . ." Bracken stopped, not wanting to bring up the green stone again. "There has to be a connection—a link—between some of the things that are beyond our comprehension."

The fog crept out as quickly as it had come, clearing the way for a cool wind that whistled in the trees. Silas shivered and began to kick dirt over the fire's embers. "Let's go."

Bracken reached for his stam, but an outcry from Silas halted him.

"Look! Up there!"

An intriguing sight in the heavens held Bracken spellbound. He had spent many nights under the stars, but this was a new phenomenon. Or was it? His mind flashed to the evening, months before, when he'd walked home from these woods with his father and Amont.

"Look how that thing moves," Silas whispered. "It can't be a sky-flyer. What is it?"

An oval disk danced in a darting, rhythmic pattern. The pattern slowed, and the disk floated downward until it hovered above the clearing where Bracken and Silas stood.

An overwhelming force seemed to pull at Bracken. A gentle hum droned from the craft. The sound seemed almost melodious, a lonely cry, like an ancient song from before the world was made.

The disk began to move. It slipped into an aerial ballet, each skittering maneuver lengthening the distance between it and Ebbern. Other disks came from the stars to join the ballet, with movements so rapid and intricate that Bracken couldn't distinguish the performers from the stars. Then, one disk broke formation and dashed back toward Ebbern. It paused, made a ninety degree turn, and darted out of sight.

Silas broke the silence, his voice couched in wonder. "What do you think it was?"

Bracken searched the sky where he had last seen the disk. "It couldn't have come from this planet."

"Right," Silas mumbled, "unless we drank too much krem."

"Hah!"

"Or, else the astro studies nuts laced those white pastries with star dust." Silas' attempt at humor fell like an errant stroke on his stam.

"Think of the intelligence behind that craft."

"Let's say that it didn't come from Ebbern," Silas proposed faintly, "could that mean that the professor knows what he's talking about?"

Bracken was lost in thought. If the space disks were real, then why not the Mingus realm? The creature Hiffornak had promised that Bracken could save Ebbern from destruction, that he could prevent the planet from being obliterated by the terminus bomb. But if that was true, then he was running out of time. The very thought of it bothered him.

The plaintive song of the disk haunted Bracken as he and Silas hiked back to Tizra. The stone's verdant tunnel beckoned. An urgency to pursue his search for truth filled his mind and fired his imagination. It enticed and challenged him, making it imperative that he explore sources of power beyond the confines of Ebbern.

CHAPTER 5

High in the barren Pillars of Rimlex, Professor Frimleter heard the sound again. He might have thought it was a footstep, someone crushing a bit of loose gravel spilled on the granite surfaces that surrounded him, except that his appointment was not with anyone whom he expected to use a heavy step.

The sound seemed to weaken his thin legs. He caught a niche in the rock wall that lined one side of the narrow trail and pulled himself up a steep grade.

His back to the wall, he peered over clusters of irregular spires lighted by Ebbern's three moons. This small group of rain-starved mountains known as the Pillars of Rimlex rose from a broad plain on which he had traveled from Tizra.

Below, the sporadic popping noises made as his trans-rig cooled in the chilled night air were long gone. He'd climbed too high, winding and twisting among the crags, to see it, even if it had been bathed in bright sunlight.

Frimleter was out of breath. The astro studies show for the school's career day had run late, necessitating a faster journey than usual. But such shows provided a fruitful method of introducing newcomers to a field of study that reached far beyond his recognized work as a professor at Tizra Academics.

Now, convinced that the disturbing noise was caused by some small animal scurrying across the rocks, Frimleter proceeded. Ahead, the trail veered from the edge. He knew from previous trips that it leveled off, passed through a narrow cut in the rock, and then reached his destination—a plateau open on three sides.

He'd waited there other nights, keeping his part of an appointment, which he had to admit was a one-way arrangement. But, he was a patient man. Surely tonight, they would come.

Anticipation hastened Frimleter's pace. Despite an uneasy shiver that rippled down his back, he entered the narrow passageway. Part way through, at a sudden violent movement behind, he whirled and saw a dark form jump from above. It crouched in the corridor, barring Frimleter's retreat, blending with the darkness, so that the professor registered only a vague feeling that it was human.

Frimleter turned, seeking escape to the plateau. But, another form now blocked that end of the passageway. Illuminated by light from the heavens, the image clicked in the professor's memory. He was looking at a Rimmer.

Fearsome in appearance, the bearded Rimmer wore a torn hide tunic and held his dark unruly hair back by a leather headband. Frimleter fought off panic with the thought that this was, after all, a human. Regardless of the wicked-looking club the Rimmer clutched, this ragged savage surely meant no harm.

Frimleter extended both hands, palms up, hoping to convey a peaceful intent. "Friend."

The Rimmer tensed, but stayed where he was.

"Friend." Frimleter took a cautious step toward the body that barred the way to the plateau.

The professor was acquainted with the existence of the Rimmers. Few outsiders explored the Pillars, but farmers cultivating fields below reported seeing rag-clad ruffians darting behind rocks. It was concluded that the Rimmers dwelt in the narrow holes and tunnels that honeycombed the mountain range.

The Rimmer stood his ground, gripping his weapon. Frimleter knew that he intruded in this man's domain. He'd heard the legend that these people had descended from a clan that once followed the Night Ruler. They had been abandoned and had retreated to this rocky citadel. They had remained faithful followers—some said slaves—and worshiped him to this day. In their barren and lonely existence, they had evolved into a vile and ferocious tribe, dedicated only to keeping the memory of the Night Ruler alive.

Of course, Frimleter disputed the validity of the legend. He took another step. "My name is Professor Frimleter. I have come to watch the heavens." He pointed upward.

The Rimmer glanced toward the sky and backed away slightly.

Encouraged, Frimleter moved near the gateway to the open plateau. "I come here often."

A deep growl vibrated from the Rimmer. "Too much."

The fact that he was now in conversation with the nearsavage did little for the professor's peace of mind.

"Never again," the Rimmer growled, and thrust the club high over his head.

Frimleter gasped, his gaze riveted on the club until, into his field of vision, drifted a far-away movement. A dot of light approached on the horizon.

"Look!" he cried so forcefully that the Rimmer turned his head toward where Frimleter pointed.

Transfixed, Frimleter's present danger paled beside this momentous happening. He whispered, "They've come."

The dot of light moved closer, assuming the shape of a bright, polished disk. A faint hum sounded. Spinning, it knifed its way toward the plateau, the humming growing louder.

Frimleter trembled with eagerness, overwhelmed by this chance that he might realize his most precious dream. He wanted to move beyond the select group assigned to the great scopes and space sensors at Tizra Academics. He was determined to become a Touch-Point, a bridge between Ebbern and the powerful force that, he believed, sought to make contact across the vast distance of space.

The Rimmer lowered his club, sharing Frimleter's preoccupation with the approaching disk.

Vague impressions began to weave their way into the professor's mind. Suddenly, as if a transmitter were activated within his brain, a voice spoke to him.

"It pleases us that you have waited patiently, Professor Frimleter." The words pulsed warmly in his head. "Your faithfulness will be rewarded. You have acknowledged our existence and have the insight to recognize the importance of our coming."

Frimleter tried to contain himself. After years of study and preparation, he would be rewarded.

"But first . . . ," the voice whirred in Frimleter's mind.

Abruptly, a blue-gray light flickered on the side of the hovering disk. A thread of energy lashed out from the spacecraft, striking the Rimmer who stood on the plateau and capturing him in a cage of light. Awestruck, Frimleter watched a continuous flow of the paralyzing ray hold the terrified man and then withdraw. The Rimmer's muscles jerked spasmodically until he regained enough control to run screaming after the other Rimmer who had escaped through the rear of the passage.

A simple explanation penetrated Frimleter's mind. "We have merely frightened them. Neither they nor their companions in the caves will bother you again."

The massive disk floated to rest on the plateau. The humming sound abated, and Frimleter heard, "Come quickly. We have much prepared for you."

Professor Frimleter shook with anxiety. He was actually in contact with beings in the spacecraft. The prospect of a tangible encounter with the aliens seemed almost beyond enduring.

A stairway descended from the underside of the space disk. Frimleter climbed the steps. At the top, several creatures met him, each one dressed in a shiny gray garment, which covered its body from the neck down. The heads appeared similar to his own in shape, except for an odd angular quality and narrow, slit-like eyes. The flesh had a grayish cast.

Again the voice hummed in Frimleter's mind. "I am Taylay. We are Trionites. We travel the universe and seek to help civilizations like yours. We have watched Ebbern for many generations. Now, it is time to reveal ourselves."

"I knew you would come. I never gave up."

"We have chosen you from millions. Yours is a sublime calling. We have many secrets to unlock for you, many new theories and methods to teach you."

Frimleter marched primly on board. "You will find me a willing student."

Inside, Taylay communicated, "We have established an accelerated evolution structure. With it, we will advance the growth of the race and save Nerkush from the certainty of a ruinous war. Touch-Points are the contacts for this process. They are being trained for future leadership. Come, we will begin treatment at once."

Frimleter's joy dispelled a fleeting fear at being led to the transition compartment where the mind-expanding operation would take place. He'd heard of the treatment from others who'd been so privileged. He knew that the simple operation would alter his mind and senses to enable him to contact the disk command center at will. He was being made a Touch-Point. He would be an agent commissioned to carry the message of galactic assistance and evolutionary restructuring.

In the transition compartment, Frimleter was assured, "The operation is short and quite pleasant."

He reclined on a chair padded with a gray leather-like material. Probes above his head lowered into place. A deep sense of well-being overcame him as he yielded to the waves of energy that surged through his brain. His thoughts and senses seemed to knit into one quivering mass, echoing with reverberations of excitement.

It ended too quickly. Words hummed in his thoughts, "The treatment is complete. You will find it easy to contact us at any time."

"When? When shall I make contact?"

"As soon as you have brought others to your level of comprehension." Frimleter was led from the compartment. "Come this way for your first lesson."

The professor fell into place behind his guide through corridors and chambers filled with what appeared to be maintenance and power equipment. Taylay offered explanations, but Frimleter understood little. Although highly educated by Ebbern's standards, he found this technology beyond his comprehension.

In the disk command center, creatures at consoles controlled the operation of the space disk. On one wall, flanked by banks of instrument panels, hung a large observation screen. Projected on it was a sector of stars. Frimleter recognized the Trion Stellar System from maps he had used in research. He was shown to a semi-circle of seats with a view of the screen.

"A familiar sight, Professor?"

"Yes, I've done much study on this fascinating sector of space, hopeful of discovering more about its unusual structure."

"We know. We want to help in your investigation. Watch closely and remember."

The screen instantly magnified the Trion Stellar System. Frimleter found himself examining it at a closer range than he believed any other scientist had been privileged. Dots of light clustered in shapes that resembled frolicking four-legged animals. Glowing planets, their multi-colored rings blending into circular rainbows, seemed to revolve around a gray cloudlike mass, which faded at the edge into drifting particles. The mass parted in the center to reveal a ragged circle of unending blackness.

Dazzled by the sight, Frimleter took rapid mental notes, despairing of capturing the wealth of information. What he saw would increase Nerkush's knowledge of the celestial network by many years.

Suddenly, the screen went blank.

"It is time for you to leave."

Reluctantly, Frimleter turned from the gray screen. He followed the disk creature to the craft's exit. Back on the plateau's firm surface, he listened to words of encouragement pulsing in his brain.

"Bring others to your level of understanding. Time is running out, but our plan will save Nerkush."

The disk began to hum. It rose rapidly into the pre-dawn sky and departed, growing smaller until it was indistinguishable from the stars.

The thoughts that filled Frimleter's mind were not so much in the form of sentences, but were as seed concepts, growing into material for speeches and papers. He descended to his trans-rig in a daze, acutely aware of his tremendous responsibility. He had been chosen! And having been selected as a Touch-Point, he would be a leader in the new order destined for Nerkush.

* * *

At that moment, on the other side of the Pillars of Rimlex, a dirty bearded man slouched at the mouth of an open cave. He stared in wonder as an object fell swiftly from the sky. It neared Ebbern, a glowing disk that followed the towering rim of the mountains for a short distance. The terrified man called to a trembling form that cowered deep in the cave and responded with an incoherent whimper.

Alone, the Rimmer watched the disk drop suddenly into a pile of rock. The humming ceased. Gradually, the disk's glow faded until it seemed nothing more than a large boulder, still and dark, one of countless other boulders on the mountain range. Except that from this one, there slowly rose gray ghost-like images. Silently, one by one, the apparitions slipped away.

CHAPTER 6

Following Lisha up the hillside, Bracken amused himself, watching her hair glisten like wispy strands of gold as a light breeze brushed it across her shoulders. They had climbed leisurely for nearly an hour. The sun was warm and the air fragrant.

Lisha stopped abruptly. "That meadow is exquisite, prettier than I've ever seen it," she exclaimed. "If only I had my paints . . . an infinite number of greens, and see the purple blossoms edging into the forest?" She pointed in delight.

"Nice," Bracken agreed, more taken with Lisha's charm.

A small brook splashed its way down the gentle rise. Kicking off their shoes, they stepped into the cool water. Bracken gripped Lisha's hand, though he had no doubt that this girl, who moved with strong athletic grace, was as steady on her feet as he. Her fingers held his tightly, and he flushed with pleasure.

Reaching the opposite bank, they sat on a grassy carpet, their feet dangling in the swirling water. Lacy branches formed an umbrella of filtered shade.

A piece of bark floated by. Lisha nudged it with her toes, speeding it downstream. "A brook like this gives me a clean feeling inside. I could stay here forever, watching it and listening to it. I guess that's the way I wish people were—fresh and changing, but somehow staying the same."

"That's my idea of real character," Bracken said, "being open to new ideas and yet uncompromising in principles."

"Most people are caught up in their own desires."

"I agree. With no time for the valuable things in life."

"My father's like that," Lisha said. "More interested in his work than in being with our family." Her cheeks reddened, as if embarrassed at the candid remark. She scooted back from the brook and went to sit under a nearby tree.

Bracken followed.

After a while, Lisha straightened her shoulders against the tree's wide trunk and said with a trace of wistfulness, "You were smart, Bracken."

"Oh? In what way?"

"Leaving Tizra when you did. I respect you and Silas for going out on your own, for experiencing what others want to do and haven't the nerve to try."

"We haven't collected any medals for bravery."

"Maybe not. But, now that you've explored Nerkush, you can finish your studies and begin a career without feeling there's something wonderful out there that you've missed."

Bracken dropped beside Lisha. "We did see most of the country. Met new people and new ideas. But, I guess curiosity is never completely satisfied."

"What place did you like best?"

"Hard to say. Spending time in the Community in Accad was probably the most exciting. People there write and sing of changes, of better times coming for Ebbern. They believe that if we all care about one another, the better times will come."

A pensive look crossed Lisha's face. "How I wish that were true. But what about the terminus bomb? How long before we're all blown to bits? Something has to change," she declared. "People must open their eyes and be willing to trust."

It was almost a repeat of Bracken's own words as spoken years before. More jaded now, he hadn't changed his basic opinion. "Yes, even though many people consider the inhabitants of the Community as strange, their believing in life and not in destruction is to be admired."

"I like that about you," Lisha said. "You don't walk the same trampled path that so many men my age follow. Their interest is limited to trans-rigs and female conquests. They act stupid and drink too much krem. But, you . . . ," her voice trailed off.

Bracken lay on his side, propped on one elbow. The other hand sifted bits of humus. "I've passed that stage."

"There's something different about you. It's as if you are—I don't know how to say it—puzzling over the stars and the sea. You have an almost child-like inquisitiveness. You want to know where the snow on the mountains comes from and why the leaves on some trees have five points. It's as if you were pushing upward, away from where most men walk, on your way to the sun."

Bracken chuckled, partly from embarrassment, but more to disguise a surge of emotion triggered by Lisha's moist lips and the warm glow in her brown eyes. "On my way to the sun? People have called it by less flattering names. It's been said that I'm on a perpetual search for the true gem."

"I don't see anything wrong with having a goal. Without goals, people stagnate."

"My family accuses me of looking for answers that are bigger and better than anyone else's. That makes me sound selfish. Maybe I am. But, I know there are realms beyond our understanding. Sometimes I think those phenomena have a common denominator. If so, I'm determined to find it."

Bracken sat up and slipped an arm around Lisha. Shadows lengthened and stole across the meadow. The purple blossoms dropped from sight and blended with the green foliage. Bracken said, "My mother believes that real truth is found in the stories of the Volume."

Lisha clasped her hands and tapped her forefingers together. "Sometimes I believe that, too. But not enough, I guess."

Her remark took Bracken by surprise. "How logical is it to rely on words in an ancient book? Why stop with legends when there are worlds waiting to be explored?"

Lisha giggled. "Worlds? Other worlds? You sound like Professor Frimleter."

"Don't laugh too hard," Bracken cautioned. "We can't continue to ignore the many reports of extraordinary happenings." He hesitated before adding, "Maybe I shouldn't tell you this, Lisha, but I've seen a space disk."

"Are you serious?"

"Silas saw it, too."

"After how many bottles of krem?"

Bracken jerked his arm from her shoulders in a show of outrage, not entirely pretense. "That has nothing to do with it."

"If you say so."

Defensively, Bracken said, "I told you about my theory, that there's a connection."

"Between space disks and krem?"

"No! Between space disks and . . . ," he stopped, unwilling to discuss his experience with the mysterious green stone, "other things. For instance, there are rumors that Mingus Stones are circulating and that they can transport a person to a level that we know nothing about."

"Is that how one boards a space disk?" Lisha smothered a giggle.

"I thought you were an open-minded woman."

"Sorry. It all seems utterly fantastic. Besides, Mingus Stones are a thing of the past."

Bracken put his arm back around Lisha. "It is fantastic. That's why I believe these unexplained phenomena hold answers that our world needs. That's why I'm going hunting on Shidow Mountain."

Lisha tilted her head and looked up into Bracken's eyes. "I think it's wonderful that the things that satisfy most people aren't enough for you. But, going off to Shidow Mountain? I'm worried. . . ."

Bracken cupped her face in his hand and stopped her protest with a long kiss.

Soft sounds of the brook's ever-moving water blended with calls of the night birds welcoming the dusk.

"Bracken," Lisha whispered. "Promise me you'll be careful."

His fingers brushed across her lips, across her delicate cheek. He sensed her response. "I'll be careful, very careful. I've found something else that's extremely important to me, and I don't want to lose it."

The water in the brook drifted downstream, its flow undisturbed until long after the sun's last rays had ceased to sparkle on the rippling surface.

* * *

A few days later, Bracken's trans-rig jerked to a halt outside his home. He strode into the family gathering room.

"You missed the evening meal," informed Amont. "Mother and I have already eaten." He confronted Bracken in a fighting stance. Bracken responded valiantly until Amont wrestled him to the floor.

Myra appeared, waving a plate. A smile wreathed her rosy face. "I made your favorite stew."

"Thanks, Mother, but I'm not hungry."

Myra looked dubious.

"As a matter of fact . . . ," he hesitated. They would probably make too much of his news.

Amont announced, "Father's coming."

Myra scolded her husband, "Kressdek, you worked late again. Sit down. I'll bring you some stew."

"Just a cup of tea."

Concern clouded Myra's blue eyes. "I wish you'd eat something."

"Just tea."

"Do you want a cup, too, Bracken?"

Ordinarily, Bracken would have departed to follow his own pursuits. But tonight he stayed, a detached observer.

After Myra brought the tea, she summoned Amont. "It's time for the evening lesson." She settled herself with the Volume on her lap and patted the seat beside her.

"I'm too old for the evening lesson," complained Amont, aiming a dark look at Bracken.

Bracken saw the wistful expression Myra tried to hide. To her, the family was all-important. She preferred not to face Bracken's independence. Ten years of roaming around Nerkush was simply ignored. He was back now. That was what counted.

As Myra read from the Volume, Amont's thoughts seemed faraway. When she paused, he said, "It's hard to believe that a man who died can return."

"Not *can*," Myra said firmly. "The Prince of Wonder *will* return and destroy the Night Ruler."

Amont looked skeptical.

Bracken didn't blame him. He had been younger than Amont when he pegged this as just another myth. He hadn't changed his mind.

Myra raised her eyebrows at Kressdek, who focused his attention on clearing a place for his empty cup. Bracken chuckled inwardly. His mother wouldn't get much help from Kressdek on that subject.

"You know the story, Amont," Myra said patiently. "The Prince of Wonder once lived here on Ebbern. He died, but he left the grave. Only those who ask the Prince of Wonder to save them will live with him forever. Everyone who follows the evil Night Ruler will die forever."

"Most of my friends say they'll believe that story when they see the Prince of Wonder fighting the Night Ruler."

Myra hugged her son, who was nearly as tall as she. "With faith, we can believe that which we cannot see."

* * *

After Amont went to bed, Bracken broke his news to Myra and Kressdek. "The man from the Currency Center contacted me. We met tonight at the Brighton Inn."

Myra's eyes widened. "Did he offer you a position?"

Bracken nodded. "Part-time at first, in their bridging program." In answer to her perplexed expression, Bracken explained, "It's a program with flexible hours that allows students to continue taking classes."

"What an honor!" Myra exclaimed. "And you'd be at the branch right here in Tizra."

"I don't know about honor. Trasent probably selected me because I'm older than the other applicants."

"Trasent. What a nice name. I'm sure," Myra said proudly, "Trasent chose you because you're the best person for the job."

"Spoken like a loyal mother," Bracken teased. He propped his chin on his hands and waited expectantly for his father's reaction.

Kressdek worked his lips thoughtfully. "Currency Center, huh? Always knew you had a head for figures. Just a matter of applying yourself."

Bracken grimaced.

His father continued. "With that kind of training, there's no telling what you can do. Why, it could prepare you for almost any kind of work, whether you moved up in the financial world or," he paused meaningfully, "if you decided to operate a small business of your own."

Bracken bit back a retort.

His mother interjected, "We're both proud of you. When do you begin?"

"Not for a couple of weeks. I have something to do first."

He shrugged off his parents' alarmed looks. "It's okay. I cleared my starting date with Trasent. He understands." Bracken got up to leave.

"I don't know," Kressdek worried, "if they want you now . . . postponing that way doesn't sound like the best idea. What do you have to do that's important enough to jeopardize a good job?"

"I'm taking a few days off. Going hiking up on Mt. Shidow." Bracken heard his father's sharp intake of breath and knew instantly what was going through the man's mind.

"What about your classes?" Myra intervened quickly.

A scale model of a trans-rig belonging to Amont lay on a shelf.

Bracken picked it up. "No harm in missing a few." He turned the model over and over. "I know what you're thinking. But, it's only a short vacation. I'm leaving tomorrow morning." He forced a smile. "I'll be back to the old grind soon enough."

"I thought this time . . . ," his father began but was interrupted by Myra.

"Of course, you'll be back. And I'm sure Trasent feels that you'll be a better employee by getting this out of your. . . ." she too stopped. "I mean, you'll be refreshed and ready to start after a few days vacation."

Bracken spun the wheels on Amont's model furiously.

Kressdek reached for it, as if to save it from demolition. "I guess you won't be using your trans-rig if you're hiking. Good thing I inquired about that repair job it needs. This will be a perfect time to get the work done." He ignored his wife's startled signals. "I'll take it in tomorrow."

Bracken dredged up untapped depths of self-control. Muttering about fresh air, he stalked out of the house, slamming the door as if blasting it off its hinges would solve everything.

CHAPTER 7

With hands that seemed experienced at what they did, the man on Mt. Shidow tightened the ignition wires to the terminals on top of a charge generator. He pulled off his hat and wiped sweat from his forehead. Carefully, he pushed sparse strands of reddish-brown hair back over his baldish crown and replaced the hat. Then, making sure that the charge generator was steady, he raised its arm. He squinted at a point some distance away. A smile creased his face.

"Bless your wormy heart, Cibbmingus! You're making me the richest person on Ebbern." The man's muscles knotted, and he thrust down the generator's arm.

It wasn't much of an explosion, but Layozz had been a miner most of his nearly four decades. He knew how to cover up a mine entrance so only he could find it again, and how to uncover it.

With the dust still settling, Layozz ran to the mouth of the excavation. Yes, sir, if he handled himself correctly, took time to build a good clientele, and above all, guarded his secret, he'd be set for life.

Coughing, he ducked his head and entered the mine. Using a small search lamp, he proceeded cautiously, examining the stability of the support beams. Nothing appeared to have been disturbed since his last visit.

He reached a metallic wall built across the tunnel to form a sealed partition. In its center was a closed hatchway. To his left were stored the protective clothing and helmet necessary for entering the chamber beyond the wall. The clothing looked stiff and worn, but Layozz knew from experience that it would give him sufficient protection. He rested his lamp on a rock and put on the bulky outfit, pausing to rub away a smudge of dirt that marred his recent manicure. Mining was untidy work.

He consulted a worn piece of paper. Carefully, he punched several areas on the panel of the recessed lock console in the wall. At once, the hatchway's oval cover opened. Putting on gloves, the miner stepped through.

Standing in the chamber on the other side, Layozz ran his tongue over dry lips. Before him lay a treasure greater than he had once imagined.

He'd had his disappointments. Played-out claims and false hopes had left him desperate for a strike. Then, not long before, he'd come across the deserted shack, its owner dead and gone. No one else had bothered to search carefully, assuming that the old man, himself a hapless miner, had nothing of value. And probably, the old man did not know about the map rotting behind a board in his shack. How fortunate for Layozz that he did not think like other people, or he would not have found the map, undoubtedly drawn by Cibbmingus himself, the map of the Mingus Mine.

Scattered over the floor of the chamber, stones of various sizes emitted a pale green glow. Fragments of green light dotted every surface, giving promise of countless other stones imbedded in the chamber's rock walls. Layozz opened the pack he had brought and removed an assortment of silver-colored boxes. If the stones weren't properly contained, he would be unnecessarily exposed to their effect.

Layozz gleefully stooped to collect loose stones on the floor. He held each one in his gloved hand, examined it through the helmet's visor, and gently placed it in a silver box, as one would deposit a precious trinket in a velvet-lined chest. Carefully, he put the boxes in his pack.

Outside the mine, he sealed its entrance again with a small explosive charge. He consulted the old map. Then, he plunged into the surrounding forest.

Let all of Nerkush think that the Mingus Mine had died with Cibbmingus. Nothing could please Layozz more, except the fact that he himself had access to the mine and thus controlled the source of the Mingus Stones.

* * *

Bracken and Silas dropped their packs and sank to the hard ground beside a little-used trail on Mt. Shidow. Nearby, the waters of a small lake lapped gently against its rocky shore.

"As soon as I can make my legs work again," moaned Silas, "I'm going to have a drink from that lake. It looks better to me now than all the krem in Tizra."

Not wanting to show his own fatigue, Bracken pushed himself up and meandered over to the lake. He drank deeply from his cupped hands. The lake rippled away from him, his reflection wobbling on the surface of the clear water.

Their journey from Tizra over open fields and across the slopes of Mt. Shidow had taken a toll. Bracken disliked the discouragement that crept along with them. He could handle the physical tiredness, but he'd hoped to find some sign of the Mingus Mine by now. They had ever enlarged their area of search, moving quickly and lightly. To their disappointment, they'd had no reason to return to their base camp for the small amount of mining equipment Bracken had hidden there.

Bracken looked across the lake, unable to shake a feeling of sadness and guilt. He'd coerced Silas into coming. In the old days, Silas would have supported him all the way. Was this what returning to society and conforming to its mores did to friends? What would it be like after they actually began their so-called careers?

Silas joined him. "Let me at that water."

"Here!" Bracken hurled a handful at Silas' face.

They shed their clothing and dived into the lake. Revived, Bracken swam purposefully. Silas was content to tread water and gaze up Mt. Shidow's massive sides toward its towering peak.

"How would you like to be on the top?" asked Bracken, gliding over beside Silas.

"Not even with clothes on. I like climbing *around* mountains, not over them."

"Hey, we've scaled plenty of mountains. Remember the time at . . ." Bracken cut off his own words and peered toward the bank in sudden alarm. He'd detected a movement in the brush where they'd left their clothes. "Hold it," he whispered.

Silas quickly twisted around, and slipped lower into the water. With the same silent communication they'd relied on for years, Silas nodded and began a slow sidestroke away from Bracken. Bracken executed a smooth surface dive and disappeared.

Silas swam until his fingers scraped the lake bottom. Seeing nothing amiss, he doubled up, then stood and headed casually for shore. He was within an arm's length of his clothes when a man emerged from the brush.

Caught between embarrassment and fright, Silas stopped short. He gathered as much dignity as possible. "Hey, fella!"

"How's the water?" inquired the stranger pleasantly. "Name's Layozz."

At that, Bracken stepped from behind a boulder near the water's edge, adopting the same friendly tone. "Hi, friend." He took in the newcomer's fine quality boots and outdoor clothing. The wide leather bracelet that encircled his wrist marked a style worn by many men a few years older than Bracken. "Bracken here, and this is Silas. From Tizra."

"What are you doing in these parts?"

"A little hiking," Bracken answered. "How about you?"

"Oh, I've been mining in this place for years."

At the word *mining*, Bracken's thoughts spun with possibilities. By then, he and Silas were getting into their clothes. More appropriately dressed, Bracken felt better able to deal with this stranger. "So, you're a miner? We heard blasting. Are you working a claim?"

"Me? I don't do much of that anymore." Layozz pulled off his boots, giving them a quick polish with his sleeve. "Beautiful sight, Mt. Shidow. Strange that more people don't travel this way." He splashed lake water on his face. Before replacing his hat, he meticulously smoothed his thinning hair. "Fine with me. I enjoy being away from the crowds."

Lulled by the man's informal friendliness and a certain likeable charm, Bracken began to feel at ease.

"Pull up a rock," Layozz invited. "Make yourself comfortable. That is, unless you've got someplace to go."

Bracken accepted the invitation, but saw Silas pacing the ground where they'd left their clothing, kicking at the lowgrowing grass. "Lose something, Silas?"

"Can't find all the stuff from my pack."

Layozz pointed a short distance away. "Is that yours?"

"How'd it get over there?"

"As I was saying," Layozz went on, "the only people besides you two that I've run into this trip were some NAFIS fellows."

"NAFIS?" Silas scooped up his belongings and hurried over.

Bracken asked evenly, "What are they doing?"

Layozz grinned. "A team of so-called experts is looking for the old Mingus Mine."

Bracken squinted, trying to control an eye muscle that twitched in excitement. "I've heard talk that it's here on Mt. Shidow."

"Could be, but NAFIS will never find it." Layozz shook his head confidently. "Nobody can find it."

"Where are they searching?" Silas ignored Bracken's cautious frown.

"They blocked off a hillside over there." Layozz motioned vaguely. "Chased me away. Hush-hush stuff."

Bracken tried to reflect only casual interest, "I heard that Mingus Stones are showing up."

Layozz pulled on his boots. "They're showing up, all right."

Silas made no pretense of his interest. "You've seen Mingus Stones, real ones?"

"Sure."

Relief shuddered through Bracken. At times, he'd nearly convinced himself that finding the mysterious green stone that day in the forest was a fantasy. But, if Layozz spoke the truth, Bracken could indeed have found a genuine Mingus Stone. He felt exonerated, forgiven for believing that he'd experienced those actions or dreams or hallucinations—whatever they were. His pulse raced at the implication that his encounter was real.

"Plenty are circulating in Accad," Layozz said, "mostly in the Community."

"Then someone knows where the Mingus Mine is," Silas declared, "unless there's more than one mine."

"Who needs a mine? I can tell you where to get stones."

"How come you'd do that for us?" demanded Bracken.

Layozz grinned. "You guys are okay."

Silas glanced at his pack about the same time it dawned on Bracken why Layozz trusted them. A peek at the identification inside convinced him that they had no connection with the Pirax or NAFIS.

Suddenly, Layozz's grin faded. His eyes, green with brown flecks, narrowed as he stared intently at a huge cinder cone off to the right. Bracken followed his gaze but could detect nothing out of the ordinary.

Layozz stood up. "Time for me to move on. I'm headed for Accad. You're welcome to travel along."

Confused at this abrupt change, Bracken turned to consult Silas.

Impatiently, Layozz said, "If you're going with me, come on, both of you. You're so interested in the stone, I'll see that you get a taste of its power once we're at Accad."

Bracken overruled Silas' silent protest by grabbing up his things and starting after Layozz. Silas looked unhappy but did the same.

Saying little, they tramped along the trail around the lake. Just before entering a thick stand of trees, Bracken glimpsed a momentary flash coming from the direction of the cinder cone. If it wasn't so unlikely, Bracken might have thought it was a reflection from a mirror or perhaps a scope.

CHAPTER 8

Layozz pulled his trans-rig past the Nerkush Hall of the Fathers in the busy metropolis of Accad. "The selfish ruling the ignorant. It won't be that way forever." He pointed to an upper story of the stately, old building. "NAFIS." He spit the word like a curse, hunched over the wheel, and turned his attention back to the crowded street.

Bracken followed his new friend's lead. "Our government is as rigid and unyielding as the stone pillars holding up its offices."

From the back, Silas observed, "You'd better be glad those stone pillars are rigid and unyielding." He craned his neck to view the slender spire on the building's roof. "Some people don't appreciate engineering skill when they see it."

They passed the wharf area, where transports coming across the Sea of Aurin entered Accad's port, one of the busiest in Nerkush.

"Silas is a structural engineer," Bracken explained, "or soon will be."

Layozz drummed his fingers on the wheel, waiting to move ahead. "That so? I hope you don't build any structures in Accad. Too many people now."

"More than the last time we were here. Huh, Silas?"

Silas grunted agreement.

Bracken tried to interest himself in the passing scene, but a different subject commanded his attention. "What about the stones?" he said at last. "When are we getting to that?"

Layozz smirked. "Patience. Got an errand or two to run first. Don't worry. I won't disappoint you."

Bracken found it increasingly difficult to wait. "This is the kind of thing I've been wanting to try for years. I've always believed there was more to existence than the limited things we perceive in this level." His warning glance reminded Silas of their hurried decision not to reveal Bracken's earlier encounter with the mysterious green stone.

"Here's the Community," Layozz said. "You'll have your chance soon enough."

Bracken recognized the unique section of Accad. Its inhabitants came from all over Nerkush, as if drawn by some hidden force and bonded by a universal desire for change.

Flower boxes hung from the exteriors of ancient houses and shops in the small neighborhood. Containers of plants dotted sidewalks and alleyways, contrasting with the rather sterile atmosphere of Accad.

Layozz parked his trans-rig near the Brazen Eagle, a favorite local shop known for spiced liquids and tantalizing foods. The three men climbed out. Layozz glanced in both directions and, after slinging his pack over his shoulder, locked the rig. They ambled along the sidewalk to the Brazen Eagle's heavy wooden door. Silas, the last one in, dragged a fingernail across the sculptured metal eagle embossed on the door.

Pleasant chatter and mellow music blended in the smokefilled air above the tables. Layozz sauntered past the customers to the service window. Behind the counter, a heavyset man filled a large earthen crock with hot fragrant liquid.

"How's business, Zactor?" Layozz asked.

The man looked up. "Layozz! Haven't seen you in weeks. Thought you decided to stay on that mountain of yours."

Layozz leaned on the counter and matched the jovial manner with a wink. "I've got good news for you."

The proprietor stroked his scraggly beard, his eyes surveying the room, lingering on Layozz' companions.

Layozz explained, "Bracken and Silas rode in with me. Met them up on Mt. Shidow." He helped himself to a stick of dried fruit from a bowl on the counter. "How about our deal?"

Zactor wiped his hands on his coarse apron and headed for the back of the building.

Layozz told Bracken and Silas, "You fellows find a table. I'll be only a minute," and followed the fat man.

When they were out of hearing, Silas grabbed Bracken's elbow and hissed, "I'm not sure that this is a good idea. What do we know about Layozz? Do you think he really has the stones?"

"If he doesn't, he's getting them right now. Take it easy. Remember, a generation or so ago, people used stones whenever they felt like it."

Silas frowned. "Ever think that NAFIS could have had good reason for outlawing them?"

Bracken ignored Silas' objection, intent on seizing this opportunity to approach the Mingus realm gradually and safely. Bracken had to reach the creature of light in the Mingus realm, and soon. As unlikely as it seemed, Bracken couldn't dismiss the fact that he'd come away from his experience in the realm of the stone with the promise that he could save Ebbern from destruction.

Layozz returned and led the way out the door, still nibbling on the fruit stick.

Bracken's excitement grew as they moved through the Community. He'd forgotten the district's extreme casualness. Turning his head at the wild colors and styles, he confided to Silas, "Maybe we've been back with the narrow thinkers too long."

"Or maybe we're getting too old," Silas grumbled. "All this isn't as thrilling as it used to be."

"You must admit the place is unique." Bracken stepped around jewelry displayed on a dark cloth spread over a walk crowded with pedestrians. A girl, her straight blonde hair falling like a curtain over her face, sat cross-legged on a corner of the cloth, stringing a necklace of beads and shells.

Layozz ducked into a used book shop, leaving Bracken and Silas outside. Two bare-chested men lounged in a sunlit doorway, listening to another play a stam. A couple stood against a wall, locked in a sensual embrace.

Layozz emerged from the book shop. He smiled at a striking girl with flowers in her hair and a tinkling bell hanging by a ribbon around her neck. She returned the smile, and Bracken feared that Layozz would desert them. But he moved in the opposite direction. Bracken and Silas followed.

They came to a two-story house with a rock exterior. "This is it," Layozz said with obvious pride.

"You live here?" Silas asked in awe.

"I need a big place. Lots of guests."

Across the street, a rectangular park formed an oasis of green in the crowded Community. A group of musicians entertained an appreciative audience.

"They're good." Bracken admired the skill and ease with which they played. "Is that the Golden Flight?"

"Sure. That's Chepa and his group. I'm meeting them across the bay in Demur tomorrow afternoon. He has a houseboat tied up there." Layozz commented dryly, "A touch of the stone would improve their sound."

Inside, the house was even more impressive. The furnishings were good quality, and someone kept the place clean. "Take a seat," Layozz invited and then excused himself. Silas sank on a couch that looked more comfortable than he did.

But Bracken paced in front of a window overlooking the park. When Layozz returned in a clean shirt, Bracken blurted out, "What about trying the stone?"

Layozz wouldn't be hurried. He passed around bottles of krem. "I feel kind of responsible for you two, and I want to make sure you understand a couple of things."

Silas took a swallow and then slammed his bottle down. "Just how safe is it?"

Bracken coughed loudly.

Layozz seemed unruffled. "Hey, Silas is right to ask. If you know what you're doing, like I do, it's perfectly safe."

"What if you don't know what you're doing?" Silas winged a challenge toward Bracken.

Layozz took a drink. "You're looking at a knowledgeable person. There is no need for you to worry. Simply put, there are two kinds of stones. The more powerful variety can lift a person completely out of this level. That's why the stones were outlawed. A few people, lacking the sense to work up gradually, got themselves lost."

Bracken cracked his knuckles and ignored a creeping sensation of fear in the pit of his stomach. This experience would be under expert tutorship.

"Lost?" Silas appeared even more doubtful.

"Take it easy. It's all in the technique, an understanding of what's happening," Layozz said confidently. "It's a matter of yielding to the effect and not fighting it. You'll start with the weaker variety. No problem." Layozz put down his krem bottle. "Are you ready?" He pulled the curtain facing the park and told Bracken, "Sit by Silas."

Bracken complied immediately.

"Like I said, you won't have a problem." Layozz removed a small silver case from his pack and put it on a low table. "These containers prevent leakage."

"Leakage?" Bracken asked, staring at the case.

"If you ever see a stone without the proper container, watch out!"

Silas squirmed to the edge of his seat. "Could one really steal a guy's mind?"

"Absolutely. You gotta know how to handle this stuff."

Silas shot Bracken a look that said, *I told you this was dangerous.*

Feeling doubts of his own, Bracken reminded himself that he'd been looking for the actual mine. Why worry about one small stone?

"Let's begin." Layozz reached for the silver box.

"Wait!" Silas cried hoarsely. "This is crazy. Bracken, we haven't any business trying this. We might have fooled around with it a few years ago, but not now."

Layozz snatched the box and replaced it in his pack.

Bracken fastened his eyes on the pack. "It's not crazy, Silas. It's a way to open up new vistas, new areas of our mind. We don't want to limit ourselves, to shut ourselves away from knowing what's out there waiting for us."

"I tell you, it is stupid. Maybe your mind is already on its way to some other level. Maybe that other time . . ."

"My mind is fine," Bracken interrupted, "and it's going to stay that way."

"Well, I'm not taking chances. I'm leaving!"

Layozz waited, removed from the discussion.

Bracken pleaded, "Silas, stay with me. I have to try this. You've always understood before."

Silas' face twisted in frustration. He clasped both hands to his head, his fingers buried in his thick black hair. "Not this time!" He broke away and stormed out the door.

Bracken sank back on the couch, trying to hide his embarrassment and disappointment. "Guess he's taking his new lifestyle more seriously than I thought."

Layozz shrugged as if nothing of consequence had occurred. "What did he mean with that remark about the other time?"

"Who knows? We don't need him anyway. How do we do this?"

"You go first. That way I can make sure you'll be all right your first time out. Press this button to open the box. Then simply remove the stone and pass it across your forehead."

"That's all?"

"I told you it was simple."

Uncovered, the stone emitted a soft green glow. Gingerly, Bracken removed it from the container. Eager now, he lifted it to his forehead. Slowly, he moved it back and forth.

At first, nothing appeared to be happening. Then, Bracken grinned involuntarily and sensed it spreading over his face. He began to feel light-hearted, then became overwhelmed with joy. He fell back on the couch, laughing uncontrollably. As the effect increased, he lost awareness, first of Layozz, then of his surroundings.

Bracken began to tumble down a furry, warm tunnel. It was soft and pleasant, and it led him into blissful oblivion.

* * *

Near morning, Bracken slowly became aware of the room, of the soft couch on which he lay. He noticed Layozz nearby, peacefully staring at a lighted candle in the center of the room. Bracken lifted his head and marveled, "That was greater than I had expected. Such beauty and color! Such dimension! It's beyond words!"

"And it's limitless . . . cosmic prairies stretching forever . . . uncharted seas of bliss," Layozz murmured in dreamy agreement. "It's the new frontier this Community has waited for."

Bracken sat up, choked with wonder. "I see now why NAFIS wants the stone under its control."

Layozz's eyes mirrored the soft candle light. "They want it for themselves."

Bracken fastened his gaze on the candle. "It's all beginning to make sense."

"Those narrow fools don't want people to get the secret. But it's too big a secret for NAFIS. It's beyond anyone's control. Something more important than any of us has a hand in what's happening. That's why we've gathered here in the Community. There's a new hope for Nerkush."

"And those boxes hold the key!" Discovery made music of Bracken's words.

"Exactly." Layozz's voice took on a tone of harmonious rapture. "Soon the whole of Nerkush will begin to understand."

"It's all fitting together," responded Bracken joyfully, "becoming clear. I'm so happy. I can't stand such happiness." He fell back and began to weep for joy.

Layozz smiled knowingly, a tear rolling down his own cheek.

* * *

Dawn was still a promise when the two men slipped from Layozz's house. They walked serenely past the park and down the quiet thoroughfares of the Community as the last morning stars blinked in the rapidly vanishing darkness. They wandered aimlessly, Layozz with his ever-present pack, leading the way. Bracken, also lugging his pack, was content to follow. They moved into a narrow street.

Suddenly something warned Bracken. He sensed danger. Trouble at this peaceful moment was unthinkable. But a heat pellet hissed by his head and burned into the wall beside him.

Bracken and Layozz bolted. They rounded the first corner. A glance behind revealed several figures slipping from the semidarkness in pursuit.

Thoughts of peace and bliss vanished. Bracken sprinted down the street, barely able to keep abreast of Layozz, who moved as adroitly as a swift-footed animal fleeing for its life.

They ducked into a sheltered alcove. Layozz pulled a hand weapon from his pack. Its burnished surface glinted in the light of a street lamp.

A surly voice shouted from across the street. "You know what we want."

Bewildered, Bracken looked to Layozz.

"Give it up and we'll let you go." This new demand came from a secluded doorway down the street.

"Probably think I'm unarmed," muttered Layozz. He pulled three small objects from his pack and shoved them at the startled Bracken.

Bracken felt the rough, oval shape of handbombs. He fingered the detonator caps. Where had Layozz gotten these illegal weapons? Was there no end to the man's resources? Bracken slipped them into his pack, keeping his hand curved around one. He knew the havoc a handbomb could cause, but he had never imagined himself using one.

The surly voice demanded, "Toss it out. If you don't, we'll come get it!"

Layozz snatched up a piece of paper trampled underfoot and a rock from a flower pot in the cramped shelter. Hastily wrapping the rock in the paper, he called boldly, "Okay! Okay! I don't want trouble. Here it comes!" He threw the package into the street.

A figure ran from the shadows and headed for the bundle. Layozz raised his hand weapon. Aiming carefully, he fired. The heat pellet rushed from the cylinder and struck the squatting figure. The figure moaned once and then collapsed.

The fire was returned instantly. Pellets narrowly missed Layozz's head. Two other figures rushed toward them, weaving in and out of doorways.

"Split up!" ordered Layozz, and shoved Bracken from the alcove. "You go that way!" With that, Layozz jumped from shelter and scrambled madly across the pavement. Bracken last saw him crouched behind a trans-rig, firing his hand weapon. A pellet hit Layozz' pursuer in the arm, spinning him about, but not taking him out of action.

Bracken scrambled in the direction Layozz had ordered. He knew that Layozz could outrun a wounded man. But Bracken wasn't so sure that he could get away from the heavy pounding he heard hot on his own trail.

Doorways passed in a blur. The few early risers dodged to escape the chase. An alleyway loomed ahead. Should he cut over and follow it, or stay out in the open?

Tiring, Bracken's vision clouded. The alleyway faded. Had he passed it? A new, indistinct substance moved ahead of him. It turned sharply. There was the alleyway. Bracken turned, too, and followed a gleam of bright color, shimmering red in the predawn light.

The red disappeared. Bracken hesitated. Then, without warning, he was jerked into a dimly lit passageway. A cloaked figure pulled him along a corridor. Behind, a volley of heat pellets struck the wall where Bracken had stood only moments before.

CHAPTER 9

Still dazed from the sudden ambush, Bracken found himself sitting in the dim interior of the Brazen Eagle, accepting a steaming cup of tea from his cloaked benefactor. The old man, who had introduced himself as Dalfang, pulled a chair to the small table. He met Bracken's confusion with a faint smile, which seemed to hint at amusing thoughts.

The gray beard and maturity gave the stranger a scholarly look. Deeply set, pale blue eyes reflected an air of wisdom. But the heavy cloak failed to disguise a strong physique, and Bracken believed that, regardless of how ancient Dalfang looked, he possessed enviable strength.

"You appear puzzled, my friend." Dalfang said.

Bracken laughed self-consciously. "I am. The probability of your being where I needed you at just the right time. . . ."

"Some would say a fortuitous circumstance."

Who was this man? Bracken stammered the first question that came to mind, "Are you from Accad?"

"I come to Accad on occasion. I live north of here, in the Forest of Zorek."

"I've never met anyone from there. In fact, I think of it as being almost a distant wilderness."

"Zorek is not far from here in distance. However, it is set apart, almost isolated, and the mountains in that part of the coastal range are surprisingly rugged for their height."

"What brings you to Accad?" Bracken grew more bold. "I mean, specifically to the alleyway behind the Brazen Eagle?"

"I have a purpose for being where I am." Dalfang's voice rang with agreeable resonance over garbled background conversations. "Others come from time to time to live in the Forest of Zorek. They realize that living here in Accad tightens the nerves and restricts the senses." The man's erect posture and confident manner exuded an air of majesty that lent credibility to his prediction, "As time goes on, an increasing number of people will join me."

The aura of genuineness surrounding this man intrigued Bracken. "What do you do in Zorek?"

"The Forest of Zorek is a pleasant place. I wouldn't want to live anywhere else."

Bracken was tempted to repeat his question, but he sensed a necessity for patience. Subdued melodies from a musician's stam hovered over the table. The scent of burning incense mingled with clouds of smoke and pungent smells of herbal teas.

Dalfang lifted a finger to his lips and slyly whispered, "I have a secret reason for being in the Forest of Zorek."

Bracken felt like an adolescent being teased by someone older and wiser. Even so, an eager curiosity consumed him until, as unrestrained as a child, he asked, "Are you going to tell me the secret?"

Dalfang leaned forward, and together with his cloak, filled Bracken's field of vision. "Have you heard of the world of Malchag?"

In disappointment and sudden wariness, Bracken glanced around the room, deriving solace that he was not alone with this man. Of course, he'd heard of Malchag but in a context that might offend this person. Bracken regarded Malchag as nonexistent, to be classed with stories about the Prince of Wonder and other fanciful tales. Fearful of revealing his skepticism, he phrased his answer carefully. "Yes. However, I've never devoted much thought to it."

"Don't be uncomfortable," Dalfang said gently. "Many people consider the world of Malchag to be a myth."

Bracken *was* uncomfortable. He drained the last of his tea.

"Of course, it's partly true, you know. But, many fail to realize that myths are often based on fact."

"Absolutely," Bracken gladly agreed.

"People are doubtful of such things as Malchag. Mostly this is because they are too preoccupied with vain pursuits. You see," Dalfang's intensity left no doubt about his seriousness, "there really is a world of Malchag."

To cover embarrassment at the outlandish statement, Bracken asked courteously, "What exactly is it? I've heard many things."

"A vast realm of beauty and peace that few have ever found."

Bracken voiced the obvious question, "If it's so beautiful, why haven't more people found it?"

"Because, from ancient times, its gates have been kept hidden."

"Gates?"

"Yes. One gate is hidden in the Forest of Zorek."

"Hidden? From whom? How did you find it?"

"Many years ago, a guardian of the door showed me the entrance. He commissioned me to take his place and instructed me to keep the entrance secret until people were ready."

"Why are you telling me this?"

"There is something in you that tells me that our meeting today has significance. Perhaps it is your searching soul."

A shiver crept up Bracken's back, rippling over his skin like an icy wind. He put his hands on his cup, but its warmth was long gone. This man's perception was eerie.

"You are skeptical of Malchag, Bracken."

I certainly am, Bracken thought, *but it's hard to resist such confidence from one who acts and looks like a fountain of wisdom.* A desire to investigate the possible existence of Malchag sprouted and took root.

"I feel you will change your mind once you stand in the Forest of Zorek."

Bracken's desire grew. He owed it to himself to investigate. "If Malchag really exists, I want to go there."

From within his cloak, Dalfang produced a small piece of paper. "Here are directions to my home in the Forest of Zorek."

Bracken held the paper to catch the morning light now streaming into the Brazen Eagle's skimpy windows. Across the top was written *The Door to the Anindi Passage of Malchag.* The information below seemed ordinary enough. He folded it and put it away. "So, if I show up at your house, you'll give me a guided tour?"

"You could say that."

"Perhaps I'll pay you a visit."

The bearded man got to his feet. "I must leave, my friend. I am sure I will see you, and soon."

This stranger had stepped between Bracken and death. Feeling woefully inadequate, Bracken offered, "I want to thank you again for saving my life."

Dalfang gathered his cloak around his body and pulled the hood over his head. His pale blue eyes shone through its cast shadow. He said, "I saved your life for good reason."

* * *

Bracken decided against returning to Layozz's house. Silas was most likely on his way home to Tizra, and Silas was the person Bracken really wanted to see. He needed to show his friend that the stone experience had not harmed either him or their friendship. But Bracken was not ready to return to Tizra.

Asking directions, he set out for Demur. He circled the Bay of Accad, accepting some rides, and reached Demur in the early afternoon. Bracken had no desire to get mixed up again with Layozz or with the gang chasing him. But Layozz was a connection to the Mingus Stone. And Layozz had said he would be at the band leader's houseboat in Demur that afternoon.

Streams of water rushed down the green surfaces of hills above Demur and spilled into the bay. At the mouth of one stream, a group of houseboats bobbed on the water, their weathered hulls creaking as small breakers lapped against their sides. Bracken was directed to a vessel, a little larger and in better repair than her neighbors. There, mooring lines dipping in the water, rested the *Sea Cradle*.

Four men sat on the deck in rope chairs. From the dock, Bracken introduced himself to Chepa, leader of the Golden Flight. "Saw you performing in the Community yesterday," Bracken said, restraining the excitement he felt at conversing with a professional musician. "I'm looking for a friend of mine that might be visiting you today."

Chepa waved Bracken aboard. "Your friend beat you here."

Silas jumped up and strode across the deck. "Thought you'd show up here, old buddy."

Overjoyed at seeing Silas, Bracken clapped him on the back. "I supposed you'd be on your way to Tizra. What made you stick around?"

"Couldn't pass up the chance to rub shoulders with a great band. Figured you couldn't either," Silas laughed, "so, I came looking for you."

"Right!" Bracken roared with exaggerated mirth, ignoring a jab of conscience that reminded him he'd actually come to find Layozz. "Sure glad to see you! I was afraid . . ."

"Nah!" Silas grinned. "You're never getting rid of me."

Chepa introduced band members Yaavin and Shor and rounded up a chair for Bracken. "Silas says that you play the stam. He's shy about giving us a taste of his own talent."

After a respectable interval of conversation, Chepa ventured, "I hear that you've experienced the stone."

Taken by surprise, Bracken only shrugged.

A brisk sea breeze whisked away gray smoke from Chepa's pipe. "The guys and I have been thinking that we'd like to add a little excitement to our life. And to our music."

Bracken still didn't know what to say. He didn't understand the power of the stone. The one he and Layozz had shared the night before had not resulted in anything like Bracken's encounter with Hiffornak on the upper level.

As for adding excitement, Chepa's life seemed to lack nothing. A voluptuous girl, dripping with beads and carrying a loaf of bread in one hand and a bag emblazoned with a local market emblem in the other, walked on board. She threw an intimate look to Chepa before she disappeared at the far end of the boat. Bracken surmised that hordes of people would envy an up-and-coming musician with his own band and this unhampered lifestyle.

Yaavin said, "There's lots of talk about the stone."

Shor fingered an oddly-shaped pendant dangling over his bare chest. "I've heard rumors that it's getting plentiful and popular in the Community. For some, it's great. But, others . . . well . . . others just haven't come back."

Chepa chewed his pipe stem.

Bracken decided to be candid. "Sure I tried the stone. It was wonderful. I wish everyone could experience what I did."

Chepa clasped his hands behind his head and leaned back. "New experiences always hold problems for doubters. A person has to be open to whatever life offers because it doesn't wait for stragglers."

Bracken decided that Chepa was deeper than he appeared. Ever cautious, Silas warned, "I hear NAFIS and the Pirax are coming down hard on anyone they suspect of using the stone."

"Sure, sure," retorted Shor. "Doesn't matter to them whether it's good or bad. Any hint of a problem with anything, and NAFIS sticks it on the controlled substance list."

More Golden Flight members arrived. Chepa watched them trudge down the pier hauling their equipment. He stood up decisively and told Yaavin and Shor, "We're falling into a dead and boring rut. I think the Mingus Stone can help lift us out."

Yaavin slapped his knee in sudden agreement. "Roon swears by it. That's my brother," he told Bracken.

"Nothing to lose," concluded Shor.

Chepa called Bracken and Silas aside. "Kind of funny the way you two got here today, and you both play the stam. I don't understand it, but I'm not a person that fights fate. What about sitting in on a couple of rehearsal numbers?"

Silas backed away. "Bracken's the one you want. He's a real musician."

"Not good enough for even a practice session with the Golden Flight," Bracken protested.

Chepa laughed. "Who knows? We may all be better than we ever imagined—after Layozz arrives."

Bracken and Silas stayed on deck when the others went into the main room of the houseboat.

Silas propped a foot on the railing. "You going to use the Mingus Stone with these guys?"

"I might. Might not."

"But you want to, don't you? So you can explore new levels, like you always say? And maybe to punch up your music?"

Bracken didn't answer.

Silas pulled his foot from the railing and idly kicked at a soft white blob dropped on the deck by a passing seabird. "Well, if you're going to, maybe I'll give it a try. I guess friends can do a little partying together."

CHAPTER 10

Layozz slipped into the main room of the *Sea Cradle* dressed in the casual style expected of a resident of the Community, even though his clothing bore the mark of custom-tailoring. Exhibiting a diplomat's skill, he greeted everyone with a firm handshake and accepted Silas' presence with, "Good to see you again, Silas." He grinned at Bracken and announced, "Bracken and I enjoyed an exhilarating morning walk."

Chepa spoke irritably, "We were beginning to think you wouldn't show."

"I've been running behind ever since that morning walk."

Chepa motioned Layozz to a seat. "Now that you're here . . ."

"Yes." Layozz slipped his pack from his shoulder and waited for the others to gather around. Silas and Bracken sat on a couch outside the tight circle of musicians. Layozz took a silver container from his pack. "Inside this is a Mingus Stone. One touch of it brings a new mind, a new life, a new person." With dramatic flair, he lifted the lid of the silver case.

Even these musicians, accustomed to stage glitter and sparkle, reacted audibly to the beauty of the glowing stone.

"How does it work?" asked Chepa.

"Right now, all of us are being touched by it, but the power will increase as you pick up the stone and pass it over your forehead."

"Increase? How much?" asked a band member.

"Don't worry. For most of you," Layozz winked almost imperceptibly at Bracken, "this will be your initial voyage. This stone is quite safe for your first experience."

"What happens to the stone after we pass it around?" someone asked Layozz.

"Once used, the power fades rapidly."

Chepa, as the group's leader, gingerly lifted the stone. "Wow! My hand tingles just to hold it." He moved the stone across his forehead. "I feel the power already."

The others took a turn. Yaavin chuckled and then began to laugh uncontrollably. The giggling became contagious. People slid from their seats and rolled on the floor.

Bracken passed the stone over his own head. Silas was beginning to laugh. The Mingus effect increased. A sense of hopelessness momentarily overcame Bracken as he realized he could not stop what was happening to him. But anxiety quickly vanished with the wonder of the world that enveloped him. Colors in the room became more vivid, his sight keener. He lifted his hand and gazed into his palm. He could almost see the individual pores in his skin. His body fluctuated between chills and warm flashes.

"This is crazy, isn't it?" Chepa called.

"Yesssss . . . ," responded Yaavin. "I can't take it all in. My whole body feels like it's gone to sleep. Your face, Chepa! It's bending." Yaavin roared with laughter, but abruptly stopped. "I'm falling!" His hands flailed the air.

The room began to pulsate as though it were alive. Color and sound harmonized in a sensual symphony. Undulating waves of warmth flooded through Bracken's mind and emotions.

Layozz offered advice. "Keep relaxing. You're going deeper. Everything is fine."

"So peaceful." Bracken heard Silas exclaim, and then contradict himself, "No, I'm afraid. There's something wrong."

"Release your fears, and leave them behind," Layozz urged gently. "It's like flowing down a river . . . drifting. We're all floating on a gentle sea. The breeze is catching our sails. We're outward bound. Relax and release." Layozz's voice became a firm, but gentle hand lifting everyone above fear. "Soon a new flow will start, and then you'll understand."

Conversations rippled through the band members. "How long will this last?" someone asked. "It seems like we've been here for hours."

Layozz explained. "This is but a brief transition phase. In a few moments, we move deeper. Your minds are now absorbing the Mingus impulses. Our voyage has begun."

Bracken felt at ease. The atmosphere seemed to glow. "A cloud of light is filling all the space. Can you see it, Silas?"

"Yes," Silas said. "Layozz . . . look at Layozz. What's going on? His face is glowing."

Bracken's gaze traveled around the room. Everyone's face was radiant. But Layozz's was brighter than all the rest.

Silas pointed to Layozz. "His whole body is platinum, hazy and soft. How could I have been so dumb? How could I have doubted him? He's shown us the way to a state of pure bliss!"

Layozz continued to guide. "Keep on relaxing. We are entering the maximum stage."

Every molecule in Bracken's body seemed to have dissolved, merging into the formless mass of love that surrounded and gently supported him. Above, the pervasive cloud of light increased in intensity. Like a rainbow waterfall, a river of light flowed into the room and spilled down over them. As each cascading color washed across his body, Bracken felt himself becoming less and less aware of the room and those in it, finally losing all consciousness of them.

Time passed. Vast webs of pastel lights collided with bright green, red, and yellow stars. Words to express Bracken's feelings were impossible. But, what need was there for vocabulary when words had lost their meaning? Thoughts bubbled to the surface of his mind and then burst with an herbal fragrance. His senses wove a lavish garment of pleasure, which covered and clung snugly to his body.

Rippling across the room came Layozz's voice, "We are about to enter the last phase. This will be the time we have been waiting for. You'll be able to play music. It will be music like you've never heard before . . . the s o n g of dreams . . . lik e a cresting wave. It's coming. . . ."

Bracken's ears tingled to the echo of a faint melody. His mind began to create song after song until riffs of poetic melody entwined his thoughts. He looked down at his body. He moved his hands, then his feet, and pulled himself upright.

The musicians found their instruments.

Bracken discovered that he and Silas both held stams. Waves of pure sound almost knocked him to the floor. "Did you hear that?" he asked. "It's beautiful! overwhelming, impossible." Never had sound been so alive.

Chepa began to play in earnest. Bracken and Silas acted and reacted with the musicians, creating a silken entity. They played old songs and composed songs as they played. Each chord in the new progression accented the preceding one. Harmony and rhythm built to a crescendo. They sang, their voices blending with the ease of accomplished vocalists.

Let us take all our fears and cast them in the sea,
Let us leave all the past.
Let us take up the key,
Open the shining door and run free, run free.
Now is the hour to let it be, let it be.

"We've never played liked this," cried Chepa above the throb of instruments. "We are in perfect unity."

"I can't believe I can move my fingers this way!" shouted Bracken.

Silas was smiling. So were Yaavin and Shor and Chepa, and all the others. All were smiling at Layozz.

* * *

The next day, Bracken and Silas hiked down the road leading to Tizra. Neither spoke as they trudged along.

The serene countryside contrasted sharply with the clashing thoughts that filled Bracken's mind. He was headed back to the bridging program at the Currency Center, his first step in a real career. He eagerly anticipated it and even looked forward to the few classes he must complete at the Tizra Academics.

Yet, the challenge of a new job dimmed in comparison with the excitement he had tasted the past days. True, he and Silas had not located the Mingus Mine, but they had found Layozz with his pack of stones. Even in Bracken's years of tramping around Nerkush, he'd never been under attack by armed men as he and Layozz had been on the streets of the Community. And that a professional group such as the Golden Flight would allow him to touch one of their instruments was almost as unbelievable as sharing the Mingus Stone with them. Besides, Bracken felt that he'd held his own in that fantastic music session, playing better than he'd ever played before.

He and Silas walked in silence, broken only by the striking of their boots on the road's surface and the flutter of an occasional field bird. Suddenly, the whine of a high-powered rig sounded from behind. It approached rapidly, the whine winding down into a low roar of energy.

Bracken and Silas edged to the roadside, turning to watch a late-model trans-speed bearing down on them. Yielding to greater power, Silas stepped off the road. Bracken stubbornly held his place.

Unexpectedly, the trans-speed came to a precision stop, veering toward the spot where Bracken stood. The iridescent red vehicle halted with its front wheel a handbreadth from his boots.

From inside came a clear feminine voice, "Get in. I'm on my way to Tizra." The tone allowed no question that Tizra was also their destination.

When Bracken could trust his legs to back away from the still vibrating trans-speed, he moved to the passenger side window. He bent over and looked into the most beautiful face he'd ever seen, and somehow knew that he'd seen it before.

CHAPTER 11

Don't I know you from somewhere? was not the kind of line to use on a woman like the one who sat beside Bracken. But, racing down the road, Bracken almost resorted to that cliche because he could think of nothing intelligent to say.

After asking directions to Brighton Inn, Tizra's most cosmopolitan accommodations, and introducing herself as Aleena, this remarkable woman flipped on music and switched her attention to driving. She handled the rig with ease, while propelling it at speeds faster than Bracken had ever attempted.

He watched her long, narrow hands on the wheel. His eyes traced the same lithe look along her arms, her torso, on down to her slim feet. The profile of her facial features, delicate except for her full lips, was overshadowed by a voluminous frame of hair, which appeared dark brown one moment and shiny black the next. Bracken sifted his mind, trying to place the striking face.

Desperate to strike up a conversation, he asked, "What takes you to Tizra?"

Aleena turned the music down, said pleasantly, "Business," and turned it back up.

Her pale, translucent complexion bore artfully-applied touches of color, its use obvious, but not excessive. This was a completely different look from Lisha's natural style.

Bracken tried again. "My family has been in business there for years." That sounded good, he thought. She acknowledged the statement with a mere tilt of her head and reduced the music's volume slightly. Bracken brought the third occupant of the trans-speed into his one-way conversation. "Silas is joining an engineering firm soon, structural engineering."

They reached Brighton Inn. The vehicle slammed to a stop.

"I guess this is where we get out," Bracken said. "Can we help you carry anything?"

"No, thanks." Aleena motioned to the entrance where an attendant deftly removed bags from another arriving vehicle.

Feeling foolish, Bracken made a final attempt to keep contact. "I'm with the Currency Center. If you need anything, don't hesitate to call."

"I'll see you there," came the tantalizing response.

"What did she mean?" Bracken demanded of Silas as they stood in the street and watched the red trans-speed roll up to the inn's glittering facade.

Silas guffawed. "What did *you* mean? *I'm with the Currency Center*!"

"I will be tomorrow," Bracken retorted. "If that woman is going to be there, so will I."

* * *

Bracken nearly lost his nerve the next morning outside the glass doors of the imposing building in Tizra's commerce district. Not only was he reporting ahead of his scheduled starting date, he felt extremely awkward in a confining dress shirt and suit.

Upon reaching Trasent's office in the Human Resources Department and seeing the sleek, unwrinkled suit the man wore as if it were a second skin, Bracken felt even more ill at ease.

Except for a momentary blank look in his dark eyes, Trasent skillfully hid any surprise. "Glad you could come on board a few days early." Here in his office, Trasent's robust physique looked more than ever like that of a trained athlete.

After routine employment procedures, Bracken was escorted to a conference room with a stack of reports to read. Soon, a man who looked about Lisha's age introduced himself as Golens from the bond department. Bracken would work under him as a first step in rotating through the Currency Center. Golens' hair hugged his head in tight blond curls. His complexion was deep pink, a blessing that helped disguise his many acne scars.

Bracken followed Golens to the extravagant public lobby. It reached to the third floor, dwarfing Golens' small stature. A sloping, multi-tiered indoor garden with decorative rocks and artificial plants was bordered with two sets of moving stairs that ran from level to level. A stream of sparkling water dropped in short waterfalls.

"Anybody else here in the bridging program?" Bracken asked Golens.

"No, that's new. Trasent started it."

Bracken made discreet inquiries. He found that, as manager of Human Resources at this branch of the Currency Center, Trasent commanded much more authority than did many managers. That seemed a sizeable accomplishment for someone Bracken guessed to be only five years his senior.

In the upper stories of the building, Golens stopped often to introduce Bracken. It was fairly easy to sense that Golens was a low level manager. Bracken was astounded at the number of employees and wondered what they found to do. He and Golens arrived at the center hall of yet another floor and entered double doors.

"Our branch has the finest employee fitness facility in the entire system," Golens said proudly.

Here was an unexpected bonus. "What a set-up!" Bracken

exclaimed. "A rowing machine, and look at that treadmill. Definitely first class equipment and locker rooms. You probably come here every day."

"Not exactly," Golens shrugged his rounded shoulders. "Of course, I could come," he hastened to add.

Outside the fitness facility, Bracken nodded toward an opposing set of closed doors. "What's a seminar station?"

"Special meeting rooms. We hold national meetings here."

"I didn't know the Tizra branch was so important."

Golens lowered his voice. "It's not talked around, but I happen to know that several global gatherings have assembled behind those doors. Mostly it's used for training sessions. As a matter of fact," Golens' drab demur brightened, "I'm soon taking a seminar there myself."

"Oh?"

"Yes." Golens lifted his chin noticeably higher. "I've been chosen to attend the next motivational seminar for managers."

"What's that?"

"Our Human Resources Department brings in an outside group to conduct seminars. We'll learn how to develop our attitudes and skills in order to reach our highest potentials."

"Does everyone go?"

Golens smiled indulgently. "Eventually, we hope to include all employees. But, for now, it's limited to key personnel."

Bracken caught the emphasis on *key*.

Back at Trasent's office, Bracken was struck again by Trasent's image of fitness and self-assurance. But the mental picture was brief because Bracken's attention shifted immediately to a visitor in the office.

Aleena created an image of her own. She wore a white suit with a red freeform decorative pin so large it could have been a piece of her red trans-speed.

"Bracken and I met yesterday," Aleena interrupted Trasent's introduction. Hitchhiking seemed out of place in this bastion of finance. So Bracken was thankful when Aleena limited her explanation to, "He and a friend graciously directed me to Brighton Inn." If she noticed Bracken's grateful look, she ignored it and turned to Trasent. "I have more calls to make."

She passed Bracken in the doorway on her way out. Looking at her full-on and at close range, he saw her eyes. How could he have missed their impact before? They were large and pale, almost colorless, as if they'd assimilated white light from the sun. Bracken searched his memory. What hidden corner of his past had Aleena touched?

When she'd gone, Trasent explained, "Aleena heads her own company. Motivational seminars for large organizations. Here, get familiar with these daily activity reports."

Bracken tried to concentrate on bond rates and yields, but his mind was drawn to a more intriguing matter. How could he become one of the chosen few to attend the Currency Center's next motivational seminar?

* * *

Bracken waited at Tizra Academics for Lisha to finish her last art class of the day. He recognized Catine, the astro studies student, sitting on the grass nearby.

"I wish you'd stop being skeptical," Catine told a friend.

"Has anybody ever produced evidence that such things exist?"

Catine challenged, "Come with us, and you'll see with your own eyes."

"I think it's dumb. Do you really believe that if all of you hang around the Pillars of Rimlex, a space disk will drop in for a visit?"

"The professor is a sensitive, intelligent man. If you were a being from another universe, wouldn't you pick someone like that to contact?"

Just then, Lisha called to Bracken. Almost reluctantly, he turned from the conversation and went to join her.

"How's the finance wizard?" She laughed, offering her face for a quick kiss.

Bracken briefed Lisha on the several days he'd spent at the Currency Center since he'd last seen her.

"Sounds as if you're getting caught up in that job." Lisha ran ahead and whirled lightly to face him, her arms held wide. "I think I'm getting jealous." She opened her brown eyes innocently and posed her lips in a pout. "And, it's going to be worse. I'll probably never see you after you finish classes here and go to work full time."

He gladly answered her invitation for an embrace. He couldn't help but contrast Lisha's openness, her casual dress, her passion for a natural appearance with the careful business decorum of most women at the Currency Center. Her ambition seemed to reach no further than her current art project. A fleeting image of Aleena crossed his mind. But, he snapped his attention back to Lisha. It was Lisha's freshness and her ideals that had first attracted him.

"Are you still Trasent's boy wonder?"

Bracken grimaced. "Don't say that. It's to be expected that he'd take an interest. I'm in his bridging program, and he wants the program to succeed. He did pay me a compliment today—that I'll soon know more about the bond department than the regulars."

"Bracken," Lisha sat on a bench, a serious look on her face. "You've been working at the Currency Center only a short while, but I'm wondering . . ."

Bracken joined her and flopped an arm over the back of the bench.

Lisha continued, "You're not forgetting important things, are you?" She twisted her fingers. "I mean, remember the day at the brook when we talked about being open to new ideas and change but not compromising principles?"

"Hey, working at a regular job doesn't mean compromising principles."

"Of course not." Lisha agreed. "But you don't talk anymore about . . . well, about . . . making things better for Nerkush."

"I've been kind of busy."

She stiffened.

Bracken gave her a one-armed hug. "Don't worry. My values are the same as they've always been."

Lisha turned a smiling face toward him. "Still on your way to the sun?"

"You bet!" Bracken said. Lisha had no reason to be concerned over his values. And he brushed aside the thought that her brown eyes glistened from any emotion other than happiness.

* * *

One morning, Golens had a headache and a desk piled high, and he asked Bracken to sit in on a fire protection committee meeting for him.

A day or so after that, a notice arrived in the late afternoon of an impromptu meeting for employees selected to attend the coming motivational seminar. Golens wasn't at his desk to receive the notice. The meeting was to be held immediately following the closing hour.

So, it was easy for Bracken to take it upon himself to go to the meeting in Golens' place. The fact that Golens had left his office only minutes before the notice came, and was probably still in the building, did not deter Bracken from rationalizing that Golens was practically on his way home; and he would want Bracken to act as his substitute.

The next morning upon arriving at the Currency Center, Bracken received an urgent request to report to Trasent's office. There, he found a hostile Golens, bubbling and boiling like a pink volcano ready to spew out pink lava.

CHAPTER 12

Bracken knew he had stepped out of line the previous night by going in the manager's place to the seminar planning meeting. Now, Golens' fury showed him how far.

Not long before, Bracken would have gladly told Trasent and the wimpy Golens a fast goodbye, but this opportunity at the Currency Center had opened new vistas to Bracken. He had not abandoned his principles, but he saw now that the pursuit of goals could be enhanced and even furthered by accepting new challenges, not the least of which was paying off his trans-rig and moving into a place of his own.

"Bracken made no effort to locate me," Golens sputtered. "I was in the research department until after closing time."

Trasent appeared ill at ease. "It's regrettable that you missed the meeting. I'll see that you receive a full report."

"I took notes with that in mind," Bracken said meekly.

Ignoring him, Golens kept his blue eyes directed on Trasent. "I will contact a fellow supervisor for a report. What we need is reinforcement of the line of authority. Bracken works for me."

And you have no intention of letting me squeeze you out of your spot in that motivational seminar program, Bracken thought. Aloud, he said, "I apologize if I undermined your authority."

Golens' face flamed. "The issue is one of adhering to accepted behavior."

In a rare show of indecisiveness, Trasent drummed his fingers on his polished desk. "Bracken, we do abide by certain protocol here."

"I'll be more aware of protocol in the future." Bracken's slight shrug indicated how inconsequential the matter was. "In representing Golens at the meeting, I acted on my own initiative. Apparently I assumed too much responsibility." Bracken guessed that Trasent disliked this scene almost as much as he did. He appealed to the seething Golens, further turning the tables on him, "And I wish we could have resolved this without letting it go beyond our own bond department." The implication was not lost on either Golens or Trasent.

* * *

One morning weeks later, Bracken walked through the double doors of the seminar station across the hall from the fitness facility. There had been an inspiring opening session of the motivational seminar, then a break. Now, it was time to begin in earnest.

Bracken found his name on a wall chart and took his assigned seat at a round table with five supervisors. More supervisors sat at other round tables. He wanted to laugh. He, a man who'd knocked around Nerkush for ten years working only when necessary, now wore a suit of the correct cut and fabric, and he was training for management. Even funnier, not only did he work for a stuffy financial institution, he regularly deposited money in one of its savings accounts.

Bracken fingered this session's packet that lay on the table and again congratulated himself on being in this select group. He wasn't sure how he'd gotten here, except that Trasent liked him. Golens' attendance was *postponed because of more pressing matters*, he'd told Bracken.

To Bracken's disappointment, someone else was absent. Aleena had swept into the opening session with an aura of glamour and excitement. Her keynote speech emphasized the purpose of the motivational seminar: "To move your thinking from the staid mode of traditional currency handling into the mind frame necessary to compete in today's global financial market." She left the program in the hands of the seminar leader.

Bracken examined the packet. The purpose statement for this exercise concerned the problem of effectively evaluating employees. After a discussion period, Bracken's group moved into a breakout room.

The group scribe stood at a portable easel. He listed levels of thought: Belief, Principle, Philosophy, Theory, Method, Action, and Evaluation.

One supervisor summarized the first level, "My belief is that all supervisors should evaluate their subordinates." The scribe recorded that and followed it with the principle stated by another, "All employees who get evaluated by their supervisor understand their roles in the company."

The group leader prodded, "What product do we want from an employee evaluation?"

Given his limited experience, Bracken was hard pressed to contribute, but he answered tentatively, "We want an employee to have a better awareness of his place in the company." The scribe turned to a new sheet of paper and wrote Bracken's product. Bracken felt elated.

Soon the group leader directed the members to the philosophy level of thought. "We believe that evaluation helps an employee understand his role in the company. Let's go deeper. Let's work on the philosophy behind that principle."

Back in the main seminar room, scribes papered the wall with sheets torn from their easel pads. They told how their groups proposed applying theoretical ideas to the job.

Someone commented, "I don't think my subordinates would appreciate being ordered to list attitude adjustments which they should make."

The seminar leader asked, "How could you avoid that problem?"

Say please? came to the tip of Bracken's tongue.

Despite an occasional sarcastic thought, he found himself leaving the on-going training sessions feeling less stressed and more in tune with the creative, productive side of his life. He began to analyze each proposal or idea in light of what its application could do for him. He was convinced that he was becoming mentally and emotionally more in command of himself. He began to understand others in such a way that brought a power to manipulate them. He played around the edges of this newly found skill, experimenting with initiating subtle games.

One night, weeks after the seminar program began, as Bracken sat alone with Lisha, she commented, "You're awfully quiet." Bracken winked, "I'm analyzing my state of energy concerning the method of a problem we are dealing with."

"Oh, Bracken. What kind of jargon is that?"

"I'm serious. We have levels of energy."

"Energy? I remember you talking about levels of thought."

"We have levels of energy, too. I'm past the *absorb and don't react* level. I may be to *assimilating and I can see it*."

"So?"

"Then I reach the responding stage, and then I'm supposed to be thinking of the next thing to do. After that, I am at an energy level of understanding. Next thing you know, I am thinking of the ultimate way it should be." Bracken shook his head. "I can't believe I remember all those levels."

Lisha frowned. "Those techniques must be making a deep impression on you. Is that some sort of a religion?"

"I hear grumbling at the Currency Center to that effect. They say the main seminar leader occasionally goes into really heavy stuff—techniques that help you unlock untapped potential in yourself. The idea of going into a trance scares . . ."

"A trance? That scares me, too."

"The mind is the key to another plane of existence. He also promises that money, power, and love can be acquired through releasing ourselves and stepping out to where we can get help."

"Tell him that you don't need help getting love. Or," Lisha eyed him suspiciously, "do you? You wouldn't be getting personal instruction from that Aleena?"

"I simply go to her seminars." But as Bracken laughed away Lisha's suspicions, he winced, remembering recent occasions when Aleena had come to Tizra on business. One afternoon she'd asked him to meet with her regarding the bond department. They ran late and adjourned to a nearby place that served Aleena's favorite seafood. "Our contact is strictly professional."

Lisha bit her lip, then said lightly, "Well, anyway, what kind of help will you get when you release yourself?"

"I don't know, but supposedly when we abandon control of our mind, we lapse into a passive thought pattern, a kind of void. Then, others out there can communicate with us. They can direct us."

"Others? It sounds awful." Lisha snuggled close to him. "I don't want anybody telling me what to do." She leaned her head on his shoulder and fingered the base of his throat. "About now, I especially wouldn't want anyone, anywhere, to know what I'm thinking."

* * *

Bracken, freshly bathed and wearing a plush robe from Trasent's guest closet, returned to the exercise room in his supervisor's home. Trasent, perspiring heavily, was just finishing. Bracken, amazed at the man's stamina, had given up long before.

Their friendship had grown rapidly. At times, Bracken suspected that if he had been in poor physical shape and unable to join Trasent in his relentless pursuit of the perfect body, Trasent might not have welcomed Bracken's companionship. Trasent seemed obsessed with being in top physical condition.

"What an experience!" Trasent declared. "Working out at the Currency Center's fitness facility is fine. But it doesn't compare to the exhilaration I get here on my own equipment."

"This is a beautiful set-up," Bracken agreed. "The whole place is beautiful." The handsomely furnished rooms of Trasent's home were in a new building in a fashionable section of town. Every time Bracken had visited, he'd been impressed by the near luxury in which Trasent lived.

It was a different world from the one Bracken had known until recently. He thought of the Community in Accad. People gathered there to assert their right to live in a world free from control of Nerkush's narrow thinkers. Trasent, on the other hand, used Nerkush's controlled and structured environment to his advantage. From his well-stocked pantry to his career to his superb body, he appeared prepared for anything. If a person agreed with Trasent's goals, he would have to say that Trasent had done everything right.

Bracken looked through a large window at the familiar streets. The Currency Center towered over a cluster of commercial buildings in the central district. Homes and businesses fanned outward from that. Soft pinpoints of light transformed the night scene into a glistening work of art. Bracken observed, "Tizra isn't this spectacular in real life."

"It's all an illusion, the good and the bad," Trasent said.

Later, Bracken sat in a comfortable chair opposite a screen across the room where Trasent adjusted the controls.

"I'll prove to you that everything is an illusion. Watch." Trasent dropped into an adjoining chair, a remote in his hand. "At first what you see will appear as beautiful scenes and sounds. But there is more to it than that—relax. Be open to the subliminal. Let happen what will happen."

Aleena's seminar had taught that there were blissful states waiting to be enjoyed. Bracken remembered the techniques he'd learned and absorbed what the screen offered. Sunlight and sea—the calming song of refreshing waves—enchanting music—drifted sand—they all played on Bracken's senses, lulling him into a readiness of spirit.

Trasent urged, "Just let yourself go. Let your higher self link with the universe."

Bracken's eyes fastened on the screen. Its messages massaged his brain. Its sounds silenced his cognizant thoughts. He floated, passive, awash on an ocean of translucent red, gently rocking, and moving upward. He sensed another presence, a magnetic, drawing presence.

Suddenly, Bracken was back in the dark tunnel of the Mingus realm. He twisted, struggling against hideous images. The golden light shone ahead, almost within his grasp. Blackness overtook him. The golden light disappeared—black . . . a flash of red . . . black . . . black . . .

The other presence, the magnetic, drawing presence pulled at him. Again, it drew him upward in a restful euphoria.

Suddenly, a stark realization sliced into Bracken's consciousness. His dominion over his thoughts was breaking down. The beatific state beyond his body lured unceasingly, begging him to release, promising him untold rewards.

Bracken lingered in a void, caught between ecstasy and reality. The void widened. The distance between him and reality lengthened. Bracken's thoughts did not respond to his command. He was losing control!

Gathering all his strength into one massive effort, Bracken pulled back from the brink. He jumped to his feet and turned his face from the screen.

Startled, Trasent flicked the remote. "Hey, you all right?

His heart pounding, his breath coming in deep gasps, Bracken stumbled to the window. He gripped the ledge until he steadied himself and muttered, "Powerful stuff."

"For most people, it's pretty mild. But, for you . . . you must be more receptive to exploring new thresholds than I'd guessed."

But Bracken didn't want to discuss new thresholds. He mumbled a hasty goodbye and left. He stomped along the dark streets of Tizra, glad for every street lamp, for each firm impact of his shoe against the solid surface.

Bracken had willingly ventured into the upper level of the Mingus Stone. But tonight's experience was different. Not only had it threatened to steal reality from him, it had dredged up painful, disturbing images that he wished to leave buried.

Although he held no resentment for Trasent, and certainly the techniques he'd learned at Aleena's seminar couldn't be at fault, Bracken could not dismiss a nagging feeling of having been tricked. No, it was stronger than that. He felt violated.

Bracken quickened his pace. He knew where to go for answers.

CHAPTER 13

From a secluded spot high on the ridge in the Forest of Zorek, Dalfang stroked his gray beard and watched a hiker tramping up the trail that led along the steep cliffs above the beach. Breezes from the Sea of Aurin ruffled Dalfang's cloak and fluttered through the trees toward the clearing where his humble cabin stood, removed from a fragmented and hectic culture.

The hiker stopped to adjust his leather pack. He tarried a few minutes, looking down at the breakers that crashed against the rocky shoreline.

The old man wearing the cloak waited serenely. *You are almost here, my son. A few more steps.* Dalfang, the keeper of the Door to the Anindi Passage of Malchag, would be patient. A little encouragement, and this one would carry his search through to pinnacles of ancient wisdom.

* * *

Bracken turned his back on the Sea of Aurin's blue waters and tackled the final stretch of his climb. His boots left prints in scattered patches of brown soil on the crusty rock surface. A ridge loomed above. By his calculations, Dalfang's cabin must lay behind it in the Forest of Zorek. Reaching the crest, Bracken looked into the old man's deeply set eyes, almost as blue as the sea below.

"So, you've come," Dalfang said. The intervening time between this and their previous meeting in the Brazen Eagle seemed immaterial. "Follow me."

They walked through heavy forest to a clearing where a mountain cottage nestled. Its wooden porch squeaked as the two men crossed and entered the main room. A breeze stirred coarse curtains that hung inside the open windows. Chairs of wood and leather clustered near the stone fireplace filled with ashen logs.

"Sit at the table," Dalfang offered cordially.

In contrast to the cabin's sturdy appearance, the table was made from handsomely carved wood. Its polished top rested on intricately sculptured legs, a delicate ornament in the simple surroundings.

Dalfang brought cups and a pitcher of spring water. A bowl of fresh fruit was on the table.

Bracken leaned back in his chair, savoring the moment. The woods and mountains surrounded and protected the cabin from all thought of care. Tizra seemed eons away in time and distance. He bit into a crisp piece of fruit. "Where did you get this? I've never tasted such flavor."

"My orchard is on the far side of the meadow."

Bracken grinned. "I see some advantages to living here: marvelous food, beautiful forest."

Dalfang nodded. "Malchag is even more beautiful."

"Oh, yes." The mythical Malchag. "I find that hard to believe."

The sage folded his arms across his chest. "Perhaps you have something to learn about believing."

This strange statement reminded Bracken that he'd traveled to see Dalfang for more than an opportunity to investigate the idea of Malchag. There was the matter of the experience at Trasent's home.

Bracken hadn't mentioned the traumatic happening again, but when he requested a few days off work, Trasent had willingly adjusted the schedule. "I promised that your hours would be flexible," he'd said.

Now Bracken looked across the table at Dalfang and asked, "What can you tell me about higher planes?"

A trace of humor crossed Dalfang's face. "How direct you are. You have not been touched by this peaceful place long enough to abandon your habit of haste."

"Some people refer to them as higher planes of existence, or blissful states, where one leaves cognizant thought behind and enters a state beyond reality."

"Am I to assume that you have had such an experience?"

"Very close to it." Bracken's fingers traced the contour of the carved table leg. "A friend was demonstrating that reality is often not what it appears. With the help of a few techniques, the demonstration exceeded the point of comfort."

"Children playing a mind game." Dalfang sighed. "People in a materialistic society often struggle to reach new heights in developing their own potential, in order to satisfy their craving for more possessions."

Decidedly ill at ease, Bracken stood up and took a turn around the cabin. "Disregarding motives, what can you tell me about reaching higher planes of existence?"

"If I were to tell you everything I know about that subject, you would not comprehend now. I will say this. The fact that you can't see something does not mean that it doesn't exist. And your failure to understand something does not mean that it isn't knowable. But one must use discernment. Seeking power to win over others can hardly be favorably compared to the nobility of seeking to further one's own enlightenment and wisdom. Travel to a peaceful parallel universe can be rewarding."

Bracken returned to the table. "You're speaking of Malchag?"

Dalfang nodded. "Malchag holds the key to much wisdom. He

pointed to a tiny insect crawling across the window ledge. "Observe. Do you think our little friend has knowledge of our plane of existence?"

Bracken snorted. "I doubt it. He lives in his own world."

"Exactly! Yet, even though this creature doesn't know it, we do exist, don't we?"

Bracken nodded.

"Now imagine for a moment that this insect was suddenly given the capacity to understand as we do. Because the realm of the insect is ordinarily limited, such capacity would be outstandingly beautiful to him, to say the least."

"I suppose it would."

"And likewise our realm is *ordinarily* limited," Dalfang said.

Bracken frowned. "Are you saying that there may be a higher realm for us as men?"

"The caterpillar metamorphoses and comes forth as a butterfly. And you and I must move on as well."

Bracken pondered. Where did death fit into that scenario? Skepticism crept in. "Which shall I compare myself with—the caterpillar or the butterfly?"

Dalfang sighed. "Comparison is not required. We can go anywhere we wish if we know how. We can become creatures of a higher realm if we learn the keys to that world."

"What kind of a world are you talking about?"

"One that is infinite." Dalfang's blue eyes took on a faraway look. "It's a world in which we evolve ever upward until . . . until we become like the one who made the world."

A wave of shock buffeted Bracken at the magnitude of that astounding theory. Man as creator!

"And then," Dalfang continued, "we can create our own worlds and fill them with what we choose."

Guilt for even listening to such an idea swept over Bracken. A picture of his mother with the Volume in her hands flashed into his mind.

Dalfang said gently, "A concept like this requires a searching soul." Sadness tinged his observation, "Perhaps it is too soon for you."

Bracken tried to push aside restrictive ties from the past. "I'll be honest. I can't completely go along with what you've just said. However, I realize that I can not get all my answers in one short conversation. I'm willing to listen."

"Of course. That is why I invited you to see Malchag."

Bracken was still not convinced that Malchag was more than a myth. But he had come to investigate. Could he perhaps find the truth of other mysteries there? "I'm ready."

Dalfang rose and took a staff that leaned against the stone fireplace. "We shall go now. The sun moves toward the sea, and we must reach the gate before dusk."

Bracken followed the cloaked figure from the cabin. Branches of great trees laced a green sanctuary around the two men as they trekked along a twisting path. Granite cliffs closed in to form a narrow canyon. Its floor sloped upward. Bracken was amazed at the way Dalfang unhesitatingly climbed and picked his way among the rubble of small rocks strewn in their path.

As if reading his companion's thoughts, Dalfang said, "I've walked this trail often. My feet are familiar with each step."

The first chill of the evening had settled when the trail ended abruptly at a solid wall of granite. Mystified, Bracken concluded that the old man had been playing out some wild fantasy.

Again, Dalfang seemed aware of Bracken's silent misgivings. "Don't be deceived by appearance. Secrets must be hidden well. Mysteries like Malchag do not unfold to stumbling fools and stubborn skeptics."

Dalfang ordered, "Now listen to me." An evening breeze billowed Dalfang's cloak, increasing his already generous stature. He pointed to the wall of stone and announced with awesome majesty, "Here lies the Door to the Anindi Passage of Malchag."

Bracken's eyes followed the granite wall to its crest. Above, fading sunlight splashed itself on clouds that had rolled in from the sea. He shouldn't have come. What answers could this strange person give him? He could leave now and head for Tizra.

However, Dalfang's commanding manner quelled Bracken's thoughts of abandoning the venture. "The key to this door lies in your tongue. A few short syllables will turn its lock. The code is simple. But, remember, it must be kept a secret."

From the leather pouch at his side, Dalfang withdrew a flat, rectangular piece of polished metal. He handed it to Bracken. On its surface was inscribed:

*IVEX * HITH * MINAE * TRAE TRAE * VO * REM*

Dalfang said, "Speak these words and the door will open."

Bracken ran his fingers over the metal piece, once again seized by thoughts of flight.

Dalfang patiently continued, "Sometimes you may speak the words only once. Other times, more. But, the door will always open if you are faithful and persistent."

The idea of making a granite wall move by repeating a mindless phrase was too much. Bracken got up and thrust the metal piece toward the old man.

But, Dalfang interrupted the words forming in Bracken's mind. "Quiet yourself, Bracken. How long before you understand that Malchag is a parallel universe? It is not in this dimension. Two worlds meet here at this rock. Simply repeat the words with me and push away your doubt. You must try."

In a reluctant whisper, Bracken joined Dalfang in repeating each word.

As the last syllable died away, a faint hum began. It continued and grew into a loud ringing. Then, without warning, the face of the granite wall dissolved.

Bracken stared, fear mixed with wonder. Moments before, he had seen only solid stone. Now, a passageway, filled with bluewhite light, yawned before them.

"Let us go," said Dalfang.

CHAPTER 14

Totally humbled by the sight, Bracken followed Dalfang into the passage. No sooner had they stepped into the corridor than it was gone. They stood on a green hillside brushed with swaths of low-growing blossoms. Sun-bathed hills dotted with trees rolled toward distant snowcapped peaks, where a lake reflected the brilliant blue sky.

Overcome by the beauty, Bracken shouted, "I can't believe it! This is real! I was crazy to doubt." He trailed his fingers through soft-petaled pink and lavender flowers. "Wait until Silas hears about this." All inhibition deserting him, Bracken dropped to his knees. He scooped up slender blades of grass by the handful and threw them in the air.

As the burst of exuberance subsided, Dalfang said, "You're welcome to remain in Malchag as long as you wish."

"You're not staying?" Bracken asked in alarm.

"You may leave whenever you wish." Dalfang indicated a nearby smooth granite shaft rising from the ground. "Simply come to this marker and repeat the code." With that, Dalfang walked to the obelisk. As he spoke the phrase, the passage appeared again. Stepping into it, Dalfang and the passage vanished.

A curious-looking creature approached. It reached about waist-high on Bracken and walked on two legs with a graceful gait. Two large eyes dominated the head. Above a high brow, bushy hair grew back over the skull. The body was dressed neatly in what appeared to be a bluish-green leafy garment.

Something like a smile crossed the face. "You are enjoying yourself." The voice had a slightly melodious tone that almost tickled Bracken's eardrums, and the head bobbed in time with its speech. "Unhappiness is rare here in Malchag."

Bracken's disbelief bordered on hysteria at the sight of this creature.

It articulated without blinking its eyes. "Dalfang's a good fellow. He's brought others like yourself here. They all wear a similar look when they first arrive."

What kind of a look? *Amazed, crazed, stupefied?* Bracken knew his face might well reflect any of those feelings. He decided to try communicating. "What . . . er, who are you?"

The creature responded courteously, "I am Dayon, at your service. Come along now. There is much to see."

Partially regaining his wits, Bracken fired questions as they walked toward a grove of trees on the horizon.

To a question about the being's race, Dayon replied, "We are the family of Finlanleys. We came to inhabit Malchag after losing our former home." He seemed dejected at the thought but quickly recovered his good humor. "We were driven from our home by a strong lord who made war against our leader. It was not pleasant here at first, because we were unaccustomed to this kind of life. However, we have adjusted."

"Who is your leader?"

"Our leader is Wissim." Dayon pointed to the snowcapped peaks. "Wissim lives high in those mountains. Perhaps you'll meet him someday."

"How long have your people lived here?"

"Ages." Dayon's answer sounded strangely distant, like a fragile echo traveling from the mountains. "I am quite old myself. At least six thousand of your years."

Bracken heard his own detached reply, "How well preserved you look," and wondered if he were truly holding this weird conversation.

"Our kind do not age in the normal sense," replied Dayon.

"Oh."

"Dalfang told us to expect a visitor," Dayon brightened. "So we arranged a party for you."

Bracken decided that either he must accept this situation at face value or admit insanity. He chose the former. He was conversing with a midget who claimed to be a Finlanley. And they were on their way to a Finlanley party.

Plaintive music drifted from the grove of trees, where a group of creatures like Dayon played strange-looking instruments.

Dayon said, "You'll be glad to know that another of your kind is present and will be a guest at the party."

Bracken looked around warily, unsure that he wished to meet a human crazy enough to think he was here. Politely, he said, "I'll be interested in seeing who else Dalfang has brought."

Dayon corrected him, "This one did not arrive through the western gate with Dalfang, as you did. This one came through the passage beneath the mountains."

Suddenly, Finlanleys broke from the wooded canopy and converged on Dayon and Bracken with cheerful greetings.

Bracken was escorted to the area beneath the trees, which was fashioned into various rooms and levels. Scattered throughout were plots of ground planted with a low-growing, large-leafed vine. White flowers and a slim, blue, gourd-like fruit intermixed on the vine.

Everyone appeared to be happy, and Bracken wondered if parties might be everyday affairs. He sat at a table and munched on one of the blue gourds, relishing its sweet, refreshing taste. The fact that it flourished without sunlight seemed no more exceptional than anything else in this incredible place.

Bracken soon saw the guest that Dayon had promised. Although this visit to Malchag could hardly be called ordinary by Nerkush standards, nothing he had seen yet was a bigger surprise than the sight of Aleena gracefully wending her way through the Finlanleys. Today, her hair looked truly black, the silky tresses adorned with a single red flower. She wore flowing white, caught with a blue sash.

She came to Bracken's side, laying a hand on his shoulder, as if their presence together in Malchag was as likely as their meeting at a Tizra social event hosted by a mutual friend.

Bracken stammered, "Wh . . . where did you come from?" This lovely woman belonged in a setting of sleek buildings and red trans-speeds.

"I came through the passage beneath the mountains." Aleena sparkled with enjoyment at Bracken's bewilderment. "Although I am acquainted with Dalfang, that is my entrance."

There was an intimacy about the way she sat beside Bracken, an intimacy that he thought would not have been possible in Tizra. But, perhaps Tizra was no longer real.

He confessed, "I would never have pictured you in Malchag."

"There is much about me that you would not suspect. I've always loved it here. Each day brings something new and unusual."

"Such as my arrival?" Bracken warmed to the developing camaraderie. He felt a kinship growing. They were pilgrims together in a new world. "I was skeptical," he heard himself telling Aleena. "I'd always supposed that Malchag was a myth. Even after I met Dalfang, even after he brought me to the Door to the Anindi Passage, I still didn't believe."

"It's exactly the kind of place we need. A dream world."

"I know. It's the kind of place everyone should have."

"Yes, it's wonderful, except," Aleena inched closer to Bracken, "something has been troubling me lately."

"What could bother you here?"

"It's a feeling."

Bracken protested. "I don't believe it. In your business, you teach others how to overcome their doubts."

"I'm puzzled too. How could anything be evil in this beautiful world?"

Bracken slipped an arm around Aleena. "Evil? You must be mistaken."

"No, there's a feeling that comes just after sunset. It's powerful and overwhelming, arriving with the evening air. Lately, it has been getting stronger each night." Aleena touched tapered fingers to her lips and looked over her shoulder. "I wasn't frightened at first. But, now that it's growing more intense, I've found myself becoming extremely concerned. Oh, Bracken, haven't you ever been afraid?"

A sudden memory chilled Bracken. He swept aside a terrifying image of serpentine jaws and unending blackness. "Each of us has his occasional nightmare."

"I'm almost afraid to go to my dwelling this afternoon."

"Have you spoken of this to the Finlanleys? Surely Dayon can set your fears at ease."

"Yes, I've asked others, but they don't seem to understand what it is." She gestured to the festive party-goers. "They appear pleasantly ignorant of anything amiss." She looked expectantly into Bracken's face. "Perhaps you could go back with me to my dwelling. Maybe you can discover the problem."

Just then, Dayon interrupted. "We wish to let our new friend know we are glad that he has come." A crowd gathered. "Bracken, you are welcome to stay as long as you like, and to bring others. We know the predicament of Nerkush and trust that Malchag's tranquility will settle many troubled lives." The Finlanleys applauded. Dayon continued, "The problems of Ebbern will multiply and rise to a climax of destruction. We offer you wisdom so that you may escape to our universe. This is our sacred pledge to you."

The Finlanleys dispersed. Aleena whispered, "Let's go now."

The trees cast long shadows across the green rolling hills as Malchag's sun dipped close to the horizon. At first, Aleena chatted happily walking across the open fields. As they progressed, she became noticeably upset.

Bracken reassured her. "What you fear is not real. It's only a fading memory of something from your life back in Nerkush."

"You're probably right," she said bravely.

They came to the top of a hill. Aleena pointed to a white cottage. "My place is there."

She escorted him through a small garden. Inside the cottage, Bracken saw pieces of handicraft and art work, which Aleena said she had made. He marveled at this new facet to her personality. Most rooms were paneled in dark wood and covered with tapestries. Against the dark walls, Aleena stood out like a dazzling ivory moving statue. She paced with increasing nervousness. They finally settled on a couch.

She fussed with the cushions. "I don't understand why I'm frightened. I never used to be."

Dusk came. She lit a candle, its light glinting on the metallic links of the heavy bracelet on her arm. Her anxiety was contagious. Bracken found himself reaching into his pack, seeking small comfort in three items at the bottom, which he'd neglected to remove—the handbombs Layozz had given him when he and Bracken were attacked in the Community.

Aleena's breath came in soft gasps through her rich, full lips. Bracken leaned close, wanting to reassure her. Her look seemed to invite more. Even in this fearful moment, an innocent softness hovered about her, as if she'd adopted the child-like qualities of Malchag. She reminded him of Lisha.

Lisha! Bracken drew back.

Abruptly, a presence invaded the room. Aleena's eyes widened. She began to tremble. "Do you feel that? It's here! There is something here."

A cold fear descended on Bracken, transcending flesh, chilling through to his marrow. He made himself stand and carefully study the room. He saw nothing unusual. But the dreadful presence pervaded everything. Where did it come from?

He peered through the window. Aleena followed him. There was a shift in the distant shadows. She screamed and pointed.

Bracken jumped to the doorway, trying to identify what had frightened her. The movement of shadows stopped. There was silence. He heard only the thud of his own heartbeat and the clink of Aleena's bracelet sliding down her arm.

"Blow out the candle," he ordered.

Aleena dropped and crept along the floor until she reached the table. The candle's flame flickered. She blew again. The smell of smoking wick wafted through the room. She threaded her way back to Bracken. A wordless eternity passed. The air was suffocating, enveloping them. Again, the shadows moved.

"Did you see that?" Bracken hissed. "It's coming!"

Aleena's slim hands closed over his arm like a vice.

An erie thumping, whirring sound rumbled through the ground. A bluish metallic glimmer, shrouded in a cloud of darkness blacker than the dusk, floated from the shadows toward Bracken and Aleena. Eyes appeared in the midst of the miasma, huge blue balls topped by fringes of red flame.

Horror gripped Bracken. He felt a force tugging at his inner self, drawing him toward the murky apparition, like quicksand sucking down its prey. He clutched the doorway. Threatening tentacles crawled from the cloud and moved along the ground toward him. Physical capability drained from Bracken. He tried to hold on to his mind.

Screaming hysterically, Aleena fled to the rear of the building.

With a strength wrested from unknown depths, Bracken conquered his paralytic state. Frantically, he searched his pack. His fingers closed around a handbomb. He pulled it from the pack and set it to discharge. Fighting a new onslaught of mesmerism, he moved clear of the doorway. He hurled the weapon at the advancing specter and then ran after Aleena.

CHAPTER 15

A powerful explosion rocked Bracken as he reached the back of the house where Aleena crouched in terror. Simultaneously, from outside, a hideous scream erupted, rose to a crescendo, and then died away. Aleena and Bracken waited fearfully in the still night air and then crept to the front door.

Pale light from the heavens revealed that the handbomb had accomplished its purpose. A direct hit to the mid-section of the creature had dismembered it and left shards of bluish, flesh-like substance strewn over the ground. Bracken and Aleena stared at the repulsive sight. Suddenly, the remains seemed to move.

Aleena gasped, "What's happening?"

Bracken shook his head, blaming the darkness for deceiving his eyes, for making him think that the scattered remains were beginning to disintegrate. He choked out a denial, "This is insane."

He and Aleena clung together, forced to believe what they saw. They watched the disappearing bits until there was nothing left of the creature except for a few ashen marks on the ground.

Bracken drew a faint breath and uttered, "It's gone."

The quaking of Aleena's body eased slightly. "Oh, Bracken, what would I have done if you hadn't been here?"

As they stood locked in each other's arms, trying to recover from the traumatic experience, an awesome sight filled the sky.

Aleena whispered, "This happens every night in Malchag."

The dark sky blossomed in a majestic display of sparkling light. Tiny luminous winged creatures spun a radiant ballet. A feeling of peace infused the atmosphere and enveloped the two spectators.

"It's the fireflies' dance of bliss." Aleena's warm breath caressed Bracken's cheek.

Entranced, Bracken's uneasiness melted away. The joy of his initial experience in Malchag began to return. Aleena drifted back to the house. Bracken remained there in the ebbing light of the fireflies.

Already the evening's terror was a fading memory. He felt secure. He reflected only on the happiness of his visit to Malchag.

This mysterious parallel universe was too wonderful to be kept to himself. He must bring friends here. He would bring them through the Door to the Anindi Passage.

* * *

In the weeks after returning to Tizra, Bracken did not forget Malchag. He often thought of the promise of wisdom and wondered about Wissim, the leader who lived in the snowcapped mountains. He also pondered the Finlanley's prediction of doom for Ebbern and the possibility of refuge inside Malchag's tranquil boundaries.

But for now, duties at the prestigious Currency Center claimed his attention. Having finished classes at Tizra Academics, he'd become a full-time employee under the supervision of Trasent.

Each day, Bracken became more aware of the power Trasent carried in his specialized job in Human Resources. This man was important, both within the Currency Exchange branches and as its representative to organizations all over Ebbern.

Trasent's responsibilities earned him access to every function of the Currency Center. Late one evening, Bracken descended two floors underground, looking for the dead files storage area. Golens had pointed it out on the tour that first day. Bracken tried the key card from Trasent's office that was supposed to fit. It did open a numbered door, the wrong one. Bracken closed the small empty office he'd gotten into by mistake, and then he found the file storage door, which was designated as such, and let himself into a deserted warehouselike space. The door closed behind him.

"Dead file storage is right," he muttered. "Almost anything could be buried here." He returned to the door, meaning to prop it open and relieve the closed-in feeling of the underground cavern.

Just as Bracken cracked the door, a movement in the deserted corridor caught his attention. A man emerged from an unmarked door. Bracken recognized him as Trasent and would have called out except that, in a furtive movement, Trasent slipped away. He paused at a corner, then disappeared around it. Bracken looked blankly at the lonely corridor, decided against fulfilling his errand, and locked the file room. He followed the winding tunnel out, but Trasent was nowhere to be seen.

Something about Trasent's manner called for discretion, so Bracken kept silent concerning the incident. He meant to retain his good relationship with his mentor.

A few nights later, Trasent invited Bracken to join him and Aleena at Brighton Inn's executive retreat for the evening meal. Aleena had taken permanent rooms at the inn, and spent much time in Tizra in connection with her business.

"So, yet another organization has contracted for your motivational seminar," Trasent said after they had ordered.

Aleena, resplendent in a white and black dress, which lent soft elegance to her professional appearance, included Bracken in her reply. "The response to our approach is marvelous. People everywhere are becoming aware of the gifts available to them. They want relief from stress. They want to reach new plateaus."

Bracken toyed with the fine table service. Dining like this marked a new plateau for him. He and Lisha usually spent their evenings together at more unpretentious establishments. Not long before, giddy with his advanced economic status, he'd invited Lisha to celebrate a special occasion in a fine place such as this, but she preferred one of their familiar haunts.

"What about you, Bracken?" Aleena asked. "Do you feel your seminar training is helpful?"

"Of course."

"Bracken's doing well," Trasent beamed. "I take credit for much of that."

Bracken laughed and confided in Aleena. "Yes, he gets credit for pushing me beyond my limits—on the exercise equipment."

"Physical well-being is important," Trasent insisted.

Aleena smoothed a red bow at her neckline. "I'm well aware of Bracken's physical potential." She ran her pink tongue over shiny, full lips. "But we mustn't neglect his inner well-being."

Bracken took refuge behind a sparkling glass of water. The suggestive tone in Aleena's words left him in a quandary. A cool business executive by day, and an efficient hostess for an afterhours business engagement, she kept her two male companions on edge with an occasional peek at a fiery vivacity smoldering beneath the surface. The child-like qualities she had exhibited at Malchag were apparently left behind in that dream-like terrene.

Bracken sought to fill the uncomfortable silence. "I rejoice with each trip Trasent takes to some far corner of the globe. It provides a respite from that rigorous fitness program he outlined for me."

Trasent ignored Bracken. His knife sliced across his plate furiously, and he aimed sharp words at Aleena. "You can take care of everyone's well-being, can't you?"

Bracken wondered what had caused that outburst.

Aleena's eyes flashed a change of mood. "You've been snappy lately, Trasent. Maybe you're neglecting your meditative exercises." She turned to Bracken. "Everyone needs a balance of energy—physical, emotional, and spiritual." She patted her lips with her napkin and said pleasantly. "Now, are we ready for something sweet?"

A picture of a frightened Aleena cowering in Malchag flashed into Bracken's mind. Had others witnessed her secret vulnerability?

The tension abated, and the meal finished harmoniously. Bracken had to admit that Trasent had been a little edgy for several days.

Later, after escorting Aleena to her suite, the two men left Brighton Inn. In the parking area, three lamps were out of order, a curious rarity for the upscale establishment.

They neared Trasent's low-slung trans-rig parked in a far corner. Trasent handed Bracken the key card. "Want to drive?"

Bracken gladly accepted, bending to insert it in the door. A sound startled him, but before he could react, a powerful blow landed on his head, resounding through his skull, and sending him reeling. He heard wheels skidding to a noisy stop. A sudden crushing pain squeezed his rib cage. He dangled helplessly, feet scraping the pavement. He caught a whiff of chemical odor and twisted his face away from it.

Through the fog, rapidly sucking him into complete surrender, he sighted the lights of another vehicle approaching. Those revealing lights illuminated a trans-max that blocked the space behind Trasent's vehicle. The power drive of the trans-max was running, and the side cargo door gaped open.

Trasent leaped from the passenger side of his trans-rig and pulled off one of Bracken's attackers, sending the huge man sprawling. Bracken shook free of the other. The lights of the moving vehicle came closer.

A voice boomed from the motionless trans-max. "Let's get out of here!"

The downed man scrambled up and ran for the vehicle. The other man whipped past Bracken, giving a parting blow that lent violent emphasis to the threat he bellowed, "We'll be back!"

With a clang of metal, the door slammed shut, and the transmax roared away. It narrowly missed the other vehicle, which continued to cruise, its driver apparently oblivious to the skirmish he had interrupted.

"Where are you hurt?" Trasent helped Bracken to his feet.

Bracken slumped against the trans-rig. "Who was that?"

"Let's get you inside. Here, lean on me."

"They were waiting for us."

Trasent rushed him toward Brighton Inn. "Hurry."

Biting back the pain, Bracken hissed, "Could you identify the rig?"

"Didn't get any numbers. But it was a dark color with two convex bubbles on top."

"Should we call the Pirax?"

Trasent looked over his shoulder. "No use. They're long gone by now."

Bracken didn't argue. His thoughts drifted to the attack with Layozz in the Community. The attackers had been after something Layozz had. They'd seen Bracken with Layozz. Could it be that tonight the same people ambushed Bracken, seeking to cart him off in that trans-max? Did they think he was privy to Layozz's private affairs? Bracken did not wish to, by some strange turn of events, be forced to explain to the Pirax his connection with Layozz.

At the inn's entrance, Trasent asked, "Can you walk by yourself?"

Bracken drew a careful breath. He took one step, winced, and nodded.

Inside, Trasent led the way to the men's room. He bent over and splashed cold water on his face. Bracken leaned unsteadily against a wall, aware that Trasent looked as pale as the white basin into which the water fell. For all his physical prowess, Trasent must be faint-hearted at the thought of a fight.

"You sure came through for me," Bracken said.

Trasent dried off, combed his black hair, and grinned weakly. "I told you physical fitness is important."

"You've made a believer out of me." Bracken tried to laugh but stopped midway, clutching his ribs.

"You're really hurt. Let's go upstairs."

They got to Aleena's floor without attracting undue attention. Taking in the situation at once, she opened her door wide. She deposited Bracken on a bed, where she and Trasent stripped him to the waist. Deftly she prodded his torso and examined the bump forming on Bracken's head.

"I can help you, Bracken, if you will let me." She dimmed the lights.

"Can you cure a powerful headache?" He whispered through clenched jaws. Breathing hurt.

"You can cure it. Your pain is a perception, not a reality."

"Believe me, this pain is real."

"You are using the discomfort to tell yourself that you are still alive. If you will let down your barriers and allow yourself to feel safe with me, you can release your pain."

Her hands roamed over Bracken's upper body. Trasent had disappeared. She leaned close, her hair a black cloud above his face. "My hands can feel your pain. Will you let me help you?"

Mesmerized, he nodded his assent.

She glided away and returned carrying a flat case, which she placed on a table beside the bed, and opened it. The contents caught the light, reflecting it in shining rays. Briefly, he wondered if Aleena had the Mingus Stone, but he saw that these were various-shaped crystals. Some were clear, others gleamed with color.

Aleena's hands gently explored Bracken's head. Her touch was replaced by a solid object. It moved over the area of his pain. He closed his eyes against a light that seemed to penetrate his lids.

"The light is flowing to your wound." Aleena crooned. "Soon you will be released from pain."

Gradually, Bracken experienced less and less hurt. He wanted to open his eyes and tell Aleena, but the call of the soothing comfort that crept over him was strong. He lay motionless.

She moved her hands to his torso and carefully traced the outline of his ribs. "It's warm here, and here," she said. "I'm connecting. I can feel the energy flow."

As the crystals moved over his chest, Bracken's resistance seeped away. Tingling sensations gradually replaced the hurt.

Later, how much later he didn't know, Bracken awoke. Startled to find himself in a strange bed, he bolted upright. Then he remembered.

In surprise, he stared down at his naked chest. He felt little pain. Aleena was gone. The crystals had disappeared.

Still leery, he carefully drew on his clothes. He went to find the others. Aleena sat, staring into space, apparently lost in thought.

Trasent, a glass in his hand, jumped up as Bracken appeared. "Did it work?"

Aleena uncurled herself. "Of course, it did."

Bracken stretched this way and that. "Something sure helped. I feel like a new person."

"Renewed," Aleena corrected.

"For whatever it is that I feel," Bracken said, "I want to thank you."

"I was only one part of the healing process," she said.

Trasent started for the door. "We'd better go. It's nearly dawn."

The two men left Brighton Inn. This time Bracken crawled gingerly into the passenger side of Trasent's trans-rig. Then, as Trasent lowered himself into the driver's seat, Bracken had a flash of insight. Earlier, it should have been Trasent opening the driver's side—not Bracken. They were roughly the same build, and it had been dark. Was it possible that Bracken had not been the target? Perhaps it was a mistake to assume that the attackers were the same men who'd come after Layozz and Bracken in the Community.

Trasent was extremely upset over the attack. Could he have another reason, one that went beyond the obvious danger of common thievery, to be worried about the incident?

* * *

As they rode, Bracken considered this possibility. But before he found a suitable way to question Trasent, they arrived at Bracken's house. Trasent's parting words were, "Don't bother to come to work this morning, Bracken. In fact, why not take a few days off? It's been rough."

Bracken stumbled into the house, only to be met by a disheveled Kressdek, who, rousing from a half-sleep, bounded from his chair and confronted Bracken.

"You all right, son?"

Caught unaware, Bracken retorted, "Of course, I am. What were you doing? Waiting up for me?"

Kressdek blushed fiery red. "Certainly not!" he snapped. "But you could consider your mother. Staying out all night. Didn't you suppose she'd worry?"

Bracken swore under his breath. "Do you sit in that chair every time I'm gone? I'm surprised it's still hanging together, considering all the years I wasn't around."

His father sucked in his stomach, his rumpled night clothes buckling. "Never mind where I spend my nights. And I'm not asking you where you spend yours."

"What are you asking, Father?"

Myra's gentle voice from the doorway cut short the confrontation. Her blue eyes were puffy, and this morning, her hair seemed more gray than blonde. "My men are up early. Who is ready for a nice, hot cup of tea?"

Kressdek ignored his wife. "How are you ever going to get to work on time?"

"That's my problem," Bracken said and retreated to his room. Over his shoulder, he announced curtly. "I'm taking a few days off—going to Accad."

". . . to the Community, I'll bet!"

Enjoying the outraged reaction to his sudden decision, Bracken added, "Yes. I need to rub shoulders with real people."

Bracken made numerous trips to his trans-rig, his arms loaded with belongings. He said good-bye to Amont, who followed him outside. Then, he went back and sat at the table with his parents.

He munched on a piece of bread and said casually, "I'm taking most of my things."

Myra's face contorted.

"I'll store them at Silas' house, temporarily." In the silence that followed, Bracken explained, "Trasent has been after me to move in with him . . . might do that when I get back."

"But," Myra said, "we were hoping you were home for good."

Bracken groped for patience. "You two couldn't think I'd always live with my family? I've appreciated having a place to stay . . . but, not forever! You must have known that."

"Nobody expected you to live here forever." Kressdek spoke gruffly. "Now that you're making money, we should have guessed you'd be wanting to move on to something better."

"It's not that!" Bracken bristled.

Kressdek slammed his cup down and snorted in his wife's direction, "Something better, like the Community."

"Oh, Kressdek," Myra rebuked, "he's not going to live in the Community." She turned a worried face to Bracken. "You aren't, are you—going to live there? You aren't giving up your good job at the Currency Center?"

Bracken stood up. "No, I'm not giving up my good job at the Currency Center. No, I'm not going to live at the Community. But," he stalked toward the door, "I am not going to live here either. As long as I do, I'll feel guilty because I chose not to work in your business, and I'll always be forced to prove to you that I can hold down a job at all."

"Bracken, don't go away like this," Myra pleaded.

Bracken sent a despairing look to his mother. "I just don't fit in around here—with your lifestyle, or with your antiquated philosophy."

"Bracken!" Myra's pleading changed to shocked denial.

Kressdek sputtered, "By antiquated philosophy, I suppose you mean your mother's interest in the Volume? Well, let me tell you, son. . . ."

"I don't need you to tell me anything, Father." Bracken whirled and stomped out, yelling over shoulder, "I'm capable of learning for myself. I have been for a long time. Whole worlds exist that you can't even imagine. And I'm not going to miss anything they have to offer."

CHAPTER 16

The road to Accad passed in the vicinity of the Pillars of Rimlex. The odd configuration of granite hills rose as jagged teeth erupting above a patchwork quilt of rolling grain fields. The Accad River meandered through the fields, like a lazy snake, in its crawl toward the sea.

Well off the main road, Bracken sat with Lisha and Silas on a small knoll garnished by a gathering of a few lonely trees. The first stars peeped through the sprawling branches, which would provide their shelter for the night.

Only by assuring Silas that they would be back in Tizra before Silas' starting date at his new engineering job had Bracken been able to coax his friend to come on this trip. The prospect of spending a few leisurely days camping en route to the Community thrilled Lisha, especially the idea of hiking. Bracken had convinced Silas that going on foot, even though they both now owned rigs, would allow a freer perspective and let them really sweep away the cobwebs. *I'll humor you in one last fling*, Silas had said.

Now, a noise down on the main road drew their attention. Lights from a caravan of three trans-rigs appeared. The vehicles turned onto a small dirt road and rumbled up the incline toward the pillars, passing a short distance from where Bracken and his friends remained secluded. The trans-rigs continued on to the base of the Pillars.

Lisha commented, "Seems odd that anybody would be out here this late."

Silas laughed. "We're out here this late, aren't we?"

"You know what I mean."

People spilled out of the rigs, lively chatter bouncing back from the bare granite walls as they began to hike up a small ravine. They soon passed from sight between two large pillars.

"I've seen a rig like one of those around Tizra Academics," Silas said. "I know! Professor Frimleter drives that kind of rig, remember him?"

"Oh," Lisha squealed, "maybe this is that funny group that people say he started."

Bracken watched until faint images showed against an exposed section of a smooth rock wall part-way up the side. Did a visit to this barren formation have anything to do with the professor's theory about life in distant space? unlikely, still . . . , "Let's go see what they're doing."

"I don't want to be with a bunch of crazies," Lisha balked. "Besides, it's too dark for mountain climbing."

"They must be following a good trail. Anyway," he indicated the rising moons, "it's going to be a bright night. We'll keep our distance and have a look at what's going on."

"There may be other strange oddities in this neighborhood," Silas cautioned. "Don't forget the Rimmers."

"They don't bother anybody," Bracken said.

"At least not anybody that lived to complain."

Lisha dismissed the Rimmers. "We don't know that they even exist. On second thought, maybe it would be fun to see what's happening."

Silas relented and followed Bracken and Lisha.

They paused high on the trail where it veered to the right and passed through a narrow cut in the rock. Bracken crept forward, lured by a buzz of conversation. Seconds later, he returned and led Silas and Lisha to a vantage point at the top of a ridge.

The group, obviously students, was gathered on a plateau a stone's throw below. One addressed a stick-thin figure who stood in their midst. "Professor Frimleter, how long do we have to wait? I don't mean to complain, but we are going to feel foolish if we sit here half the night and don't see what you promised."

Frimleter answered patiently, "As I told you, it may be hours. Or, merely a few minutes." The professor smoothed his dark hair down from its center part. "This is an excellent opportunity for firsthand observation of the heavens." His index finger extended toward a bright configuration shaped like a soaring sea bird. "Can anyone tell me the nature of that system?"

Bracken recognized the girl who identified the constellation as Catine, the astro studies student he'd seen several times. "That's the Trion Star System." She spoke in an odd twang, which Bracken hadn't remembered. It mimicked the Professor's high-pitched speech. "The best estimates are that it contains at least seven hundred stellar bodies, although no one has arrived at an exact figure because of an unusual phenomenon that leaves whole sections in a cosmic cloud."

Up on the ridge, Silas whispered, "This is nothing but a dull astro studies field trip. Let's go."

"There might be something more." Bracken resisted leaving. How valid was the professor's contention that intelligent creatures from outer areas of the universe sought contact with Ebbern?

Lisha and Silas were already backing away from their perch. Bracken started to follow when he was startled by a plaintive sound so foreign to the natural sounds of the region that it seemed to be a strange entreaty from another age. He froze, captured by its appeal, puzzled by its familiarity.

Someone shouted, "Look! Professor!"

The students reacted in wild confusion, some pointing at the sky and others screaming. Lisha and Silas scrambled back to Bracken.

Traveling rapidly, skimming over the distant fields, came a shining disk of light.

"See," Frimleter shouted. "It's just as I told you. They always come, now that I've been made a Touch-Point."

Arms outstretched, stature swollen with pride, he basked in the glory of the approaching revelation. "They've homed in on my mind waves. Soon they will speak to you through me."

One student found his voice. "Aren't they going to talk to us directly?"

"They don't generally communicate through vocal language. Until mental contact is established, I will be their mouthpiece. That's because I'm a contact, a Touch-Point."

From their observation platform, Bracken, Lisha, and Silas watched stupefied.

With a loud hum, the space vehicle filled the near sky and hovered to a stop on the plateau. A beam of light shot from its surface. The light focused on Frimleter's now entranced face. His whole frame appeared suddenly metamorphic, glowing in the light of a new-found energy. He began to speak.

"Be restful friends!"

The students' attention shifted in amazement from the space disk to their professor. A deep tone issued from his vocal chords, replacing their normal squeaky dissonance.

"We are among you for your own good." The soothing modulations being issued through the professor's mouth played a peaceful tune for the apprehensive watchers. "As Professor Frimleter told you earlier, this is a contact gathering. Some of you did not believe him. That is understandable."

Bracken crept closer, fascinated by the sight. Frimleter stood like a gleaming sentinel of another dimension.

The voice continued, "You are not the first to question, but now is the time to vanquish all destructive thoughts."

Catine looked at the disk nervously and then back to the professor. "Who are you?" she asked.

Frimleter turned toward the girl, and the voice responded sonorously, "Your instructor has told you. We are Trionites, inhabitants of the Trion Stellar System."

"Then you've really come to help us, just like he said."

The Trionite responded through his oracle. "Certainly, and let this be a lesson to you. Such men as Professor Frimleter are of great importance to your world. Trust them."

Catine's moon-shaped face reflected light from the glistening form before her. "Can we be like Professor Frimleter? Can we touch other worlds?" Her voice quaking, she clasped her hands to her breast. "I mean, will we be able to contact you?"

"All of you may become contacts if you so desire," the voice instructed smoothly. "There is little time remaining for your race if you and others do not respond." A series of clicks and whirls sounded from inside the disk. "In a moment you . . . ," the voice stopped abruptly.

Slowly, as if mounted on a swivel, Frimleter turned and faced the top of the ridge. "Our sensors perceive the presence of observers."

The trio crouching there shielded their eyes against a second beam of light, which shot from the disk. Bracken edged ineffectively in front of Lisha. On an alien's whim, they could be exterminated.

The voice intoned with increased firmness. "Come out! You will not be harmed. We intend only peace."

They had no choice but to climb down to the plateau.

Bracken looked from the professor to the disk, and then back to the professor, unsure how to address the faceless disk. "We didn't mean to interfere."

Silas added eagerly, "We're leaving. We won't say a thing about this."

The oracle stood motionless, as if its attention were distracted. It resumed, "Our memory scanners tell us that you have heard the previous conversations."

Silas promised, "We'll forget everything."

The voice issued a curt invitation, "Perhaps you desire to join these people who are becoming contacts tonight."

An overwhelming curiosity struck Bracken. No, more than curiosity, he felt irresistibly drawn toward this strange and spectacular power. He put aside rational reservations. "I want to know more. I'm interested in anything that can stop our planet from its senseless drive toward destruction."

Lisha hissed, "Bracken! What are you doing?"

Bracken ignored her, speaking as if pressured by some inner creed. "I'm open to hearing about any method of ensuring peace for this planet, even if that information comes from an alien force."

The Trionite responded courteously through the professor. "Very well, you may come aboard. Your friends will remain behind. We have no desire to force our way on your people."

"Bracken!" Lisha begged. "Don't go. This is weird."

"She's right." Silas put himself between Bracken and the disk. "Anything can happen if you go inside that thing."

Bracken brushed him aside. Here was a chance to see firsthand what he'd only glimpsed previously. "No one in that disk wants to harm us, or they would have," he told Silas. "Zapping us out of existence must be as easy as snapping their fingers."

"How do you know they have fingers?" Silas muttered.

The alien voice came to life again. "Your friends worry needlessly. You will be returned safely." Frimleter was already moving toward the glowing craft. "Please follow the professor."

The outline of a rectangular opening broke the smooth surface of the disk's underside. A gleaming metallic stairway emerged and extended slowly to the ground. Frimleter stepped up the stairs confidently.

Bracken reached the craft's entrance last. A faint grayish light illuminated the corridor stretching into the craft's interior. A human-like creature stood at the entrance, its body layered with a glistening gray garment. An extended arm beckoned Bracken forward. Bracken took a final look at Lisha, and Silas huddled below and stepped inside. The stairway retracted and the hatch closed, hissing to a tight seal.

Aboard the ship, fierce doubts plagued Bracken, but a sudden increased hum of its power source told him that already the craft was underway. His body pressed heavily into the seat that had been assigned to him.

The professor and his astro studies group sat with Bracken in a semicircle facing the Trionite who had welcomed them aboard. Here, the alien no longer used the professor as an oracle, but with a placid smile on its gray lips, implanted words directly into the listeners' minds. "My name is Taylay."

Taylay explained that the chamber where they rode was the disk command center. Its walls were mostly covered by gray panels overlaid with opaque rectangles of cool light. The pale illumination cast an ethereal atmosphere over the chamber. A large viewer screen hung on one wall. Trionites seated at consoles faced blinking readouts. Bracken deduced that here were the controls for monitoring speed and navigation. A lone alien near the doorway operated a hexagonal panel studded with buttons mounted beside squares of colored light.

Taylay's mental conversation rose like sparkling bubbles in Bracken's thoughts. "You will soon see your planet on our viewer screen. It will appear to be a lovely place from here. In sad reality, this is not the case. We have discovered several planets that are near self-destruction." Taylay's smile drooped in sympathy. "Their inhabitants have unleashed technology that they are neither willing nor able to control."

A student asked, "Do you use the same tactics in dealing with the problems of all these planets?"

The alien's answer filled each listener's mind spontaneously. "We are but one unit of an interstellar assistance force sent to aid races such as yours."

Bracken had come for information. He asked, "What exactly does your program involve?"

Deep in the heart of the craft, the lumbering of its energy force changed noticeably. The Trionite host said, "We have reached observation level. Turn your attention to the viewer screen."

The splendor of Ebbern filled the screen. "This is some field trip," exclaimed one student.

The Trionite spoke, "To answer the question asked, we hope to raise the overall consciousness of your sphere, to make the people of your race aware of their position in the global structure."

Bracken tried to read the alien's eyes, which were mere slits in the angular head.

Catine asked, "How long will that take?"

"Perhaps a generation. But, as the contacts increase and our presence becomes accepted, we will exhibit an open display of our purpose."

A student questioned, "I don't understand. If we are presently at a crisis point, do we have time to wait for another generation?"

Professor Frimleter appeared to emerge from a trance. "Don't you realize that our friends are able to hold back the release of destructive weapons anywhere on our planet in order for Nerkush to reach a state of maturity? This capability will allow us to dismantle our own arsenal and put our technology to more fruitful use. They want to teach us their advanced evolution structure. They will guide us—you and me—as Touch-Points to mold the thinking of the entire race and lead it in the proper direction."

With a loud sizzle, Ebbern faded from the viewer screen, replaced by a shimmering gray. Two flashing hexagons appeared.

"There is no cause for alarm," the Trionite assured. "That is the signal that our leader is ready to address you."

Shock registered on Frimleter's face.

"Yes," Taylay said, "this is a momentous occasion, even for Professor Frimleter."

Bracken repressed a surge of fluctuating emotion that careened between exaltation, fear, and humor. He had just been introduced to the Trionites. Now, he was to meet their leader. He'd never even met the leader of Nerkush. He could hardly wait to get Silas' reaction.

The screen crackled to life. Amazement rippled through the students as the faint outline of the upper part of a body appeared on the screen. It was shrouded entirely within the folds of a gray veil.

Taylay explained, "The energy veil you see covering our leader's body is necessary for his protection. His life is of the highest importance. It must be preserved while our expedition is in this primitive section of the universe."

"Please receive my warmest greeting," came the voice of the leader. A strong sense of authority and power emanated from the screen. "I congratulate you on being chosen to assist us in this program. It is my wish that all of you take the treatment and become Touch-Points, as Professor Frimleter has done."

Bracken gripped the arms of his chair. His heart pounded. This was the first he had heard of a treatment. Everyone else seemed familiar with the idea.

The leader's voice filled the chamber, the audio monitors straining under its resonance. The message was thrilling, enthralling, commanding. "Dedicated people like yourselves are a great asset to your country. Your cooperation ensures that our purpose will be more easily and speedily triumphant. After you become Touch-Points, and as the program evolves, our forces will be in contact with you. Remember, through you, a new order will sustain quality life for your race."

Without warning, the shrouded image vanished.

Catine's twangy whisper broke the ensuing silence. "He's awesome. Can we talk with him again?"

"A strong possibility, for those who become contacts," Taylay replied. "If you will all come with me, we will proceed to the transition compartment for the treatment."

Bracken's feelings of doubt picked away at a titanic urge to join this magnificent undertaking. The leader was powerful and seemed capable of almost any accomplishment. But, was there a price to accepting this program? Bracken felt mentally seduced. He tried to clear his head.

He lagged behind the students going down a passageway. In the transition compartment, each was shown to a softly-padded chair. Suspended above each chair was a set of metallic probes.

Taylay said, "If any one feels hesitant, please speak up. We do not desire to force people into this treatment."

Did no one share Bracken's apprehension? The others must be more informed. Feeling almost ashamed of his wariness, he slipped into a seat.

Taylay adjusted it to a reclining position and looked down at Bracken through narrow, unreadable eyes. "Sit back. We will begin shortly."

The Trionite disappeared from Bracken's field of vision. The apparatus above Bracken silently glided downward. He felt it lower over his head, felt the touch of cold metal on his scalp.

A soft hum acknowledged the beginning of its cycle.

CHAPTER 17

At the first sensations emitted from the probes, Bracken's defenses began to drop away. His muscles relaxed. His eyes grew heavy. They were nearly closed when a startling sight jarred him from his stupor.

Tingling with sudden alertness, he watched in disbelief as the surrounding walls of the ship lost their sophistication. The winking lights and complex readouts were slowly vanishing. In their place emerged curving walls of rock. Taylay, visible in the distance, appeared changed, looking fearfully hideous, like some kind of small, gray monster.

Desperately confused, Bracken reached above his head and pushed away the probes.

At once, Taylay appeared, again the courteous Trionite host. "Is something the matter?"

Bracken shook his head, not wanting to admit what he thought he'd seen. "I don't know," he muttered. "Everything looks different here in the transition compartment." He drew deep breaths and tried to focus his eyes. The polished walls and winking lights returned. Once more, Bracken felt that he was on a genuine space disk. "I'm okay now. I must have gotten a little dizzy."

"Shall we continue the treatment?" inquired Taylay unemotionally.

"No!" Bracken said. "I've decided to wait." The momentary shock of the unexplainable illusion was gone. Nevertheless, he wanted only to get back to Ebbern.

"Very well. Please sit quietly until the others are finished. Once on the ground, your equilibrium should return quickly."

The compartment now looked as Bracken supposed a space disk should look. He admonished himself for having let his imagination run awry.

As the probes lifted from the heads of those around Bracken, the chamber filled with talk of the beauty of the experience.

Taylay congratulated them. "You are the hope of your planet. And, now we have landed. You may return to the contact location."

Taylay bestowed a parting promise to the students. "You will be contacted for future assignments." To Bracken, the alien merely said, "Farewell."

Lisha and Silas ran to meet Bracken as he reached the bottom of the craft's steps. "What happened?" they demanded.

"I'm not sure. Not at all sure. Can we talk about it later?"

"I was afraid you wouldn't come back," Lisha cried, "that we'd never see you again."

Professor Frimleter hailed Bracken. "I don't know what inhibitions restrain you. But, I hope that nothing will keep you from following through on this. We need more like yourself who see the urgency of the hour."

"I'll have to think about it," Bracken said.

Behind them, the stairway retreated, the door sealed, and the glowing disk spun away.

* * *

The next morning, the sun streaming through the branches above woke Bracken. Thoughts of the previous night invaded his mind until he stifled them. He wanted to forget that experience and would continue for now to refuse to answer questions from Lisha and Silas.

Beside him, Lisha's face remained peaceful, her long lashes gently resting against the smooth skin of her cheeks. "You're beautiful," he whispered, and was rewarded by a sleepy smile as Lisha stirred. He leaned over with a tender kiss for her lips. She rolled away, not yet ready to come fully awake.

In the distance, a field bird warbled. The call traveled with the breeze that gently rippled stands of grain. Silas still slept. Bracken felt a deep bond with his friend. Despite the previous evening, he hoped Silas shared his joy at their being out here together, a renewal of their camaraderie during past travels.

Silas moaned and stretched. He cupped his hands beneath his head and studied the canopy of leaves. "Was last night a dream?"

To Bracken, it was indescribable. A mystery. He'd knocked on a door to another realm. "Let's call it that."

Awake now, Lisha declared, "Fine with me." She sat up and hugged her knees. "I'm just glad you're not orbiting in space." She inched closer and curled against Bracken. "I want you here with me, on solid ground." Something near the main road below caught her interest. "Look!" She pointed to a large vehicle pulled off to the side, its power drive cover propped open. "Such a big trans-max. I wonder if it's anybody important."

"Whoever it is has trouble," said Bracken.

"Let's go see." Silas began gathering up his gear.

Later, as they approached the stalled vehicle, Bracken quickened his steps. "Hey, Chepa! What are you doing out here?"

Chepa came to meet them. After he'd greeted Bracken and Silas, the musician adjusted the brightly-colored scarf tied around his head and gave Lisha a long look.

At Lisha's nudge, Bracken said, "Lisha, this is Chepa."

"Chepa from the Golden Flight?" Lisha frowned at Bracken. "You didn't say you'd met *that* Chepa."

The musician grinned. "We're on our way to Demur. Playing

there tonight, providing," he tipped his head toward the raised power cover, "we get there."

"Want me to take a look?" asked Bracken. "I've fooled around with a few power drives."

Chepa led the way. "We can use any help we can get. Hey, somebody bring something to eat for these people."

A pretty girl stuck her head out of the trans-max. "Sure thing, Chepa."

Silas and Lisha found a shady spot to sit. Yaavin and Shor ambled over and joined them. Sounds of music and laughter blended in the peaceful morning.

"Nice rig." Bracken admired the vehicle's sleek metal body lined with tinted convex windows. The interior had been sectioned into living quarters and a traveling lounge.

As Bracken worked, he listened to Yaavin and Shor countering one another on their instruments. Out of the corner of his eye, he saw Lisha's body swaying freely with the sounds. How like her to slip into the mood of the music and the moment.

The sun grew warm. Bracken wiped beads of perspiration from his forehead. Seeing Chepa brought strong memories of using the Mingus Stone. "How's the music these days?"

"Great! Our playing has come alive, if you know what I mean."

Bracken knew.

"Say, do you people need a ride?" Chepa pointed to the three packs at the side of the road. "We'll take you to Demur if you're headed that way."

Demur was across the bay from their destination, but what was wrong with that? They could go to the Community in Accad whenever they felt like it. Bracken backed out from under the power cover. "Sounds fine—and I've about got this energy generator going again."

"Funny how you came along. I was afraid we might not make tonight's performance. But, it must be in the cards for us to play at the Sea Sphere."

"The Sea Sphere! I hear that place is really something. Never been there."

Chepa clapped Bracken on the back. "Well, you're going tonight. You and your friends will be my guests."

"The Sea Sphere," Bracken marveled. "Can't turn down an offer like that."

Before long, Bracken stood back and wiped the grease from his hands. Chepa's driver started the power unit. It jumped to life with a loud roar.

Lisha was delighted to board the trans-max. "I've always wanted to go to the Sea Sphere," she whispered to Bracken. "Sea Sphere," she repeated, drawing out the words. "I love even saying the name."

Food and drinks were passed. Silas grinned his approval at

Bracken and settled back to enjoy the luxury of their new mode of transportation.

Lisha leaned against Bracken, fitting her body snugly next to his. "Isn't this wonderful?" she whispered.

He gave her a quick kiss and squeezed her hand tightly.

After the trans-max was underway, Chepa reached for his stam and handed one to Bracken. Admiring the expensive instrument, Bracken plucked the strings. Warm tones vibrated from the touch of his fingers. With Chepa listening, Bracken wanted to play his best, which was easy on that instrument.

"Not bad." Yaavin chuckled. "I wouldn't have guessed you could play that well without a visit from Layozz."

"We'll have Bracken sit in with the Golden Flight on a number tonight," Chepa said over the melodies. "I think the people will love him."

"Especially after he's had a touch of the stone," Yaavin added.

The trans-max lumbered down the road, a hive of melodic sound and pounding rhythm. Bracken doubted that even a touch of the stone could make him happier than he was at that moment.

* * *

The Sea Sphere floated on the sheltered Bay of Accad near Demur. Giant mooring lines, like threads of a silver web clutching a round ball, held the globe firmly beside a wide pier. Bracken had never seen anything like this performance hall. A transparent floor fanned out from the front of the platform and covered the entire diameter of the globe. A look downward revealed the lower part of the sphere falling away. Above, the walls of the sphere swept upward in a curving arc. Fixtures hung from the top of the dome, ready to turn the sphere into a glittering ballroom.

"See that transparent gauze-like material draped near the walls?" Chepa pointed to a covering stretched over, but not touching, the interior face of the sphere. "Behind that lining are special atmosphere producers. Tonight, when they're activated, you'll see what a fascinating world this place can become."

Someone called from the entryway. "Chepa!" A man strode toward them across the glass-like floor.

"You're just in time, Layozz." Obvious relief warmed Chepa's greeting. He eyed the pack on the newcomers shoulder. "I was counting on your getting here early enough so we could have some time together before this evening's performance."

Layozz acknowledged Bracken and Silas but quickly gave Lisha his full attention. Moving close, he looked down into her face with unabashed interest. "Somebody introduce me to this lovely lady."

After Bracken did so, Layozz continued his haunting gaze. Lisha and he exchanged a few words. She blushed.

Layozz headed off the floor, asking over his shoulder, "Bracken, have you told Lisha about our little secret?"

Bracken and the others followed. "Of course," he said, "but she's never . . ."

"Then, you know," Layozz said confidentially into Lisha's upturned face.

Bracken said, "Lisha isn't interested. I tried to tell her she should try it."

"Its effect is perfectly safe, Lisha."

"I have thought about it."

"With me to help you, there isn't a thing to worry about." Layozz spoke as if he and Lisha were the only two people in the Sea Sphere.

She said, "I don't know how I feel about something that is supposed to alter one's awareness of reality."

"Not alter," Layozz corrected gently. "The stone enhances reality."

Chepa nudged Bracken. "He's absolutely right, isn't he?"

For Bracken's part, he wanted Lisha and everyone else to experience the stone. He would even share it with the Pirax force or NAFIS if they'd accept it. He hoped Lisha wouldn't be put off by Layozz. She wasn't a woman, say like Aleena, able to handle almost any person or situation.

"There's more to life than meets the human senses and, I believe, there is much you have yet to understand," Layozz said with an abundance of charm. Lisha listened intently. "The stone is able to unlock treasures."

The other Golden Flight members had finished unloading the equipment and were sprawled over the stage. Chepa motioned to them. They fell in behind.

The group walked leisurely across the Sea Sphere's transparent floor, their footsteps tapping a slow marching rhythm on its hard surface. Layozz, his neatly manicured hand now resting firmly in the small of Lisha's back, led everyone through the double doors that marked the entrance to the musicians' lounge.

CHAPTER 18

Entering the music hall later that evening, Bracken was confronted by an overpowering sight. With the atmosphere producers activated, he had expected the room to be spectacular. But, as he mounted the stage, what he saw before him exceeded the limits of his imagination.

People dressed in a rainbow of colorful clothing clogged the massive floor. Splayed on the gauze-like surface of the curving walls were mixed hues of amber, violet, magenta, and vermillion. Dancing pigmentations spilled over the onlookers as a kaleidoscope of spotlights beamed down from above. Every action of the people swelled into fluid motion. Every tint of light shimmered with life.

Chepa had invited Bracken to sit in on rehearsal and the concert's first number. Now, basking in the effect of the Mingus Stone, and overwhelmed by the Sea Sphere's beauty, Bracken's heart bloomed in awe. At Chepa's signal to begin, Bracken erupted with song, as if ignited by the blaze of a hidden fire. His fingers sprinted on the strings of his stam, detonating an explosion of arousing sound.

Leaning into the crowd, he sang. His voice, unleashed, exalted in song like a chorus of anthems.

Wanderer, find your home,
Depart your vacant tomb,
Grasp the stars to take your flight,
Shake away the webs of fright,
And soar. . . .
Straggler, set your course,
Break the binding force,
Place your feet upon new ground,
Listen closely to the sound,
And roar. . . .
You are new, you are now, you are the breath of life.
You are free, you are here, you are the death of strife.
Hate will melt beneath our gaze
In the loving nights and endless days.
No more the fist of hate, gone forever suffering's gate.

The crowd thronged closer, begging for what the Golden Flight could give. Bracken eagerly offered the mass of people all that was within his power to grant.

The room began to glow with a radiance that bathed everyone in a gentle light. A shower of ethereal stars fell onto those swaying on the floor. Each person twisted in delightful response. Bracken watched with an aloof sense of knowing. He saw brilliant points of energy dancing over the heads of the people, stars of light, which he beheld as visible only to him and others on stage. Throwing his head back, Bracken laughed loudly with an exhilaration he'd never known before.

Suddenly, his laughter caught in his throat, stopped short by a sight high in the gauze-like veil covering the dome. There, a vortex of swirling, brilliant color began to splinter. As he watched, the rainbow palette melted under the hot lights. It seeped away and revealed dark, shadowy forms curling within the radiant lights, hiding safely behind the filmy veil.

But the crowd beckoned louder. Hundreds of bodies swayed, coupling, spinning, caressing. A rippling ocean of desire linked everyone in the Sea Sphere in a bond of fellowship. Voices called to Bracken from every side, asking for more, whispering for further blessings.

Riding a wave of pure ecstasy, Bracken left the stage at the end of the first number and joined Lisha and Silas. In melodic union, the Golden Flight played on until the early morning hours.

Chepa called Bracken back for the final number. Heart bursting with pride, Bracken gave his all to bring the concert to a sublime climax.

A resounding ovation echoed through the dome as Bracken and the others descended from the stage and pressed through the mass of admirers. Silas and Lisha greeted Bracken with almost reverent astonishment.

In the relative quiet of the musicians' lounge, Silas cupped his mouth and told Bracken, "The Mingus Stone has changed you."

Bracken smiled in agreement and drew Lisha close, defending her from the pressing crowd. Her brown eyes held an adoring look. He could feel the soft warmth of her love.

Layozz took Bracken to meet Yaavin's brother, Roon. "Roon has a place nearby, in the hills outside of Demur. He's invited us to go there and unwind where we won't be bothered by strangers. I can guarantee you a night like you've never experienced." Layozz looked to where Lisha and Silas eagerly watched the behind-the-scenes happenings. "Of course, the invitation includes Lisha." He caught her attention and flashed a wide smile. "Silas, too."

* * *

Roon's place turned out to be an isolated estate, spread over a private mesa, and situated at the end of a narrow, winding canyon road. A forest of low-growing trees covered the surrounding hills.

Lisha was ecstatic over the natural setting. After parking the trans-max, they made their way along a cobblestone trail. Lighted by burning torches, it led to the huge wooden door of their host's sprawling dwelling. Silas gazed approvingly at the thick open rafters, which gave a massive feeling to the main rooms of the house. Bracken could almost hear Silas thinking in terms of foundations and load-bearing beams.

A spacious gathering room dominated the floor plan. There, Roon introduced his mate, Rovalla, a buxom woman with straight black hair hanging to her waist. She wore a long, violet gown printed with abstract designs and tied with a silver cord.

Rovalla acknowledged the others, but she fastened her small dark eyes unwaveringly on Silas. His usual cheery greeting failed him, and he extended his hand, which she ignored. The silence became more and more strained until, at last, Rovalla said tersely, "Our guest is a man who will travel to untried domains."

Silas choked out a half-hearted laugh. "That's me! Always the adventurer." The look he gave Bracken suggested emphatically that their hostess suffered from mental illness.

Later, Roon's guests assembled in a circle near the huge, rock fireplace in the gathering room. Lisha sat under the protective eye of Layozz.

Soon, Layozz produced a glowing Mingus Stone from his pack. It was passed from person to person.

Bracken felt good. His new friends from the Golden Flight admired him. It would be a great night.

The instruments came out of their cases, and music enveloped the room. As a united body, people swayed and rocked. Unbound by others' values and traditions, they had their own lives to live and proclaimed it in song.

I've been forced in a mold like an ingot that's been cast.
I've kept the empty rituals and worn them like a mask.
But it's become an empty foolish task.
Let us leave them, not believe them,
We're free, free at last.

Undulating bodies echoed the words, pleading for freedom and liberation. These people sought their own world. Moving with the pulse of the music, they rode the increasing cadence to its peak.

Then, as Bracken played his stam, he felt a strange force begin to flow through his body. It added ease to his playing, but it became a sweet seducing power, gradually consuming him. He let himself go with it, yielding further and further.

Roon rose to his feet and began to dance around the room. His tall body rolled and jerked with the music's tempo, casting multiple shadows on the walls from the flickering firelight. Soon, Roon slowed his movements, his chiseled features dark, his eyes fixed intently on the fire. Then, from his throat came a deep wailing chant, rising and falling as he rocked in place, back and forth from foot to foot.

A sudden confusion and overwhelming apprehension swept over Bracken.

Roon began to laugh—a shrill, fiendish laugh that chilled the air. The laugh died away. Roon's face froze in a terrifying gaze. In his hand was a pole. Roon began to dance again. The pole swept along with him, bobbing and weaving, his intimate partner. Riding on the top of the pole was a stark white skull.

The music played incessantly. Bracken's confusion increased. His hands dropped from the strings of his stam. Hidden surges of energy stroked him, tempting him to play again, to play and never stop, to lose himself in the music. He resisted, not understanding the battle.

Bracken saw Silas across the circle. Suddenly, Silas jumped to his feet, his eyes filled with something that could only be described as raw terror. He looked around, like an animal seeking a route of escape, and ran for the front door.

The music beating in Bracken's head grew louder. He shoved away the stam as if it burned him. He sprang up and ran after Silas.

Once outside, Bracken's heartbeats slowed, his thoughts ebbed toward a more normal state. What had happened in Roon's house? Silas had fled in desperation. Why?

In the distance, Bracken saw Silas alone, staring at the darkened sky. Bracken moved carefully toward his friend, not wishing to startle him. The stars winked as if they knew a secret. Light rays from the sky refracted. The universe seemed to bend and twist.

Over pleasant melodious sounds, which filtered near, Silas must have heard Bracken's steps. Standing at the rocky edge where the mesa dropped away into a deep canyon, he said, "I don't know what's back in that house. But I saw evil in Roon's eyes."

Bracken reached out with a cautious gesture. "Come back from the cliff, Silas."

"The evil was pulling at me, smothering me."

Bracken inched closer. The drop over the cliff was long. The bending light from the sky revealed spike-like rocks jutting upward from the canyon floor.

"I'm sorry, Bracken. I just had to get out of there. Can you understand?" His voice trembled.

"It's all right," Bracken said as evenly as his own shattered state would allow. "Come back here by me. Everything will be fine."

"Everything will be fine," Silas acknowledged.

The pleasant, melodious sounds gently swirling over the mesa gave way to whirling tones and hypnotic rhythms. Bubbling, bouncing, rumbling sounds churned in Bracken's ears.

With them, a stream of ethereal fog began to drift from the house. Pushed by the rhythm, it billowed toward Bracken and Silas, ballooned around them, and then cascaded over the edge of the canyon, forming a large pool of glistening light.

A movement startled Bracken. "Silas!" he yelled. "What are you doing?"

"The pool of light!" Silas worked feverishly, stripping off his clothes. "Look, he's calling me to join him. Don't you see him, Bracken?"

Suddenly a glowing, enchanting face appeared, speaking out of the swirling fog below. "I am comfort, I am home."

Bracken tried to question. *What is that? Who is calling?*

Other voices coming from every side urged Bracken to trust, to be at peace. The face compelled him to look at its fascinating beauty.

It entreated, "Come, I will help you. You have no need to fear."

Bracken felt himself drawn toward the face. He desired its warmth and security. His whole being wanted to surrender to its power. It pulled at him, pulling him closer to its peace, closer to its rest.

"The pool of light," cried Silas. "It's beautiful. Don't you see it, Bracken? So sparkling . . . I must dive in."

Bracken tried to break free. *It's some kind of spell. I have to stop Silas.* But, perhaps the inviting, shimmering white before them was a carpet, lovingly laid on a real and solid surface.

Silas stepped forward.

In a violent burst of effort, Bracken wrenched free from the seductive mesmerization that cloaked his mind. He reached out for his friend.

But, Silas stepped again, toward the glowing face, stepping forward into nothingness. The cliff was behind him now. Briefly, he hung in the air, suspended like a bird. Then, in a graceful dive, he plunged into the pool—the pool of light.

For a moment, all was quiet, before the fantasized bubble of beauty burst, punctured by Silas' scream as his body crashed to the rocks below.

CHAPTER 19

"Sorry we had to handle things the way we did." Layozz came around the side of Roon's home and up the steps to the wooden sun deck where Bracken and Lisha sat. The deck, anchored by giant beams, hung out over the canyon. Layozz, his face gaunt from lack of sleep, plopped on the top step and took a long draught from the glass in his hand.

It was early afternoon. Many of the Golden Flight members and those who had accompanied them to the forest hideaway were inside, obscuring in a cloud of sleep the previous night's tragedy.

Bracken slumped on a lounge, where he'd been most of the long hours since Silas' death. He avoided the sight of the twisting gorge below the sun deck. "I can't believe he's gone." How many times had Bracken said that? There seemed to be nothing else he could say. Even with Lisha beside him, Bracken had never felt so alone.

She squeezed his hand. "Silas was my friend, too. I want to think that he really isn't gone. Somehow, I feel that even though his body is dead, somewhere he's still existing." She added tearfully, "Maybe he's even happier than we are."

Layozz swirled the ice in his glass. "I hope you understand why we couldn't let the Pirax know Silas had used the stone."

Bracken was torn by guilt at having collaborated in the false story that Silas, acting on a dare, went too far, and still mystified that the investigators had been taken in by it.

"It was wiser not to bring up the subject of the stone," continued Layozz. "The Pirax have been suspicious of me for some time now. They would jump at any chance to pin me."

Bracken lashed out on impulse, "They surely know you're a supplier."

Layozz narrowed his eyes and leaned back against the building. "Sure, I have a few stones."

Bracken probed. "The Pirax must hear the same rumors that everyone else does. That you're the main supplier, maybe the sole supplier."

Lisha gasped. "Bracken, be careful what you say." She looked around as if a NAFIS agent might lurk beneath the deck.

Layozz sent Lisha a smile of thanks. She returned it with one signifying that she would offer her support to Layozz under almost any conditions.

"Intangible rumors," Layozz sniffed. "The Pirax would like

enough hard evidence to lock me away. They want to crush everything that defies their limited sense of reality."

Lisha walked to the sun deck's railing. Her delicate profile silhouetted against the blue sky provided a moment's rest for Bracken's troubled thoughts. She appeared as fresh as the wild flower bouquets growing at the mesa's rim and reaching precariously over the edge to wave at the canyon below.

"I know" Bracken said, "still . . ."

Layozz interrupted, "Thanks to the Mingus Stone, the Community in Accad is already discovering a positive alternative to the regulated life. In another few years, it will have spread over most of Nerkush." His eyes followed Lisha. "If they trap me, it will cut off the supply of stones. That could have more far-reaching effects on human freedom than the death of everyone of us here."

"So, you are the sole supplier," Bracken accused.

Layozz bit his lip and then grinned. "Let's just say I have my source. Lisha, can I get you a glass of something?"

Lisha shook her head, but she went and sat on the step beside him.

Yeah, thought Bracken, remembering how he had first met Layozz on Mt. Shidow. *You have your source, all right, the Cibbmingus Mine.*

But, Layozz might have a point. If there were a way for anyone to learn from the Mingus Realm how Ebbern could be saved, then perhaps it was wrong to deprive people of the stone's use.

"It's just hard to accept that Silas isn't going back to Tizra with us, that he's never going to build those magnificent structures he dreamed of." Bracken buried his head in his hands. "If the stone," he moaned in despair, "helps people find happiness, and if it holds freedom and knowledge we need, then why did Silas die?"

"Oh, Bracken," Lisha breathed. "Try not to think about it."

Layozz spoke paternally. "Using the stone is a form of pioneering. And pioneering has never been free of mishap."

Bracken tried to think of Silas as a pioneer. If Silas' death could have been for a reason . . .

Layozz drained his glass. "I've seen enough phenomena in the Mingus level to know that there are powerful forces working out there. They may seem strange to us. Nevertheless, I am convinced that they are working for our good."

"I know that using the stone has made me feel completely free and at peace," Lisha said happily. "I hope we'll all be able to try it again before too long."

"You'll have to come and see me at Accad soon. You would love the Community."

"I'm sure I would," replied Lisha.

Bracken dropped out of the conversation and wandered off. He must wipe from his mind the part he played in introducing Silas to the stone. Bracken consoled himself that, maybe when he understood more about the workings of the stone, he could solve puzzles like Silas' death.

Not long after, he and Lisha climbed in Layozz's trans-rig to leave Roon's estate. At the bottom of the hill, the trans-rig stopped at a crossroad.

"This is my turn for Accad," Layozz said.

Bracken climbed out, carrying his and Lisha's packs. Before he could open the front door for Lisha, she lowered the window. Her face wore a strained expression.

"That's okay, Bracken. I'm not getting out."

Bracken gaped. "What do you mean?"

"I mean, I'm going on to Accad. I've always wanted to spend some time there." She beamed at the man beside her. "Layozz has invited me."

Layozz raised his eyebrows, accenting a faint twinkle in his eyes. "Lisha wants to see what goes on in the Community, and maybe try the stone again."

Caught in a flood of surprise and anger, Bracken stood beside the trans-rig holding the two packs. He felt rejected and foolish.

Lisha whispered, "You mean so much to me, Bracken. But, don't you see?" Her brown eyes opened wide. "I have to do a little exploring for myself, just like you do. I'll be fine—honest. Layozz can show me around."

"Lisha." He wanted to grab her face between his hands and tell her she couldn't go with Layozz. But, he had no right. "I thought we . . . I mean . . ."

"Neither of us ever made any promises."

"I know that. But, the Community isn't the best place for somebody . . . you're young and pretty. . . ."

"Young!" Lisha jutted out her chin. "You're not my father."

Bracken knew he'd made an immense error. He could almost hear Layozz snickering. "I didn't mean that the way it sounded, Lisha."

"Give me my pack, please."

Bracken had no choice, but he hated to let Lisha leave this way. "It's not that I want to hold you back," he said. "I'm just concerned for you."

Lisha softened. "Don't worry about me. I'll be fine." She gave a little wave as the trans-rig pulled away.

* * *

Bracken threw himself into his work at the Currency Center. Trasent obliged by heaping assignments on Bracken, so that there was little time to think about the loss of Silas.

Bracken was forced to visit Silas' home. Silas' mother followed him closely as he went into her son's room to retrieve his own belongings stored there just before leaving for Accad. Although she showed him kindness, her eyes were full of questions.

Now, living with Trasent, all Bracken's waking hours were occupied by his career or spent among people connected with it. He filed the memory of Lisha away as a remnant from a past era of his life.

Trasent seemed heavily preoccupied. He continued his frenzied exercise routines. During evenings at home, he appeared absent-minded, and conversation with his new roommate was limited. This puzzled Bracken, but he attributed it to increased pressures at the Currency Center.

Bracken saw little of his parents. When he did, their eyes were full of questions. He took gifts to Amont several times, and once flowers for Myra, but the visits were short.

He took to walking alone in the evenings. One foggy night, he paced a lonely back road leading out of Tizra, struggling with a tortured conscience and searching for an explanation to Silas' death. He hurried feverishly through the mist-shrouded twilight, determined to escape the guilt nipping at his heels.

Suddenly, a trans-speed exploded out of the fog. It flashed past Bracken, a blur of red, its power-drive growling like a harnessed animal. Abruptly, the roar changed to a rumble. The sound of popping gravel signaled the vehicle's turn. The trans-speed rushed toward him and slammed to a stop.

Bracken peered through the curtain of fog, trying to identify the driver by the softly-lit panel that illuminated the interior. The door swung open, and the overhead light revealed Aleena tilting her head toward him from the driver's seat.

"Want a lift?" The syrupy voice added a freshness to the ordinary invitation, even a hint of adventure.

Taken aback, Bracken blurted out, "How did you find me?"

Aleena's throaty chuckle put him in his place. "What makes you think I was looking for you?"

Bracken sputtered, "I meant, how did you happen to be out here?"

Aleena tossed her black hair and laughed her forgiveness. "If you must know, Trasent told me you'd probably be on this road. Well, aren't you going to get in?"

Bracken hesitated. "I think I'll walk a while yet."

"Look, Bracken, being alone isn't always the best thing to do when a person feels the way you do."

She often knew the way he felt. "If you don't mind, I'd like to be alone anyway . . . been thinking about Silas." She would know that, too.

Aleena got out of the trans-speed and grabbed Bracken's hand in her own strong ones. Firmly, she drew him around to the passenger side. Tonight, her professional demeanor had shifted to the background, and she seemed determined to accomplish something more venturesome than promoting her business. She cocked an eyebrow and waited for him to open the door and get in.

Although the idea of an after-hours adventure with Aleena was certainly attractive, Bracken was not in the mood to explore it. "Thanks anyway. I do appreciate your concern."

"You are not the only one who's ever lost a close friend, you know. I realize that it's hard to deal with the pain and the emptiness. But, looking at this from Silas' viewpoint, he is probably better off."

"Easy for you to say." Bitterness tinged Bracken's words. "You're still alive and breathing. You can see and hear and touch. . . ."

"So is Silas!" Aleena interrupted. "But, he's touching another world."

"Even if he was, how would I know that?"

Aleena opened the trans-speed door herself, and firmly shoved Bracken inside. She returned to the driver's seat and faced Bracken with a subtle lift to the warm curve of her mouth. "Perhaps there is a way you can know that. Perhaps I can show you."

Her eyes, two glistening points mimicking the darkness outside, contrasted with her light complexion. They held Bracken's gaze, compelling him to share her confidence in the well-being of Silas.

"Come Bracken, come back with me to Trasent's," she said. "Let me help you. We'll find some answers together."

The trans-speed, restored to life, sped toward Tizra.

* * *

In the gathering room at Trasent's home, Bracken lay on the plush floor-covering. Aleena had ushered him in with barely a word to Trasent. The lights were dimmed, the window-coverings closed. Showing no surprise, Trasent joined them as if it were an everyday occurrence for him to lie on his back, head to head on the floor with his roommate and a guest, their bodies spread as spokes on a wheel.

The soothing tones of Aleena's voice poured over Bracken, immersing him in melodious comfort. "Trust me, Bracken. Please trust me."

Bracken closed his eyes, determined to be receptive to whatever was going to happen. Aleena had promised to prove that Silas was presently in a more satisfied state than he was before plummeting to his death at Roon's place.

"You do trust me, don't you, Bracken?" Aleena entreated.

Trasent squirmed impatiently. "We all trust you."

Aleena's slender body stiffened.

Bracken answered, "Yes, I trust you."

"It won't be long," Aleena assured them. "The light-leap technique was perfected by the ancient ones. It has been passed down through the generations. Trektra was my teacher. She was the last in her group to carry the ancient wisdom to our age. She is still my guide, even though she has passed beyond our present sphere. She will come and lead us. We must relax and make ourselves ready."

Aleena's words melted Bracken's anxiety. His thoughts were

gradually replaced by lifeless leaves that swirled in circular winds. They crackled and crumbled and blazed bright red, fueling a fire to vanquish the chill of the evening. The flames grew brighter.

Then, through the flames, a voice spoke. "Realize the truth budding within." The voice was different, no longer Aleena's satiny tones. "You have banished some of your best ideas. Now, let them return."

Deeper, older vibrations echoed from Aleena's mouth like mellow notes from a seasoned musical instrument. Poetry and the language of music whispered against Bracken's heart, tapping for admission, reached into the hollows of his ears and reverberated within his head.

"Words will soon come from the one you seek," the voice continued out of Aleena. "But first, you must build a bridge through the shadow-barrier. Focus your mind. Let your higher self lead the way. Tread lightly, but with confidence, between the worlds."

Bracken lay, listening without effort.

"Ultimate perfection greets those who shake off the dust of their body," he heard. "Perfection is for those who make their way to self-realization. All is one—one is all."

The voice repeated, "All is one—one is all." Then, it said, "Welcome."

Suddenly, almost rudely, Aleena's body lifted off the floor. It jerked to a stop at a level above Bracken and Trasent. Slowly, her form rotated in place until Aleena was looking down on the two men.

Except, the face gazing into Bracken's bore little resemblance to Aleena's face. Her image changed form and function. Different faces appeared, superimposed over hers. Some were familiar, but not quite recognizable. Others were strange, some almost fierce.

The metamorphosis ceased. Bracken saw the face of a friend. It was Silas. The face looked down and smiled. It spoke. "Bracken."

Bracken stared, unable to comprehend.

The face spoke again. "What a journey I'm on!"

"That can't be you, Silas! Your voice sounds so odd."

"Sometimes, I seem to be moving through millennia in moments." Silas' words sounded reassuring, and yet . . .

"Is it you, Silas?"

In answer to Bracken's question, a torrent of assurance rushed over him as the voice became familiar—Silas' warm and cheerful tone.

"Other times, I'm moving as slowly as the tiniest creature. But, it is peaceful here. I am evolving. I am growing up."

An immeasurable joy swept over Bracken. Silas was here!

"Next time I come back to your world," the familiar voice continued, "I'll be different. I'll be better. I've learned from my mistakes. Don't feel sad. It was time for me to go. But, soon it will be time for me to return to your world, and then it will be better. I will be wise. We will meet again."

Bracken's joy began to slip away. Sorrow invaded his body. He was separated from his friend by a vast gulf between dimensions. Pain tore through him, twisting his emotions. Now, another sense marched in, overshadowing the twisting war within. The feeling was so strong that he could not contain it. He groaned mightily. "How do I know you are real? Maybe this is an illusion, a trick."

Instantly, Bracken knew he'd done something terribly wrong. Without warning, the body above him moved swiftly. It plunged downward, only to jerk to a stop inches from Bracken. He looked into the oracle's face.

Silas stared back at Bracken. Then Aleena. The two images seemed to sweep to and fro, like fragile wings of a giant insect in slow motion, until the picture of reality froze once again on the endearing face of Silas.

"Don't doubt what you feel, Bracken. This is another step for you. Others will come to teach you. Listen to their wisdom. Trust Aleena. She has walked with the ones who know all secrets. We will meet again. We will. Don't be sad . . . I'm happy. You will be happy, too. Trust me . . . trust in them."

The voice was fading. Bracken willed himself to reach Silas, not to lose him again. A grim purpose seized Bracken. Perspiration rolled from his body. He wrestled, helpless to stop the voice from fading completely. Powerlessly, he watched the image of Silas flicker from Aleena's face and then return for one brief moment, only to vanish completely.

Gradually, Aleena's body rotated back over. It moved to Bracken's left and, like a feather descending on a gentle updraft, floated downward, settling gracefully on the soft covering of the floor.

CHAPTER 20

In the days following the strange meeting with Silas, Bracken was reluctant to admit that the event was more than a spell woven by fascination with Aleena's eclectic personality. Then, as time elapsed, and Silas' death preyed less on his mind, Bracken reasoned that there must be something to the business of contacting people who had passed on to another sphere. The thought that Silas was happy comforted Bracken. The thought that his friend might somehow be reachable reinforced Bracken's philosophy that there were worlds to explore, and he was the one to do it. Unlimited knowledge and vast realms of truth awaited him. There was power to be had.

Bracken found a new dimension in the power structure at the Currency Center when Trasent introduced Arnaman, a silver-haired man who directed International Human Relations.

This executive from the upper echelons of the Currency Center exercised control and influence. His dark eyes appraised Bracken, who felt as naked as the man's high forehead. Bracken's gaze, usually unwavering, shifted from the deep horizontal creases above the heavy brows and dropped to the neatly trimmed silver beard below Arnaman's full lips.

Arnaman appeared often for short visits. One afternoon, when leaving the dead file storage area on the sub-floor with Golens, Bracken came face to face with Arnaman and Trasent. Bracken suppressed a wayward urge to salute. After a brief acknowledgement, Trasent and Arnaman continued down the corridor. Golens and Bracken waited just long enough to see the two men pause before an unmarked door across from the file storage.

Golens turned away. "Don't stare. Come on upstairs."

"Why the hurry?"

"I'll give you a tip, Bracken. Don't hang around when anybody's going in or out that door. It's top secret company stuff. We're all supposed to pretend that door doesn't exist."

"What's in there?"

Golens snorted. "I know a lot of what goes on around here. But I'm not privy to that area."

"Can't be that important."

"Oh, yeah? Do you know that no one goes in there without an escort? I mean, no one!"

Now safely removed from the object of their discussion, Bracken probed. "Of course, a high-level manager—say, like Trasent—can go anywhere, can't he?"

"Not if he values his job. No one goes in there alone."

Arnaman departed before the day's end. Bracken put the finishing touches on a report for Trasent, trying not to think about the unmarked door below and the time he'd seen Trasent there—alone. It wasn't significant, he told himself, a man like Trasent sometimes had to bend rules in order to get a job done. Besides, Golens could be wrong.

"Bracken," Trasent interrupted Bracken's thoughts. Bracken jumped guiltily, sending the last page of the report fluttering to the floor. "There's a message for you. The new clerk put it on my desk." Trasent frowned at the paper in his hand. "It seems to be important."

Bracken snatched the paper. It was a message from Lisha. *I need transportation. Urgent.*

* * *

Bracken had no trouble locating the site of Chepa's concert in Accad's largest park. He hurried toward it, hoping to find news of Lisha. A stop at Layozz's empty house had proved fruitless. Again, he thanked his good fortune to work for a supervisor who willingly granted time off for personal business.

The Golden Flight's trans-max gleamed in the sunlight. A stationery object, it reigned over a sea of hundreds of erratically drifting people waiting for the concert to begin. Bracken surmised that a large percentage of them were already under the effect of the Mingus Stone, and many had plainly been intoxicated by other means.

But he was not prepared for what confronted him as he reached the stage area and approached the trans-max. The door swung open, and Lisha stepped out. Her brown eyes reflected a distant and elusive fire. She smiled almost remotely at Bracken and brushed by him with a light embrace.

He caught her arm. "Lisha, it's me."

She let her arm go limp until he released it.

Bewildered, he said, "You asked me to come, remember?"

Lisha walked toward the stage.

Considering their last parting, Bracken hadn't known what kind of welcome to expect, but having responded to her plea for help, he did not like to be ignored. Chepa and his musicians ascended from the rig.

"Hey, Bracken's here," said Yaavin. "Somebody give him a stam."

"Yeah, we could use you today." Chepa grinned. "One of the guys is, shall we say—indisposed."

As the musicians mounted the stage, Bracken heard a voice at his side. "Lisha wanted to see the park through new eyes."

Bracken recoiled at encountering Layozz, the man who'd brought Lisha to explore Accad and the Community. Granted, Lisha had made her own decision. But, Bracken could well guess what went on once Layozz had Lisha to himself.

"She used the stone," Layozz said cheerfully, "with particularly exciting results this time."

Bracken swallowed his bitterness. He had no hold on Lisha, who stood staring at the sky in apparent captivation. "Is she going to be all right? She's acting kind of strange."

"She's fine," assured Layozz, casting an approving eye toward Lisha. "She's a beautiful woman, and I believe she's beginning to discover a part of herself she never knew existed. Don't worry. I've been watching out for her."

"I bet you have!" Bracken muttered.

"Hey! Nobody forced anything. She's a special person. I wouldn't hurt her. I've helped many people through this." Layozz pulled a silver box from his pack. "We haven't forgotten you, Bracken. Go find a spot in the trans-max."

Bracken crossed his arms firmly. He rocked back on his heels and spat into the grass, his eyes riveted to the box. Then, eagerly he grabbed the container. Hating Layozz's knowing smile, he catapulted up the steps into the trans-max.

Inside, he re-considered. He had more at stake now. Getting caught using a substance on NAFIS's controlled list could conceivably cost his job at the Currency Center. That would bring an ugly end to his newfound life—his salary, his living arrangements with Trasent, his career. He pictured explaining to Aleena he was jobless and homeless. He snickered. No use fooling himself—if tested, Aleena's loyalty might be as changeable as her volatile personality. He hoped not.

The initial sounds of the entertainment winged their way from the stage. Chepa needed Bracken for this performance. The stone would help Bracken play his best. The people waiting deserved the finest concert the Golden Flight could give. And today, Bracken was again a part of the Golden Flight.

Besides, Bracken thought, Lisha had asked him to come. She needed him, and she was using the stone. A touch of it might help him understand what was troubling her. He opened the silver case.

This time when Bracken pressed the stone against his head, something new happened. A dreadful shudder traveled through his body. It must be more powerful than the others, Bracken told himself, already slipping under its spell.

Later, Bracken detected that the effect was leveling off. Physically unsteady, but confident in his euphoria, he stepped from the trans-max and walked toward the platform where Chepa's group was performing. He wanted to be on the stage. But he wanted Lisha, too. Where was she?

Soon, mesmerized by the driving sound waves and the swaying

crowd, disorientation overcame him. He sat down on the grass, his body tingling delightfully. The separate parts of his environment began to flow into one. Caught up in his joyous surroundings, he was only partially aware of a growing derangement. Soon he was hopelessly overwhelmed.

Confused and slightly fearful, he got up and struggled against the flow of the crowd, searching for Lisha. His movements clumsy, he bumped into people. He made equally clumsy apologies, meeting vacant stares or hostile glances. He paused, spraddle-legged to keep his balance. His gaze fell on Lisha.

In seeming ecstasy, she spun around and around, her body entwined with that of a man who held her in an embrace meant for a private time and a private place. Bracken edged closer, until a stark realization knotted his stomach and brought tears to his eyes. The man Lisha embraced was Layozz.

Pain like that of a knife blade twisted in Bracken's heart. He wanted to run, but he had no strength to run.

He wove his way forlornly back toward the trans-max. Struggling with the hurt of betrayal, his mind a flurry of hatred and bitterness, he climbed into the trans-max and collapsed.

Did Lisha care for him? Exciting, unpredictable Aleena must care for him. Maybe she cared desperately. Maybe Lisha had never cared, even before she went off with Layozz. Maybe she would never care for Bracken again.

Bracken felt himself approaching a danger point. His emotions were engaged in violent war, trapped in a cage with ferocious beasts. Suddenly, an odd sensation interrupted the agonizing battle. Miraculously, the bars of the cage parted. Something resolved itself, mysteriously setting him free. Free from Lisha. Free from himself.

Overcome with relief, he slipped into sleep.

When Bracken awoke, it was dark outside. Peering through the window, he saw a quiet residential street. Footsteps sounded beside the vehicle.

Chepa climbed aboard. "You're awake." His voice held a note of concern. "We weren't sure you'd come around before morning."

Bracken's head whirled. "Where are we?"

"The Community. Parked near Layozz's house."

"Guess I wasn't much help on stage today . . . don't know what happened."

"We managed okay."

Bracken stood up, holding his head. He felt different.

Chepa gave Bracken a wary look. "We're staying in Layozz's home tonight." He fingered a large ring set with a coiled serpent. "I guess you know Lisha is with Layozz."

"I know." Bracken was strangely unmoved by Chepa's statement. Lisha was free to be who she wanted. Now he could accept that.

* * *

Sometime during the night, Bracken awoke with a start, hearing the unmistakable sound of sobbing. Cracking open the door of his room in Layozz's home, he saw the downstairs corridor leading to the stairway. There sitting on the bottom stair, he found a trembling Lisha, her head buried in her lap.

She raised up and gasped, "Bracken! I thought you'd gone." Her face, wet with tears, glistened in the passageway's faint light. Her golden hair was disheveled, her clothing in disarray, as if she'd dressed in a hurry. In her hands, she clutched a small bag. "I looked for you in the trans-max, and it was empty."

"I'm staying down the corridor in a room with Chepa." The pitiful picture Lisha presented had little effect on Bracken. "I hope you've had a good time these past weeks with Layozz."

"Oh, Bracken!" Lisha cowered. "Please don't say that. I made a terrible mistake. That's why I asked you to come."

Still aloof, Bracken said, "You really didn't need me. I admit I was concerned, but I understand much better now."

"No you don't. I'm sorry that I ever went with Layozz," Lisha whimpered. "I don't know why I did. I'm ashamed."

"Hey, you're your own person. You have to find your own way, and Layozz is part of that way."

Shaking her head in silent denial, Lisha reached out to Bracken.

Bracken stepped back. "Honestly, I'm glad you two can enjoy each other." It felt good to hurt Lisha. Her vulnerability only increased the sharpness of his tone. But, he was being honest, too. "Remember, neither of us ever made any promises."

Lisha's face contorted. "Layozz is horrible. It was beautiful and seductive at first. Now it's different." Her shoulders crumpled in dejection. "He doesn't care for me. He just deceived me so he could use me."

"You have it all wrong, Lisha. Layozz cares. I care. The problem is you. You've got to learn to let go. Quit holding onto your emotions. You have to erase superficial feelings before you can learn to really care."

Lisha recoiled, her brown eyes wide with shock. She hissed, "What are you saying? It's like you weren't yourself. You're distant and cold." She retreated, feeling her way up to the second step. "I told you I was sorry. What do you want? Please help me."

"Calm down. I am trying to help you," Bracken assured her. "But you must loosen up. Layozz can make you happy again. Go on back to him."

"You're so different, Bracken." Lisha shook her head. "I'm confused. Something is terribly wrong with everything. I have to get out of this place."

"Lisha, let me explain. The stone released me. Now I'm free to care for you without clinging to you. We don't need commitment. Commitment would only smother our emotions for each other."

"No! I don't want to hear that. I'm afraid." Her eyes, flitted to the shadowy corners of the passageway. "I want to leave. There's something bad here. Don't you sense it? It's evil!"

A violent tremor shook her, as if the evil had overtaken her. Then, in a sudden rush of motion, Lisha darted like a frightened deer, past Bracken and down the corridor. Flinging the front door wide, she ran into the night.

* * *

Bracken stared after Lisha long after the padding of her footsteps faded away. His old affection for her conflicted with his newly formed resolve that remaining uncommitted was the best course for both of them.

Early morning fog swirled through the doorway. Distracted by his thoughts, Bracken paid little attention to a disturbance outside until startled by a frenzied flurry of activity. Feet clattered along the walk. Four armed figures materialized in the haze. They swept through the open door and overpowered Bracken. He fell to the floor, shielding his head against a barrage of blows.

Bracken lay stunned, helplessly aware that his assailants tore through Layozz's house, rousing the sleeping occupants and forcibly assembling them in the gathering room. A grizzly looking man roughly pulled Bracken to his feet and shoved him to where the others were crowded tightly against one wall.

"We're not taking your word this time, Layozz," growled a voice that seemed vaguely familiar to Bracken.

The intruders turned lights on their captives while they themselves remained in the dark. The speaker appeared to be a short, squat man with a bulbous nose. He clutched a hand weapon, its blunt snout pointed at Layozz's head.

"We want the map, and we'll get it if we have to take this building apart." He jerked the hand weapon toward Bracken and the others. "And we'll take you and your friends apart while we're at it."

"Violence won't be necessary." Layozz appeared unruffled. "I'm a miner. Of course, I have detailed maps of this whole region. Which area? . . ."

"He's playing games," interrupted a towering hulk with arms like tree trunks. "Shall I set him straight?"

The first man snarled, "One more chance, Layozz. We want the map to your source. And then you're going to take a little hike with us up to Mt. Shidow."

"I'll give you the map if that's what you want. But it won't do you any good."

"Hah! I thought there might be more involved than that ancient map. That's why we're taking you along."

"No," Layozz insisted, "it's just that the stones won't do you any good. I mean, what do you intend to do with them once you find them? You surely know the effect they have on people."

"Do I know?" A coarse laugh echoed through the room. "Stop jabbering and hand it over."

Layozz continued with incredible poise. "Then, you must realize that once you're exposed to the Mingus Stone, you will look at reality in a changed way. Your perspective will be so different that you'll no longer desire to carry on this foolish life of crime."

"A possibility—if I was planning to use the stones myself."

"If you're not, then what interest could you have in the stones?"

Bracken noticed Layozz's eyes roaming purposefully, taking in their assailant's positions.

The portly man smirked, sucking in his protruding stomach. "Money, Layozz—the same motive you have. Quit stalling."

Layozz had slipped back slightly and now began to edge along the wall. "Oh, but you're wrong. If financial gain was my motive, you wouldn't find me freely distributing the stones."

Layozz's opponent sneered. "Those free samples are a perfect come-on. Try the product a few times, and then you drag out the price list." The chubby man's patience evaporated. "The map, Layozz, and no more talk!" He panned the barrel of his hand weapon down the line of prisoners hugging he wall.

"All right," sighed Layozz. "You win." He pointed to a picture hanging on the wall by his right shoulder. "It's here, behind this. . . ."

Suddenly a loud explosion shook the room. Bracken ducked, thinking that the intruders had opened fire. But, the blast had come from the front of the house.

The fat man and his cohorts whirled in surprise as a Pirax assault squadron stormed down the hall and into the gathering room, their boots clacking on the floor, their weapons ready. The two armed groups eyed each other.

Taking advantage of the distraction, Layozz completed his movement to the wall and touched a control panel behind the picture frame. From between the ceiling beams, a thick gaseous cloud showered down on the trespassers. The chemical triggered violent coughing and choking and at the same time enveloped its target in a foggy screen.

Layozz and his invited guests pulled their clothing over their faces to ward off fall-out from the released chemical. He herded them out of the room, down a narrow passageway, and through another door.

A power drive whined beneath the floor. With tearfilled, burning eyes, Bracken saw Layozz jerk a worn pack from a concealed compartment in a wall unit. The power drive churned to a stop, and Layozz pulled back a thick floor covering.

"Give me a hand," he ordered.

Bracken sprang to help. Together they lifted a section of flooring, revealing a dimly-lit stairwell dropping away below.

"Quick," Layozz yelled over the sound of the nearby battle, "this passage leads to an exit in the park." His companions balked. "Go on!"

Layozz shoved the man nearest the stairwell, sending him below. "The Pirax have nothing on me. Probably hoped that gang would lead them to something. But I'll have to disappear for now. And so will you." Over muffled explosions resounding from the main room, Layozz commanded, "Go through the tunnel and then split up into small groups. Lay low."

"We have to meet somewhere," Chepa cried.

"At Roon's house." Layozz hissed.

"Get the trans-max off the streets," Chepa called to the Golden Flight's driver scrambling below.

Last, Layozz dropped through the narrow opening. He reached up and pulled at the dislodged piece of flooring and the rug. Deftly, he slid them into place. As the sliver of light from above was cut off, Bracken ran down the murky tunnel, trying not to stumble on its rough surface.

Behind him, Layozz vented a stream of curses and yelled, "Move!"

CHAPTER 21

Bracken and Chepa stood at the trail's end in the Forest of Zorek. Again and again, Bracken read from the flat metal rectangle Dalfang had given him, repeating the cryptic formula that was supposed to open the Door to the Anindi Passage of Malchag.

Chepa slouched against a boulder and smirked. "I admit that this is a unique rock formation. But the entrance to another world? Not a chance!"

"Shut up! I don't need your sarcasm." Bracken tried once more, remembering Dalfang's admonition to remain faithful and persistent. "Besides I didn't hear a better suggestion from you for avoiding the Pirax." Bracken wished he'd never left Tizra. Nothing could describe how foolish he felt at this moment, begging the side of a mountain to let him in. Half-heartedly, Bracken gave a last try, with no results. "Let's go! I'm no good at moving mountains."

"My son, you are much too impatient."

Bracken whirled toward the voice, startled, but thankful to encounter Dalfang.

* * *

Later, the three men sat in Malchag, viewing the evening splendor, which slowly enveloped the landscape.

Bracken finished the final sweet bite of a blue gourd fruit. "This place is more enchanting the second visit. It is hard to remember that there is even the word *trouble* in our vocabulary."

"Is it any wonder," Dalfang asked, "that Malchag becomes a refuge for many from the other world?" He added thoughtfully, "Someday, it will be the only refuge."

Chepa yawned. "I don't know about it being the only place to go, but the way I feel now, I'd like to stay here forever."

Bracken disagreed. "I'm not ready to sequester myself anyplace, no matter how tranquil and beautiful."

Dalfang fingered the smooth bowl of his unlit pipe. "The wisdom to recognize Malchag as the one true parallel universe is here for the taking. Not everyone is willing to learn this." He paused with a perceptive look at Bracken. "Some leave, still searching, always searching."

Dalfang's insight made Bracken uneasy. "I lost a friend not long ago. My best friend."

"Sad, for you." Dalfang's blue eyes reflected sympathy.

"Bracken's buddy, Silas, was killed." Chepa said.

"It was strange, and terrible." Memories flooded over Bracken. "Everyone used the stone that night, but Silas just dived off into space. He saw a face and heard someone calling him to jump into a pool of light. The next thing I knew, he lay dead, crushed at the bottom of the ravine. And . . . and, before Silas jumped, I saw a face, too."

Dalfang, eyes half-closed, sat quietly for a time. "Layozz opens the vistas of the Mingus Stone for many."

"You know Layozz?"

"Yes, I brought him here." Remorse couched the old man's expression. "I hoped to convince him of the higher virtues of the world that lies in Malchag, as opposed to his method of reaching another level. Unfortunately, he left unimpressed. Like you, Bracken, he failed in his first attempts to open the passage and, therefore, he chose an easier alternative."

"You must agree that Layozz's method has some value," Bracken said. "The possibilities of the Mingus Stone appear to be unlimited."

"No doubt," Dalfang said. "I would never discourage anyone in his quest for truth. Even before Layozz, I knew Cibbmingus. He was my companion on many journeys by way of the stone."

Bracken stood up and walked a little apart, wanting to hide his surprise at this news.

Dalfang stroked his beard. "There is good in the awareness of that upper level. But, there is also evil. Today, you and Chepa entered the gateway to something far greater than anything offered by the Mingus Stone."

Bitterness crept into Bracken's voice. "Silas deserved the best."

"Unfortunately, for a person like your Silas, who obviously knew little of what he toyed with, tragedy is not uncommon. Within the flow of the Mingus Stone is concealed a tyranny not easily recognized."

"Tyranny? Are you saying that some entity might have been in control of Silas' actions, that his death could have been deliberately caused?"

Dalfang's shoulders lifted, then dropped. "Perhaps. Perhaps not. If it was a premeditated act of destruction, it would not have been the first."

"Murder? That's hard to believe," Chepa commented skeptically.

"For years now," Dalfang defended his position, "I have been aware of the depraved aspects of the stone's power. The effect can bring about good, but many have turned it to evil."

"How can evil and good mix in the same instrument?" Bracken argued. "It doesn't seem possible, unless somewhere there is a source, a central place where the power originates."

"You have spoken wisely." Dalfang seemed pleased. "Most certainly there is a central source of power, an energy which holds this great universe together. Some choose to use that energy for good.

Some use that energy for evil. The source is in all of us, and we are part of one another. Each of us creates his own destiny."

"Perhaps, but . . ."

"I know," Dalfang finished for Bracken. "You have a passion to search. Well, search on, my friend, but be careful in your wandering. There are those who hate eager souls such as yours."

* * *

Far from Ebbern, Professor Frimleter sat on the edge of his seat in the space disk watching the viewer screen. Taylay waited beside him, an apparent smile on the alien face.

The screen's surface buzzed to life, displaying two flashing hexagons. Then, shrouded by a gray veil, the form of the leader materialized, presenting a majestic picture in a location that seemed to be the command center of a mother ship.

Frimleter's heart pounded. Although still obscured by the gray veil, the leader appeared more clearly than the Professor had seen before. A host of bustling Trionites served as aides, and Frimleter blinked in awe at the array of technological devices that lined the ship's interior. He could only guess at the number of other space disks that must be linked to this mother ship by the mystifying equipment.

The leader spoke in authoritative tones. "I have an urgent matter to discuss with you."

"Do you want me to hold another contact meeting?" At the thought, Frimleter's pulse raced even faster.

The leader clasped his hands, leaning his elbows on the arms of his command chair. The veil seemed to grow thinner, revealing more and more of his movements. "This time, I hope to make our purpose known to a much larger group."

"I think you will be well-satisfied at the number of my newly-recruited potential Touch-Points." Frimleter wished he could see the pleased smile that must have graced the leader's face at this announcement.

"We want you to arrange a contact gathering of several thousand people."

Frimleter drew back, aghast. "Several thousand . . . I could never . . . I mean, how would I assemble that large a group?" Did the leader realize the magnitude of what he asked? "Thousands? That's impossible . . . ," Frimleter broke off, fearing impertinence.

"Assistance has been arranged." An aide handed the leader a gray portable panel. The leader consulted it. "A music group based in Accad is known as the Golden Flight."

Frimleter nodded. He'd heard of it.

"We want you to contact them and arrange a concert at the Pillars of Rimlex."

"A concert? In a place like that? Why would they consent to leave Accad?"

"The Community in Accad is presently being hindered from its normal activities by a Pirax restrictive which forbids large gatherings. The Golden Flight will welcome an invitation to hold a concert elsewhere."

Frimleter cleared his throat. It had developed a scratchiness.

"The Golden Flight is in hiding now. But shortly, the members will be looking for a way to restore their following. An envoy will contact them and convince them that a huge gathering at the Pillars will accomplish exactly that."

Frimleter swallowed furiously, willing his dry throat not to start him in a coughing fit. "What about permits and . . .?"

The shrouded form on the viewer screen grew in size. Its hands knotted on the command seat's arms. "Certain officials in your area understand our cause."

Frimleter bit his lip. The challenge began to sound less intimidating. To be entrusted personally by the leader with a project of this size was an overwhelming honor. Frimleter's thoughts pushed ahead, mentally outlining his first chores.

But the leader was not finished. He stood up and moved so that his upper body filled the screen. "When those who have become discontented are confronted by the potential we offer their race, they will be willing to help us institute our evolutionary restructuring program."

The professor's attention fastened on the screen, his head jerking in short, quick nods.

"At this concert, we will inform thousands of our purpose."

Frimleter's thin lips silently formed the word *how*.

The overpowering image answered the unspoken question, "During the gathering at the Pillars of Rimlex, we shall manifest ourselves."

Manifest ourselves . . . manifest ourselves. The words seem to repeat, even as the image on the viewer screen disappeared, replaced by gray darkness. Frimleter felt faint, as if he, too, were being replaced by gray darkness.

CHAPTER 22

After a few days, Bracken and Chepa left the refuge of Malchag. They hiked along the road that led to Roon's place.

Suddenly, the silent trek was interrupted by a violent attack that swept both men off the road and into the ditch. Entangled in a scourging net of brush and bodies, Bracken struggled wildly until a repeated command made itself heard.

"Keep down! Stay out of sight!"

The voice sounded familiar, but there was nothing friendly in the strength that bent Bracken's arm near the breaking point.

"Yaavin!" shouted Chepa, spitting dirt. "You guys crazy?"

"No, just saving you from big trouble." Yaavin rolled off Bracken's back and squatted in the ditch.

Shor eased himself off Chepa. He pointed to a crossroad ahead. "There's a Pirax rig behind the big boulder on the left and another across the way."

"Yeah," Yaavin said, "they're watching the road. It's better that they don't see any Golden Flight people going to my brother's house. After one guy dying on the property, Roon doesn't need more Pirax snooping around."

Chepa sneered, "Since when is it a crime to visit a friend?"

Shor answered, "I don't know where you two have been the past week, but NAFIS has cracked down, putting people away for any reason."

Except for the statements he'd given the Pirax investigating officers the night of Silas' death, Bracken had escaped notice and wanted to remain in the background. "On what charges?"

Yaavin shrugged. "Whatever they can make stick. They want the Community to fall apart. They aim to get anybody like a leader out of the way."

"Meaning Layozz?" Bracken asked.

Yaavin grinned. "You bet. But he's already here at Roon's. So are most of the guys."

"We brought the trans-max in before things got critical," Shor said. "You two cut up through the forest. Keep away from the road. Layozz has a plan."

Later, Bracken stalked over the grounds around Roon's place, angry that this role of fugitive—however temporary—had been forced on him. He turned away from the sight of the deep gorge running beside the house, shuddering at the memory of Silas' body diving into its depths. Somewhere, someplace, there must be answers. With Aleena's help, he had met Silas, but that strange encounter had raised new and mysterious questions.

He smiled grimly. He could almost see his mother turning the pages of an ancient leather book and saying, *The answers are all here, Bracken.* Perhaps for her, Bracken thought.

Ebbern was on its way to destruction. More than pretty phrases were needed to stop that.

Bracken whirled and marched back into Roon's house. Nothing he'd experienced in the Mingus realm since first finding the silver box in the forest had matched that initial touch of the stone. He wanted whatever ultimate knowledge, whatever truth, the Mingus realm could offer. And he wanted it now.

He sought out Layozz. "I want to use the strongest stone you have."

Layozz's eyes narrowed. "Your timing is rather poor. We're leaving tonight."

"Leaving, for where?"

"I know a fellow in the Valley of Raka, in the desert." Layozz waved vaguely inland. "His place is no resort. But, he always needs people to work for him." Layozz snickered. "High turnover in personnel out there."

"I've got a job. I can't work for your friend."

"Shad is more of an acquaintance than a friend. It's a trade-off. We do a little work for him. He'll help us out."

"You mean, he'll let us hide there?"

"That's the idea."

Bracken weighed that prospect against a chance of being questioned about matters he didn't wish to be involved in. He could delay his return to the Currency Center a few more days. Surely, things would cool off soon. Besides, he needed something badly from Layozz. "So what if we're leaving tonight? I can still use the stone," he insisted. "The strongest one you have—now."

"You're not ready for it."

"I'm ready."

Layozz stared out the window and across the gorge. Finally he relented. "Okay. But at your own risk."

* * *

"Welcome once again to the Mingus realm." Hiffornak emitted a hypnotic tone that drew Bracken closer and closer to the creature of light. "I've been waiting. But, where are those you were to bring with you?"

The shroud of brightness drifted gracefully before Bracken. A rush of anticipation reinforced the already indescribably pleasurable vibrations massaging Bracken's body. Here was a friend, a friend who possessed intelligence and abilities far beyond those exhibited on Ebbern.

"I came by myself."

"This time you have advanced to a new level." The being applauded the achievement.

Confidence flowed through Bracken, and he challenged Hiffornak, "You warned me that Ebbern will be destroyed."

"And so it shall."

"You promised me knowledge and awareness so that our planet can be saved."

"With time, you will realize the answers you seek."

"I need answers now."

"But do you not wish to share with others this new level of existence? Would you deprive them of that which you enjoy?"

"You told me there is little time left for Ebbern."

"Then, why do you trouble yourself with your friend's death?"

The pleasurable vibrations changed momentarily from soothing fingers to tiny charges of pain. Bracken peered into the heart of the light, seeking to penetrate its effulgence. "Silas is dead, killed in this realm. You exercise vast power and knowledge, and yet, you were either unable or unwilling to protect him."

Hiffornak retreated a short distance. Low hums, punctuated with an occasional fluttering buzz, indicated that the creature might be consulting with an unknown source. The hums ceased, and Hiffornak returned. "We were aware of your friend's destiny, but to interfere is simply not our way."

Angry at this heartless lack of concern, Bracken tried to see around the creature.

"As you have learned, if one leaves your world, he is not gone forever."

"But Silas spoke of evil. What about that?" Bracken edged in a circular direction. If only he could get beyond Hiffornak. Perhaps a greater being was within reach.

"Some venture into regions in which they should not tread."

Determined to discover all he could, Bracken boldly dodged around Hiffornak, but the view was blocked by a veil of darkness. He charged toward it.

The darkness thickened and grew, extending until it formed a black pit, with Bracken teetering at the edge. The pit seemed to fall in an endless black void. Bracken looked for the benevolent creature of light. It had vanished.

Driven by a nameless terror, Bracken sprinted away from the black pit. He ran faster, and still faster, but gained nothing. In fact, he seemed to slip backward as walls of darkness rushed forward around him. He was being left behind, constantly retreating to the pit.

Laughter rang in his ears. Shimmering bubbles of light popped around him, revealing a sinister army of bat-like creatures. Flying, turning, swooping in formation, their wings screaming through the air in a loud whine, they fell toward Bracken like huge birds of prey. Larger bubbles of light exploded in violent bursts that sent shards of glass whistling toward Bracken, pricking with greater and greater intensity.

His legs felt heavy. He began to stumble. His heart pounded. The scream of winged creatures drew closer. Bracken's agonizing steps became slower and slower.

The pit was closing in. A thick, greenish-black substance crept up his feet, his legs. His arms flailed, beating away the winged creatures. He slipped downward. The dark green substance swallowed his chest, his shoulders. He strained to raise his face above the surging prison.

As his last breath neared, through the swirling cloud of beating wings above him, Bracken saw two tiny points of light. They were set close together, each rimmed with black, an iridescent black only slightly discernible from the utter blackness that filled the void left as the beating wings parted and formed a larger vibrating circle.

The points of light with their iridescent rims beckoned Bracken. They silently called to him, offering safety, promising sanctuary, another chance.

A ribbon unrolled from above, dancing, bobbing before Bracken's outstretched arm. He grabbed it. Like a band of metal, it looped itself around his hand and began to lift him. It carried him up, out of the pit, past the winged creatures, and into a swaying, pulsating chamber that had no walls, no floor, no ceiling. Yet, the chamber enveloped him so completely that it assumed even the task of breathing for him.

* * *

Bracken stirred, his body going from numbness to tortuous writhing. He was alone, his surroundings a blur of color overlaid with a greenish glow.

Through the massive confusion that filled his mind, he remembered the tiny points of light above the pit and their promise of safety. He tried to understand. Had he encountered them another place, another time? Concentration was futile. He dipped in and out of consciousness as if dangling from the end of a ribbon being rolled and unrolled from the known to the unknown—a red ribbon.

CHAPTER 23

"Bracken! Get up!"

Rough hands shook him. Blurred images adopted human shapes. Roon was there. This must be Roon's house. The softness of the bed beneath Bracken beckoned a return to oblivion.

An insistent voice hammered into his hearing. "We're ready to leave."

He saw Yaavin's bushy hair. Yaavin and someone else lifted him to a sitting position. Sleep tugged, relentlessly pulling him back.

"The Pirax are gone. On your feet!"

Shadowy forms half-carried Bracken to the trans-max. The door of the rig swung open. Someone pulled him inside. The power drive lumbered to life. The rig moved off into the night.

* * *

Dawn came to the Valley of Raka. Pale sunlight streamed across the flat desert from the distant mountains. The darkness slowly withdrew to reveal a desolate landscape sparsely sprinkled with dull green and blue foliage. The preceding day had been hot and dry. This one promised to be the same.

Within a small mud-patched shack, Bracken groaned and stretched the full length of his narrow bunk. It had been days since they had fled from Roon's house. Days of slave labor, caring for Ebbern's most repulsive creature—the gippen. How Bracken hated the sight of those squat, gray bodies covered with matted stripes of hair and the sagging, tusk-filled mouths that swagged from side to side.

Bracken sat up and looked out his window. The feeding pens were quiet. A few whirlwinds stirred the sand. Beyond the pens, a massive rock building dwarfed decomposing shacks like the one Bracken occupied. Shad, the owner of this gippens ranch, lived there.

Bracken wanted desperately to leave this nightmare of a farming operation. The smell, the sweat, and the barrenness were almost too much to take. But, he would never survive hiking alone across the desert that surrounded this loathsome place.

Depressed, Bracken lay back down. He considered it a miracle that he had been released from the Mingus realm. All his theories as to his escape narrowed into one bit of unexplainable, slender, red ribbon.

A faint sound came from the distant hills. It grew insistently louder, and Bracken ran to the door. Slipping over the horizon, came three black dots. Pirax sky-flyers, moving rapidly.

Shouting a warning, Bracken snatched his clothes, pulling them on as he dashed to the center of the workers' compound. He grabbed the leather thong at the bottom of the muster-bell and rang it frantically. Men began to stagger from their bunks.

Layozz flung open the door of his shack and yelled, "Why all the noise? The blasted gippens will want to eat soon enough without you waking them up." Snorting from the gippen herds proved the animals were already stirring in their pens.

The compound's loud speakers came to life. "This is Shad," the brittle voice crackled. "Layozz, the Pirax must have heard that you were here. Take your men and run for the cave." The ancient broadcast instrument popped. "Hurry if you want me to cover for you!"

As the sky-flyers closed in, Bracken sprinted with Layozz and the Golden Flight members toward a rocky hill. They scrambled into a large cave, where the trans-max with the group's equipment was already stored out of sight from prying eyes overhead.

The lumbering rotors of the Pirax sky-flyers beat the air. Three craft hovered above the workers' compound amid a storm of dust and settled to the ground in front of Shad's house.

Bracken watched from a secluded niche in the rocks.

Uniformed Pirax deplaned, their helmets glinting in the sun. A brawny officer strode to the gate to the courtyard of Shad's house. "Come out, Shad! We have questions for you." The words bounced off the rock facade of the building.

Its heavy wooden door opened, and Shad leisurely ambled out. From his hiding place, Bracken strained to hear the exchange.

"What do you want with a desert rat like me?" complained the leathery old man. "I'm just living, minding my own business."

"We don't want you, Shad. We want to talk to some rebels from Accad."

The rancher spat on the ground. "What makes you think any rebels are here?"

"We heard they headed this way. Leader is a man called Layozz."

"Can't recall anyone by that name," Shad lied. He pointed to the remaining workers standing sullenly in the compound. "You're welcome to check, but I don't think you'll find anybody named Layozz."

The officer turned to an aide. "Take two men and inspect their identification." As the three broke away and paced quickly to the compound, the officer turned back to the ranch's owner. "Shad, you couldn't keep this ranch going without hiding rebels." He gazed at the milling herds of gippens, and Bracken could imagine the officer's nose twitching in disdain. "No sane person would live here unless he was trying to hide."

Shad pushed his crumpled hat back on his forehead. "Ain't that way with me. I find this place enjoyable."

The officer swore. "How do you stand the smell of those beasts?"

"It ain't so bad when you consider how much their meat sells for on the Accad market." Shad deliberately drew a slow, deep breath and exhaled. The ugly gippens milled about, pressing against the rails of their pens.

The aide returned and confirmed that the search of the workers revealed nothing. Dismissing him with a grunt, the Pirax officer spun slowly on his heel, studying the entire horizon. Bracken shrank back as the man's eyes bored into the rocky formation that sheltered the Golden Flight.

Then, decisively, the officer ordered, "Let's go, men! This place stinks!"

In a cloud of dust and grit, the sky-flyers lifted off.

Shad watched until the noise of the impatient gippen herds became louder than the roar of the departing sky-flyers. He disappeared into the house. The speakers crackled. "Layozz, you and your buddies get down here. Rotten Pirax!" His voice boomed toward the fugitives. "Hurry, you slow-bellies! The gippens are having a fit."

Bracken scrambled from the rock-covered hill with the others. "How did they know we were here?" he asked bitterly. He was tired of hiding like a criminal.

"It's no secret around the Community that I know Shad." Layozz squinted against the sun's glare. He jerked his hat lower and gave a half-hearted pat to tufts of hair that jutted below its rim. "I think they're through looking for us for a while. A trip out here had to be the last resort."

Bracken kicked at a rock in his path. "Does that mean we can leave this hole soon?"

Layozz took off his tattered shirt and tied it around his waist. "Nothing could keep me here any longer than necessary."

As the men reached the feeding pens, the milling herds grew excited. The mechanical feeding equipment was broken down more often than it functioned. And today, the crews would be required to shovel the yellow grain into the feeding troughs for the herds with only a slight break between shifts.

Great clouds of dust and sand rose from the desert floor as the first herd advanced, pushing one another to reach the feeding troughs. The crew labored furiously to keep up with the appetite of the ravenous beasts.

Bracken's eyes burned, irritated by grit sifting into them. His body itched from the paste of sweat and dust that covered it.

After the first herd had been fed, the workers had a momentary respite. Exhausted, Bracken jerked his bandanna down from his face, and dropped to the ground.

"What I wouldn't give for some clean clothes," Layozz grumbled, joining Bracken on the sandy soil. The small leather pouch hanging from around his neck swayed on his heaving chest. "Besides, I've got to get back. If the Pirax force has its way, there soon will be nothing left of the Community." Layozz blew hot breath over the metal studs on the wide leather bracelet he wore. Idly, he rubbed them to a shine with his shirt, carefully polishing the metal plate in the center of the bracelet, which was inscribed with his name.

Bracken didn't respond. It was hard to get worked up over the Community's welfare when his own and the planet's were at stake.

"But, if the Community should be destroyed, we will start over. What we've got between us is priceless—the feelings, the love, the brotherhood." Layozz's voice, hoarse from clouds of dust, rose in conviction. "The leaders of Nerkush are trying to hold onto an outdated dream. Well, it's our turn. When we take over, they'll be just like we are now—on the outside."

Bracken closed his ears. Layozz was spouting the same philosophy as did most others in this group, the same philosophy that Bracken had once spouted. Bracken was weary of it.

The next herd of animals rammed up against the feeding troughs. Groaning, the crew returned to work. The heat increased as the sun rose higher. Workers cursed at each other and at the beasts. Bracken's muscles ached under the load of his shovel. The rank smell of the animals was nauseating.

Suddenly, Layozz yelled. Another fight had started.

Without warning, Bracken was struck in the back with the blade of a shovel. He sprawled, face first, on the sandy ground, caught in the middle of a violent brawl. He rolled over and met fistfuls of feed heaved toward him from a raging Yaavin. Bracken's hands dug deep in the grit beneath him. He came up throwing it at Yaavin's eyes.

"Stop! You fools!" The ranch foreman yelled, pulling Layozz away from Shor. Yaavin grabbed a hunk of wood and headed for Bracken. At the foreman's snarl, he hurled it across the compound. "Get back to your bunks!" yelled the foreman, at the same time signaling the next crew to take over.

Blood trickled down Bracken's back where the shovel left its mark. He trudged toward his shack with his fellow fugitives. *How do we stand being together?* he muttered to himself. *What strange force binds us, even though we've begun to despise one another?*

* * *

The final ebb of the evening sunlight emblazed the sky with gold as Bracken and Chepa sprawled on the porch of Layozz's shack. Idly ripping a splinter from the rough plank floor, Bracken forced his thoughts from the miserable surroundings. They flitted from one dissatisfying subject to another. If Silas had indeed gone on to a higher existence, why had he screamed before his body was crushed on the rocks at the bottom of the ravine? Why did the glowing creature of the Mingus realm procrastinate in its promise to reveal how destruction of

Ebbern could be stopped? Perhaps Bracken could find answers if he could go to the Mingus Mine itself.

When Bracken's thoughts returned to the present, Layozz was expounding on the subject dearest to his heart. "The Community is a delicate brotherhood. To remain spontaneous and vital, it needs attention and care."

"And an occasional touch of the Mingus Stone?" Chepa winked at Bracken.

The Mingus supplier ignored the ill-disguised challenge. "The longer we go without some form of unity, the less chance we have of restoring what's been lost since the Pirax cracked down."

Chepa pulled off a boot and inspected a blister. "I've got my own group to hold together. This engagement at Shad's ranch isn't doing much to build the reputation of the Golden Flight."

"I said we'd be here a while," Layozz reminded him. "Shad wouldn't be happy about losing a work crew early."

Bracken said, "Shad doesn't own us. And if we stay much longer in this hole, we'll be killing each other."

The rotted post supporting the porch overhang creaked. The three men snapped to attention. A figure sidled up, outlined in the growing twilight. Its hat was pulled low over its face, and it wore a jacket much too heavy for the desert climate.

"Chepa?" the stranger asked.

"Here," Chepa answered.

"Can we talk?"

Strangers came and went on Shad's ranch. Bracken assumed this one had arrived with a group that showed up earlier that day. Chepa slipped his boot back on and moved off with the man.

Bracken and Layozz sat in silence. Bracken was exhausted, too tired to turn in, even if his bunk had been an inviting bed.

Chepa soon returned, charged with a spark of energy that had lately evidenced itself only in their sporadic fights. "The Golden Flight has a date, a big one."

His new attitude immediately infected Bracken and Layozz.

"What? Where?" Layozz asked.

"Heard of the Pillars of Rimlex?"

Bracken bit back his answer. He'd heard of the Pillars of Rimlex all right. He'd been there.

"Sure," Layozz said. "What about it?"

Chepa squatted on the ground, facing the other two. "That guy is some sort of agent. He represents a man promoting an outdoor concert at the Pillars. A big-time concert."

"Yeah?" Layozz snorted. "Who's coming? The Rimmers?"

Chepa spat in disgust. "The walking dead? They'd better not. This is going to be a real show. Frimleter has promised that some big celebrity will make an appearance. Of course, the Golden Flight is the main attraction."

"Frimleter? Professor Frimleter?" Bracken barged into the conversation.

"A professor?" Chepa asked.

Bracken nodded. "He's an instructor at Tizra Academics. Didn't know he had an interest in booking bands."

"How are you going to pull off a concert without a lot of harassment?" Layozz asked.

Chepa grinned. "More good news. The pressure is off. The Pirax have backed away."

Bracken let out a yell of pleasure and swatted at Layozz. "How about that? You're no longer on the most wanted list."

Layozz frowned. "Yeah, the pressure is off from the Pirax. But, remember," he sent a guarded look toward the ranch house, which stood like a fortress between them and the road to civilization, "if we try to leave here before Shad thinks we've paid him back with enough work, we'll all be on his wanted list."

CHAPTER 24

The roots of lonely shrubs clawed at the rocky terrain over which Bracken crept. The scrawny vegetation, suggestive of gruesome creatures, seemed to move with him, as he slipped through the predawn light to the cave above Shad's house. Others from the Golden Flight entourage materialized, migrating in a silent exodus, like foot soldiers deserting the battlefield.

Inside the cave, whispering, they scraped away a layer of dirt adhering to the windows of the trans-max.

Bracken refused to believe that this subterfuge was necessary. "We aren't prisoners."

"You're welcome to stay and tell Shad that an entire work crew has absconded," Layozz offered, "after you help push this rig out of here."

The driver climbed behind the wheel. Chepa motioned. The vehicle crunched over the cave's sandy surface. At the top of the incline that wound down toward the desert floor, the men clambered aboard. Silently, the driver released the brakes and guided the lumbering trans-max along the narrow road.

As if anxious not to miss the morning's drama, the sun rose rapidly. In its pale light, the runaways saw a group of armed men blocking the road near Shad's rock-walled house.

Bracken exploded. "He can't mean to hold us here by force."

"Run them down," suggested Shor.

"Don't be stupid," Layozz snarled. "Let's see if I can appease him. Who knows when we'll need him again? He's not desperate or he'd have found a way to sabotage our rig."

Layozz climbed out and ambled toward Shad. Chepa followed.

Shad brandished his weapon. "Didn't hear no good-bye from you fellows. You ain't meaning to skip out on our agreement? After all I did for you?"

Bracken stepped from the trans-max, listening to the performances of the conniving old man and his slick younger counterpart.

"Shad, we didn't mean to rouse you out of bed. The guys here took a vote. We can't repay you for your hospitality in a proper way. So, we decided that the least we could do was leave without making a fuss."

"Well, the guys here," Shad indicated his comrades-in-arms, "decided that we would hate to let you go off all by yourselves. Seemed heartless not to show you how much we want you to stay."

The speeches continued, undercurrents of potential violence rising and ebbing. Just as Bracken feared it might overflow, the exchange was interrupted by the sound of four sleek trans-rigs tearing over the rough road toward Shad's house. The caravan skidded to a stop, stirring up clouds of dust. Well-dressed men and women alighted, talking and fanning themselves.

A leader emerged. "I'm looking for a man named Shad."

Shad's weapon had already disappeared, and at his emphatic gestures, his men vanished. Shad's coarse speech tilted toward graciousness in homage to the prospect of well-filled purses.

One stranger, a slim female clothed in sand-colored, stylish jacket and expertly tailored pants, came to where Bracken stood in the shadow of the trans-max. She exclaimed, "Whatever are you doing here?"

"Aleena!" Bracken swiped at his clothes, aware of the decrepit picture he must portray. "Just . . . just passing through."

She raised her eyebrows delicately and adjusted the sheer scarf that encircled her wide-brimmed hat and tied beneath her chin. She looked as if she'd planned her attire to blend with the desert's palette, except for her red lips and an artificial red flower, which perched jauntily on the hat brim.

Bracken forestalled her further questions with one of his own. "What about you? What brings you to this remote desert?"

"The alignment," she answered. At Bracken's blank stare, she repeated, "Alignment—there's going to be a stellar alignment."

"Here?"

"On Mt. Shidow. We stopped at this ranch to take care of a mundane matter—food for the gathering." She nodded toward the group's spokesman. "We've been at his place in the desert for days."

Mystified, Bracken asked, "A party in this desert?"

"Not a party. We've been planning the stellar alignment. We're preparing. Anyway, I love to spend time in the desert. It's so peaceful and refreshing. You should try it, Bracken. You can't believe how your feelings of hostility just melt away."

Bracken was spared having to answer when Chepa and Layozz took advantage of Shad's distraction and climbed into the trans-max. A brisk tug on his shirt-sleeve informed Bracken it was time for urgent departure. He told Aleena, "My friends are leaving."

Aleena smiled from beneath her hat brim. "Isn't it remarkable how we happened to meet here, practically in the midst of the most important event in history?"

Bracken nodded, backing up the steps of the trans-max. As the vehicle roared toward the main road, he watched Aleena's delicate figure fade into the desert landscape. But, her intriguing smile lingered with him, like the fragrance of a flower. He pondered over the red flower clinging to her hat and asked himself if it might be real after all.

* * *

The roadway from Shad's ranch to the Pillars of Rimlex rolled by slowly, a monotonous repetition of desolate sights. Bracken rode with the driver, who conversed in nods and grunts.

Bracken wondered if Lisha had returned to Tizra. He couldn't understand why she had bolted that night. She'd first gone to the Community of her own choice. If she'd only realize how the Mingus Stone had enlarged his view of their relationship, she'd agree that he'd been right to encourage her to stay and expand her horizons. Irritated, he turned his thoughts to Aleena. There was a woman who would understand how the Mingus Stone could broaden one's perception.

At last, the tedious journey ended. Bracken had gladly accepted Chepa's invitation to tarry at the Pillars long enough to participate in the concert. They turned off the main road and drove to an open spot at the base of the Pillars. Twilight revealed clusters of early arrivals sitting around a growing number of campfires that dotted the hillside.

A man approached them, propelled by thin, swinging arms. "Which one of you is Chepa?" The high voice belonged to Professor Frimleter.

Chepa introduced himself, and the two men left for the performance area.

Bracken could see that a stage had been constructed for the next day's concert on a large flat rock at the base of the Pillars. On a level above the rock, a mesa extended back, carving a niche in the Pillars, forming a high, natural auxiliary stage. The agent's information had been correct. This set-up was planned for a major concert, and somebody had invested a lot of money.

Later, Bracken sat apart from the others. Steps hurried through the grass. It was Professor Frimleter.

"Bracken, isn't it? You and your friends visited one of my contact gatherings."

Bracken was glad the professor hadn't used the more accurate description, *spied on*. "We were camped near here. Curiosity got the best of us when we saw your caravan drive by."

"I believe you were also curious about something else." The professor coughed against the evening's chill.

Bracken assured himself that no one was within hearing distance. "You mean about the space disk."

Frimleter squatted beside Bracken, his knees popping loudly. "As I recall, you chose not to become a Touch-Point. I had expected to hear by now that you were ready."

"I haven't completely resolved some misgivings about that night. Until I do . . ."

The professor rubbed his hands briskly. "After tomorrow, any questions you have will be answered."

"Oh?"

"Tomorrow, the disk people are planning to manifest themselves." Frimleter's voice cracked with anticipation. "Their leader will address this gathering."

Bracken stifled an outcry. "The Trionite leader is the surprise celebrity? He's showing himself in front of these people?"

"Yes. And, if I request it, I know he'll be happy to give you a few moments time."

"Me? With this crowd, why would he grant me a private interview?"

"You don't understand the benevolent nature of the Trionite leader. He will want to set your mind at ease. If you wish, I'll arrange it."

"Sure. I want to talk with him."

Frimleter rubbed his knees and eased himself up. "I must get out of this night air."

* * *

The next day, a constant line of rigs and hikers streamed into the area. Campsites pieced together a multi-colored collage on the meadow. Smoke mingled with the scent of cooking food. By mid-day, Bracken estimated that five thousand people had assembled, some from the far corners of Nerkush.

Long before the Golden Flight's first vigorous notes sounded, the massive assembly hovered close to the stage, waiting expectantly. At the musicians' appearance, unrestrained cheering resounded against the pillared backdrop. Chepa signaled the group to begin.

The gigantic broadcasters hummed to life and purred in subdued anticipation. The first note from an amplified stam discharged with the ear-shattering impact of a handbomb. The other musicians joined in, creating the tight, uniform sound that characterized the Golden Flight's style. Stimulated by the surges of sonic harmony, the crowd responded, sending back waves of praise and energy that magnified the output of the group.

Throughout the afternoon, this reciprocation grew in intensity. As the sun began to dip below the Pillars, the exchange between performers and audience reached a climax. The complex melodies blended to become one note. The note resounded, like the ringing of some cosmic bell. Its tone droned on and on. It called to the sky, beckoned to the stars, a pleading cry.

In that moment of clarity, the space disks appeared.

CHAPTER 25

At incredible speed, five glowing space disks slipped over the top of the Pillars. They slowed abruptly and settled down on the mesa directly behind the stage.

Bewildered, the performers and the crowd watched the crafts simultaneously open their portals. Gleaming metallic stairways extended to the ground. Rank upon rank of alien figures descended and formed two parallel lines a short distance apart. The Trionites looked almost angelic, clothed in shiny gray garments, their angular faces radiating an unreal essence. The lines snaked to the stage, turned in one unified sweep, and faced the entrance to the largest disk, the mother ship.

Bracken stared with the same blissful awe as those around him, paused in a field of wonder, suspended in a moment that belonged to a force outside their existence.

The leader stepped through the rectangular opening in the underside of the largest space disk. He marched down the stairs and over to center stage. The protective, luminous energy veil cloaked his entire face and body. A mere outline of indiscernible facial features was evident. Chepa stepped aside and yielded the platform to this imposing celebrity.

The leader addressed the spectators as a king speaking to his subjects, "I am Nebuzarr."

A shudder of excitement surged through the crowd in response to the majestic presence.

"This is an important day for your planet," the voice announced confidently. "You stand on the threshold of a new era. We have come to assist you in your quest for a higher life. All the efforts of war must end. You must turn yourselves toward the stars. The old ways are dying. The future belongs to you."

Eager faces pressed closer, drank in his words.

"Open your minds and let our energies touch you." As the leader spoke, rippling waves of light radiated through the near darkness, flowing from the alien to wash over the audience. "Receive the essence of the universe. Become children of the cosmos, sons and daughters of eternity."

Some in the assembly near the stage fell back, as if entranced by unseen visions.

"You are making another step in your evolutionary process. Soon you will be a new race."

A faint melody blending the sound of flutes and cymbals drifted through the air. Bracken searched for the source of the peaceful tune until he realized that the entrancing music came from the alien leader himself.

Gradually the music faded, and Nebuzarr spoke again. "You have heard a melody from the ancient past." His words seemed ringed with melancholy, his manner almost lonely, as if the leader were remembering another time. "I've been waiting for you to hear this melody."

Then in a sudden reversal, Nebuzarr's voice regained its magnetic nobility. "We will meet with you again—all of you. Wait for our return. We have much more to teach you."

A chilling breeze swept over the crowd. Bracken shivered. People huddled together for warmth.

"Do not believe the lies of those in power over you. Stay in unity." Nebuzarr raised both hands in benediction. "Goodbye, my friends." He strode swiftly back to the space disk. The crowd roared. Caught in the emotion of the moment, Bracken joined the outpouring of approval and gratitude.

Frimleter appeared and beckoned Bracken to follow him. They passed the lines of Trionites retracing their steps to the space disks. Frimleter confidently identified himself to a Trionite near the base of the largest ship. Immediately, clearance was granted and Frimleter proceeded up the stairs, his face bathed with pride. In numbed silence, Bracken followed him aboard the mother ship.

They entered the disk command center and found Nebuzarr at a large silver-topped table. Frimleter and Bracken sat across from him. Bracken's heart hammered. He was close to answers—real answers.

Frimleter reviewed Bracken's previous experience with the Trionites. "Bracken claims to have unresolved questions regarding the mission."

The proximity to this great personage reduced Bracken to a state of distress. He wiped perspiration from his forehead and fingered his pack nervously. Persistent qualms nagged him, but he was exhilarated at being on the verge of unimaginable discovery.

The leader addressed Bracken cordially. "I will be happy to enlighten you." To Frimleter, he said, "It is best that you return to the group outside."

Keen disappointment shaded the professor's gaunt features. "I had hoped to meet privately with you?" The statement ended in a question.

"Many new prospects need your counsel." Nebuzarr left no room for negotiation.

Frimleter backed away from the table. His bony shoulders drooped, but he dredged up a thin smile for Bracken, a show of bravado, which did little to disguise the embarrassment of being summarily dismissed. The humbled professor departed.

Nebuzarr's tone again became congenial. "So? You apparently

have muddled perceptions concerning your last visit with us?" The energy veil hummed with each movement of Nebuzarr's head.

The alien leader's presence was overpowering. He sounded benevolent. Yet, Bracken had a troubled premonition that something was wrong. What visage hid behind that glowing veil? What thoughts did it conceal?

Aloud, Bracken answered, "Yes. Things seemed to change just as I was about to receive the treatment. Even our Trionite host appeared different." Bracken felt disloyal. "There must be an explanation, but I actually thought for a few moments that the interior of the disk seemed to be breaking down." Even now he could not make sense of his recollections of the previous trip. They were obscure, except for fleeting images and the feeling of terror that accompanied them. "I've told myself that it was as the Trionite suggested, merely the effect of the flight."

"I suspect that you have a dangerous conflict. Unless resolved, this conflict will hinder our cause." The form beneath the gray veil swiveled and issued sharp commands, which Bracken could not understand. The space disk came swiftly to life. "Perhaps another journey will bring you to a positive conclusion."

Bracken gripped the arms of his chair. "I have no desire to hinder anything that will change the destiny of my planet for the better." He tried to remain calm, but inside, fear took hold. Where were they taking him? A terrifying thought seized him. *Maybe they know what I'm thinking.*

With a flurry of acceleration, the disk soared in flight. Even before Bracken became accustomed to the sensation of motion, the craft suddenly came to rest again. It settled with a rumbling and scraping that tore at Bracken's nerves. Eying the viewer screen, he surmised that the space disk had looped back over the top of the Pillars of Rimlex and dipped down to a lonely spot away from the concert's location.

The space disk became still. A cold grayness filled its interior. Bracken felt like an object on display, as readable as one of the lighted instrument panels. Mocking snickers echoed through the grayness, taunting him with the possibility that all on board were watching him.

"Why did we stop here?" Bracken demanded.

In answer, the gray energy veil covering Nebuzarr glowed brighter momentarily. But, soon it began to lose brightness and to shrivel. It shrank into a filmy netting, growing more and more threadbare, until suddenly, Bracken could see through the veil. He saw the face behind it.

The face was at once both beautiful and frightening. It was mysterious, yet somehow familiar. Had Bracken seen it before?

"What's going on? Who are you?" Bracken shouted.

"Enough of your questions, you meddling fool!" Nebuzarr's words ripped like daggers. "You must be terminated."

Bracken struggled against paralyzing fear. This was a nightmare. He must not give in. He grasped at logic. "I thought you were going to help me."

A hideous grin covered the leader's face. "You have believed a lie, a very old lie." The face rolled, folds of flesh undulating, distorting its appearance. "This is almost a pity. You would be an effective tool if properly controlled."

"Is this how you mean to help our race? Eliminate us?"

Heinous, vibrating laughter swirled around Bracken. Nebuzarr's huge body stiffened. The laughter ceased.

"Members who meet our high criteria will be selected to perpetuate and mold the race." Nebuzarr's breath fumed hot. "But, we cannot allow those members to search beyond acceptable bounds."

The face so close to Bracken changed. It became again beautiful and radiant. Its power pulled at Bracken until a painful memory cut through the magnetism, and Bracken knew why the face seemed familiar. This was the same captivating image he had seen in the shimmering pool of light at Roon's place. This face had called Silas to his death.

Instinct told Bracken to run, to escape. But, he was helpless to do more than whimper, "Who are you?"

"Surely you have heard of me. Somewhere in your past you have been told of me and my plan." The heinous laugh foamed forth again. "But you did not believe I was real."

Vague memories stirred in Bracken's mind. He tried to connect intangible, elusive bits. "This space disk? Is it real?"

The laugh grew louder and more threatening. "Your race has grown sophisticated, so I employ intricate forms of deception to carry out my lie."

Bracken's faculties seized up with terror. He was trapped. His life could be snuffed out at any instant.

"Your torment is my pleasure." Nebuzarr's mocking gaze tore at Bracken. Fiery eyes plucked him apart bit by bit. "Your desire for truth makes this all the more satisfying."

With that closing taunt, Nebuzarr vanished. A gray cloud rolled over Bracken. The cloud was thick, suffocating. A faint glow appeared to one side. It could have been the flashing of a red light on an instrument readout panel. The leader's image returned, his face contorted in a mixture of anger and impatience until a glimmer of the beauty Bracken had seen earlier broke through and transformed the face. The beauty tarried only a moment, and then it and Nebuzarr's image disappeared.

Silence filled the space disk. The Trionites were gone. Bracken was alone. Slowly, the gray cloud in the craft's interior misted away, replaced by gradual blackness. Panic gripped Bracken. Why had he been left alone? His teeth ground into his lip. He tasted blood.

Suddenly, the structure beneath Bracken dissolved. He plunged downward, falling until his feet smashed against an immovable expanse. Stunned, he sprawled upon a cold, hard surface. Where was he? Some unknown, dreadful event was wiping out his life.

In faint diffused light from above, it appeared that the substance beneath him was rock. The surface of this rock moved and started to rise. It spread outward and upward. Sides took shape and began to surround him. In horror, Bracken realized that he was being rapidly entombed.

The sound became unbearable, like an explosion of the universe with him at the center of combustion. There was no flame, only darkness in the hollow tomb. Bracken jumped to his feet, wild with fear, searching for a way out.

Then, a silver sphere, small enough to fit in his hand, appeared. The sphere became a red bubble, bright and glossy. Bracken reached for it. It popped, shattering into shiny red fragments which whisked out of sight, leaving his fingers closed over his empty palm.

Suddenly, Bracken remembered. He moved his empty hand toward the pack slung over his shoulder. He reached inside. His fingers closed around the handbomb hidden there. Quickly, he withdrew it. Holding one arm straight out to protect his face, he ran blindly through the darkness until he collided with a rock wall. He set the handbomb to go off, put it against the wall, and raced back.

Moments later, the side of the tomb erupted in a flash of light and concussion that sent Bracken flying. He pushed himself to his feet and sprinted toward the jagged opening made by the explosion. He crawled through, just as the massive boulder collapsed upon itself.

In physical and mental shock, Bracken lay twisted across the granite surface where he fell. But, fear would not let him rest. Tumbling, sliding, he groped his way down the side of the Pillars of Rimlex, far from the concert site. Reaching level ground, he headed through the dark to where he hoped the road might be.

In his confused state, Bracken nearly stumbled into the side of the red trans-speed parked by the road.

"Bracken, is that you?"

Weak with relief, Bracken slid to the ground. Strong, cool hands lifted his head, and he looked into the welcome face of Aleena.

CHAPTER 26

Near dawn, Bracken stumbled into the quarters he shared with Trasent, amazed to find his roommate still awake.

The gathering room was dark except for the bright cone spreading downward from a reading light by the chair where Trasent slouched. His usual impeccable attire in rumpled disarray, Trasent bent his dark head over something he held on his lap, totally engrossed. Obviously startled at Bracken's entrance, he jumped up, letting the object fall into the chair. "You're home!"

Bracken mumbled, "Talk to you in the morning," and shuffled to his room, too exhausted to ask questions, even why his door, normally closed, now stood wide open. He fell into bed, his head churning with thoughts of the evening's events.

Bracken slept fitfully. Once, he roused, half-seeing a shadow slip out of his room, and a wedge of light as if the door he vaguely remembered closing had opened again.

He awoke to bright sunlight, and unwound his still tired body from the tangled bedding. He squinted and went to close the window covering. A stack of bookshelves ran beneath the window. There, Bracken collided with an object that sent pain stabbing through his foot. He cursed, and hopped back to the bed. While nursing his bruised toe, he saw protruding at an awkward angle from the bottom bookshelf a thick volume, its ancient leather binding cracked and peeling.

Despite the misery in his foot, Bracken smiled. His mother had slipped that book in with his others. He discovered it after moving here and had read her poignant inscription inside the cover about it being part of the family's heritage. He had stored it on the bottom shelf, where, until now, it had lain undisturbed. He sighed. Myra never gave up. He wondered idly if she had some secret means of arranging for that book to make itself noticed.

Bracken had to talk to somebody. The previous night, collapsed in Aleena's trans-speed, he'd told her that he'd wandered away from the concert and gotten lost. She seemed to require no other explanation for his ragged clothing and bewildered state of mind.

But Trasent was gone when Bracken emerged from his room. Suddenly, it seemed important that Bracken find his roommate. Trasent was for the most part stable. He had an ambitious vision of the future, but was smart enough to keep an eye on the present. Like Aleena, he sought wealth and success, yet, there was a solidarity in Trasent that was missing in Aleena's adventurous, exploring spirit. Aleena was to be admired and desired, but Trasent had a practical streak that, at that moment, Bracken needed.

Bracken sat at the table and stared at the tea growing cold in his cup. He swirled the brown liquid, watching it sloshing around the cup's glossy perimeter. His father always swirled the last of his tea. Bracken drained the cup. He would visit his family one evening soon.

* * *

At the Currency Center, the silver-headed Arnaman always had priority on Trasent's time. Today, the high-level executive was cloistered in Trasent's office.

"How long do you think they'll be?" Bracken asked Golens. "Too bad the day I return happens to be a day when the big guy comes visiting."

"Visiting? You've been gone a while. Arnaman has moved in." Golens tossed his head smugly. "I always said our branch was important. I was right. They've centered the entire global operation here. And Arnaman is in charge of it."

"Global operations? I thought he was Director of International Human Relations."

"That's his title all right." Golens' sallow complexion flushed with pleasure at this opportunity to inform Bracken, "but, the word is that the scope of Arnaman's human relations department is limitless."

Bracken kept watch, hoping to catch Trasent as soon as Arnaman left. When time for the noon meal came, a new employee, a dark-skinned man Bracken hadn't seen before, carried a tray into Trasent's office.

"They're in there for the day," Golens volunteered cheerfully.

Bracken frowned and left the building in search of his own food. When he returned, Trasent was coming out of his office and hailed him.

"Bracken, got a minute? I'm going up for a workout. Let's discuss the productivity report due next week." Trasent walked rapidly to the fitness facility, saying nothing.

Bracken waited for a private opportunity to bring up his own topic, still not knowing how to approach it without appearing to be out of his mind. How could he discuss with his supervisor an alien leader who promised a peaceful world, but whose face was indelibly linked with Silas' death, a being also intent on effecting Bracken's demise?

They changed into exercise clothes and joined three men from the commercial division already at the gleaming equipment. Trasent set a pace that taxed Bracken's endurance. Their companions drifted away.

Alone now except for Bracken, Trasent let up only slightly. Perspiration glistened from every pore. He seemed truly stressed. Bracken wished he'd ease off more.

"I've reached my limit," Bracken said, slowing the treadmill's speed.

Trasent, now on a stationery wheel, said between ragged breaths,

"Your mother . . . she's pretty sure about things . . . about her beliefs, I mean?"

Bracken thought he'd misunderstood. "My mother?"

"Yeah . . . you know, the old-fashioned stuff . . . like the Night Ruler . . . and the Prince coming back . . . that stuff?"

Bracken stopped. Blood pounded in his ears. Too much exertion. His hearing was affected.

Just then, a group from the bond department came in. From fiery red, Trasent's face paled. He bent his head, his chest heaving, working harder than ever.

Alarmed, Bracken left the treadmill, pretending exhaustion. "Okay, okay, I give up. Let's quit."

Trasent did quit. He gasped. His hands tightened on the handlebar, then flew off, groping wildly at nothing. He slumped and began to fall. Bracken watched in horror as Trasent crumpled, his head bouncing off the handlebars, hitting the frame, and finally the floor, his feet still tangled in the pedals' stirrups. A trickle of blood oozed through Trasent's dark hair.

Heart attack ran through the building, almost faster than the medics who wheeled Trasent to the medical transport after giving emergency care.

Bracken related the incident to security as Trasent was whisked away. He dressed and headed for the medical facility, mystified. How could such a perfect specimen of a man be struck down without warning?

Frosty icicles formed and crept through Bracken's veins. Would Trasent die, too, like Silas? Should Bracken try to contact anyone? Trasent had said he didn't have a family. The thought of his friend lying helpless was ludicrous. Except for some recent moments when he seemed preoccupied, almost uneasy, Trasent seemed so in charge of his life. Bracken rushed through the medical building's entrance.

After a long interval, a receptionist directed Bracken to a station on an upper floor. Behind the counter, a girl interrupted her conversation with a grinning technician long enough to tell Bracken that he could not see the new patient. When Bracken persisted in being allowed to wait, she waved him toward an alcove across the hall from Trasent's room.

The tiny waiting area was deserted. "Can't somebody do something?" Bracken pleaded under his breath. He couldn't keep his mind off of death. Aleena's view was simple, *When it's time for one to leave this life, there is no reason to fight it.* Bracken dropped his head in his hands. He tried to tell himself that if it were meant to be, Trasent would die, but he would go on to a better place. Silas had done that. Hadn't he? Bracken clamped his hands over his ears to shut out the memory of the scream that had echoed over the ravine as Silas fell. He clutched at thoughts of the night when Aleena's guide had led the way to the meeting with Silas. Trasent had been there, too. He must have believed in Aleena's philosophy. If a person believed hard enough . . .

Arnaman arrived. He was escorted into Trasent's room by a medical official and came out a few minutes later. His neutral expression shed no light on Trasent's condition. He didn't seem to notice Bracken slumped in a chair in the shadowed alcove.

An aide, his soft shoes slapping at the hard floor, crossed the expanse leading from Trasent's door. The hallway had cleared. "Your name Bracken?"

"Yes!"

"That guy over there is asking for you."

Bracken braced himself for the worst. But, his friend's room was quiet and strangely bare. Only the bed and an uncluttered table kept Trasent company.

Trasent's dark eyes were open, and he seemed fairly alert. A bandage swathed his head.

Bracken forced a smile and held up the little bag he had stuffed with Trasent's street clothes from their joint locker at the fitness facility. "Figured you'd need these soon."

Trasent's eyes opened wide. "Good." His voice was thick from medication.

Bracken looked for a cabinet to store the bag. He opened a door and saw Trasent's exercise clothing lying in a heap at the bottom.

"No!" Trasent strained to make himself heard. His hands fluttered, his fingers motioning Bracken close. "Inside . . . take it. You take it. Don't let them have it."

Puzzled, Bracken saw that the injured man indicated the bag in Bracken's hands. Anxious to appease him, Bracken opened the bag. Trasent lay back, exhausted by the effort. His eyes appealed to Bracken to search the bag, frantically urging him on when Bracken paused.

Bracken held up each piece of clothing, but Trasent only looked distressed. Finally, Bracken's inquiring fingers discovered a small lump that seemed to have no purpose in the waistline of Trasent's neatly tailored pants. In response to the silent pleading of the man on the bed, he examined the waistline. After insistent prodding, a slim, hidden fastener slid away and revealed a small pocket.

Trasent nodded his head weakly. "You take it," he whispered. "There's no one else. Hide it. No one but you."

Bracken's fingers pried out a small, ruby-colored object a little larger than his thumbnail. It looked like glass. No, this was more beautiful than an ordinary piece of glass. The ruby-colored, faceted crystal, splendid with color and brilliance, would do justice to the finest ring mounting. Bracken held it up for Trasent to see. It swung in slow rhythm, suspended by an almost invisible thread only slightly thicker than a human hair.

Trasent nodded. "The secret . . . ," Trasent's whisper faded.

Bracken put his ear close to the white face. "What secret?"

Bursts of warm breath brushed Bracken's cheek. "The global plan is only the beginning. I know the real secret now . . . the second phase . . . I found it. . . ."

The words fell back into Trasent's throat, lost in an agonizing raspy breath.

Horrified, Bracken looked for a way to call for help. Why had this critically-ill man been left alone? Where was the monitoring equipment? Why wasn't he on life-support? The call button was out of reach. Bracken lunged for it. But, before he could touch it, he glimpsed Trasent's face. A peaceful look had transfixed it. Trasent opened his eyes and gazed at Bracken with an expression that could only be called joy. His gaze wandered upward focusing on some unrevealed vision. A smile glimmered on his lips. Then, Trasent closed his eyes. The smile faded, and Trasent's face became a still, pale mask.

Bracken jabbed the call button again and again, with no response. He shook Trasent's limp form, refusing to believe that death had overtaken his friend.

He whirled from the bedside and burst into the hallway shouting, "Medic! Here! This man needs help!" He ran back to try to restore the heartbeat.

A rush of attendants swept Bracken into the hallway. The door closed behind them. Still holding the bag of clothing, Bracken could only stand aside.

The aide who had let Bracken into Trasent's room sidled up. "Sorry about your buddy," he said. He sucked his lower lip and knit his brows intently. "Do me a favor. Don't tell anybody that I let you in there."

"Okay. Sure." What difference did it make?

"He wasn't supposed to have visitors," the aide explained.

"They're going to help him, aren't they?" Bracken's eyes riveted to the wide door to Trasent's room. For the first time, he noticed a *No Visitors* sign hanging below the number. "Aren't they?" He turned ready to shake an answer out of the aide. The young man had vanished.

Silver-haired Arnaman came to take his place. "Such a shame—it happened so quickly. No one expected it. Trasent had a brilliant future."

Bracken turned his face to the wall. He'd known without Arnaman's confirmation that Trasent was dead. Trasent had died at the moment of that last peaceful smile. A deep sense of loss overcame Bracken. His small comfort was that he had been there with Trasent. How glad he was that he'd seen the look of readiness on the dying man's face.

Arnaman put a fatherly arm across Bracken's shoulders. "Death is often hard for the survivors to accept." After several respectful moments, he said kindly, "There are things I must do."

Bracken nodded.

Arnaman stroked his beard and indicated the bag Bracken held. "Trasent's?"

Bracken nodded again.

"I'll see that everything gets where it belongs." With a final sympathetic glance, Arnaman walked down the hall, the bag in his hand.

Bracken jammed his fist in his pockets. The affairs of the medical facility continued without interruption. Wasn't anybody interested that a life had ended? Must the daily routine be more dependable than human life?

Frustrated, Bracken hurried downstairs and out the door of the medical center. A distance away, he veered into a stretch of open space. Stopping beneath the lacy branches of a low spreading tree, Bracken sank to the ground. He pulled from his pocket the tiny ruby crystal and blew a particle of lint from its gleaming finish. He dangled it from the slender thread, letting it swing free, watching it catch the light. Trasent had given it to him, hadn't he? He'd said there was no one else to have it.

Sometime later, Bracken got stiffly to his feet. Trasent had talked of a secret in those last minutes. Bracken closed his fingers around the ruby crystal. Unexplained changes had come over Trasent since Bracken had met him, changes that multiplied and finally climaxed with death. Bracken decided that, for now, the crystal would remain his secret.

CHAPTER 27

Instead of returning to the Currency Center, Bracken went home, thinking that perhaps he should do something there. He didn't know what. Vaguely, he remembered his mother helping grieving friends with gifts of food. But, Trasent had no family to grieve for him.

Feeling lost and bewildered, Bracken let himself in. Wearily, he turned from the door, ready to collapse on the nearest seat. But, his sigh of relief caught in his throat, and he reeled at the sight before him.

The gathering room looked as if a herd of Shad's gippens had used the floor for a feeding pen, upending furniture, tearing pictures from the wall, and rooting through drawers in a frenzied search for food.

A shadow, fell across the doorway leading from Bracken's bedroom. He grabbed a weapon, a short-legged stool.

"Bracken!" came a startled voice. "I didn't know you were here!" Aleena flung herself toward him, crying, "Isn't this awful? Who could have done such a thing?"

Dangling the stool from one hand, he awkwardly put the other arm around her. She buried her face in his chest, sobbing, exhibiting a new pinnacle of emotion. Her voluminous dark hair caressed his chin. Her white arms slipped around his waist.

Bracken tossed the stool onto the debris-covered floor, and held Aleena close. He whispered, "It's all right. Somebody must have heard about Trasent and supposed his house would be empty. Ghouls!" Ghouls seemed an appropriate choice of words. This destruction appeared beyond what humans could have accomplished in the short time since Trasent's death.

Aleena pushed away. "I came as soon as I heard because I thought you'd need a friend. And, here I am, crying on your shoulder." With the point of her shoe, she nudged a picture frame on the floor, its backing torn to shreds. "But, when I walked into this terrible mess, I just went to pieces."

Bracken righted an overturned lamp. "What could they have been looking for?"

"Valuables. Trasent is—was—a successful executive. It would be common knowledge, at least at the Currency Center, that he was well-paid."

Bracken stepped through the rubble to Trasent's exercise room. The sight of the equipment, which meant so much to his friend, brought a renewal of grief. He cleared a spot on the couch and sank into a disemboweled cushion.

"If they wanted currency," Bracken moaned, "why didn't they look in a sensible hiding place? Trasent wouldn't hide valuables in a pillow!" He hurled a wad of the soft filling toward the wall. At a sudden thought, he jumped to his feet. "What does my room look like?" With quick strides, he crossed to his doorway.

Aleena assured him, "It's hardly been touched. See?"

Bracken picked up several books, which lay open on the floor. The book his mother had given him stood undisturbed on the lower shelf. The crusty volume with its cracked leather cover, valuable for its antiquity, might be a more likely source of currency than finding treasure hidden in his room. The graverobbers probably deduced correctly that Bracken owned little of value. He turned away. "They didn't waste much time here."

"Would you like me to make arrangements for getting this cleaned up?"

"I should probably call the Pirax."

Aleena shrugged. "What good would that do?"

"Not much, I guess. I wouldn't know if anything were missing. And, Trasent can't care."

Aleena made a space and snuggled beside Bracken. She lay a slim hand on his leg. "You shouldn't have to face prying questions from the Pirax. You've been through enough."

He put an arm around her. "I can't believe anyone at the Currency Center could have done this. People liked Trasent." He tightened his hold, rubbing his fingers over the smooth folds of her sleeve. "I'm grateful they were gone when you arrived. If you had walked in while they . . ."

"Could it have been employees from the medical center?"

Bracken sighed. "Maybe. But, I don't see how. They would have had to hear of his death, get here, rummage through rooms of stuff, and still have time to get away. And it was for nothing. Trasent believed in keeping accounts at the Currency Center. After all, he did work there."

"Did he ever talk to you about any valuables? Anything he might have wanted to hide?"

Bracken shook his head.

"Maybe it wasn't currency. Maybe he had valuable documents or papers or . . ."

"Not to my knowledge."

Aleena leaned into the curve of Bracken's arm. She looked up at him, her changeable eyes taking on the grayish-blue color of the blouse she wore. "He never talked about anything he wanted to keep secret?"

Again, Bracken shook his head, finding it hard to speak while caught in the spell of those magnetic eyes.

Aleena tipped her face upward and brushed her lips against

Bracken's cheek. "Remember, he was my friend too, and I'll miss him, for a while."

"Of course you will." Bracken admonished himself. "I'm so clumsy, thinking about myself, when you knew him longer than I."

"Trasent was a good friend. But, Bracken, you are a special person. I wonder if you know how special you are."

Bracken hunted for an answer. Aleena meant a great deal to him. But, she was a delightful, out-of-reach fantasy. He did not allow himself to imagine that she might have a genuine personal interest in him.

"You know," she continued, "there is a reason that we have been brought together. We were meant to join forces, you and I. You have a marvelous searching spirit, and you never abandon your hope for an Ebbern without oppression. I've come to recognize that you are one of the elite inhabitants of this planet."

Bracken hunched forward, his elbows on his knees, slightly disconcerted at being designated as elite.

"It's true, Bracken. A day is coming soon, quite soon, when the bondage of archaic ideas that bind this planet will be broken."

"Just like that? On one specific day?"

"Don't be skeptical. There are those of us who have waited a long time for that moment when the chosen ones will meet and call forth a new era. And that moment is not far away."

Bracken recalled the morning at Shad's ranch when Aleena talked of a gathering. "Does this have anything to do with your alignment plan?"

Aleena waved his question aside impatiently. "Not an alignment plan, Bracken. It's a stellar alignment."

"And I'm supposed to know about this?"

Aleena crossed to a cabinet standing with its doors wide open and its contents raked to the floor. She rummaged until she found what she wanted. "Come, help me clear off this table."

Bracken did as he was told. They sat down, and Aleena opened an intact deck of cards. She shuffled them expertly.

She turned a card over and placed it on the table. "This card represents one of the enlightened tribes of Ebbern." She turned over more cards. "Now we see that tribe and other tribes joining forces with the heavens."

Fascinated, Bracken watched Aleena's strong hands deftly maneuver the cards.

"This tells us that there are power points. But, here," and she snapped over another card, "is the very center of power, at Mt. Shidow. You will be at Mt. Shidow, Bracken, in the heart of the stellar alignment. You will be an essential link."

"But, I don't see. . . ."

"You have been chosen, Bracken, because of your wisdom and

your sensitivity, and your courage." Aleena turned cards rapidly now, their colorful patterns blurring in a psychedelic display. "Here, Bracken! Here is proof! I see you beside me in the new dawn. The crystalline dawn!"

Bracken puzzled over the cards, drawn by Aleena's enthusiasm, wishing he could read them as well as she.

"Don't you understand?" Aleena demanded. "This is an exciting moment! The cards confirm that you are one of the chosen few."

Aleena's face gleamed like a delicate portrait framed in black. Bracken wanted her to tell him more. But, she gathered up the cards, shaping them lovingly into a perfect rectangle. "I must go home now."

Bracken nodded. "Brighton Inn?"

"No." She replaced the cards in their packet and put it on the bare shelf of the stripped cabinet. "I'm driving to my house over on the coast."

Bracken remembered something. "Didn't you tell me last night that you were leaving for the coast early this morning?"

Aleena bit her lip. "How could I have told you that? I'm still here, aren't I?" She picked her way to the door.

Bracken shrugged. "Actually, I'm not sure about anything I saw or heard last night." Gathering darkness transformed the room's ugly clutter into an assortment of shadowy forms. "Aleena, I'm grateful for your support." He looked back on the demolished rooms. "Losing Trasent is a tragedy, but this . . . this invasion is outrageous."

"You have untapped strength," Aleena encouraged him. "You'll survive this."

Bracken, toying with the door's hardware, suddenly bent closer and examined it. "I just realized. This isn't broken. How did those ghouls get in?"

"Some kind of a master key," Aleena said cheerfully. "At least you won't have to repair it. Just have it re-keyed."

Still looking for damage, Bracken pondered, "But it was locked when I came home."

"Of course. I locked it after I let myself in." Aleena kissed Bracken lightly on the lips. "Oh, it's wonderful that we are partners in the crystalline dawn. What a marvelous day that will be."

Bracken watched Aleena's lithe form disappear around the corner. The nearby parking spaces must have been occupied when she'd arrived. If her sleek trans-speed had been parked in front, he would have noticed it when he came home.

* * *

The next day, Bracken waited outside the art gallery where Lisha worked. Just before closing time, he cautiously climbed the steps. He'd had an emotional meeting with his parents and wasn't sure he could handle seeing Lisha. Yet, he ached for contact with these people who represented his less complicated past.

His mother made no secret of her delight that he stayed several hours. Kressdek was reserved, but he welcomed Bracken with emotion-filled eyes that promised that, despite differences and hostilities, their raveled family ties still held. Bracken was surprised at the large measure of comfort he derived from that silent promise.

His parents provided what Bracken needed at the moment, someone to talk with about Trasent's death. Without meaning to, he found himself relating his friend's last moments. Myra began drawing philosophy straight from the Volume to explain the peaceful death. She clasped her hands in wistful joy and spoke as if Trasent were a close friend. *Somehow, that man learned the truth before it was too late.* What astounded Bracken most was Kressdek's staunch support of his wife's theory.

Now, Bracken stood in the gallery, partially hidden behind a large canvas, watching Lisha patiently discuss a painting with an inquisitive visitor. A rush of longing flooded over Bracken at the sight of Lisha's brown eyes. He remembered the fresh smell of her golden hair and the smoothness of her delicately freckled skin.

Apparently, the visitor was also captivated, either with Lisha or with the painting. Bracken suspected it was both, as Lisha recorded the sale.

After Lisha walked the customer to the door, Bracken stepped out where she could see him. A shocked look passed over her face before a polite smile softened her expression.

Encouraged, he said awkwardly, "Hope it's all right for me to come here."

She shrugged.

"I'd like to talk a while, if that's okay with you."

When she didn't answer, he continued, "Sorry I haven't done a better job of keeping in touch."

Lisha reached under the counter for a bag and spoke briefly to an older woman in the gallery. Then, she told Bracken, "You can walk along with me, if you want to."

"I was watching you back there," he said, as they left the gallery. "You're very good in that job."

"It's a nice place to work. They let me show some of my things."

"I mean, the way you spoke with that man. He bought a painting, and he loved you for selling it to him."

Lisha bristled. "I didn't coerce him into anything."

"I didn't mean that," Bracken said quickly. "I was simply complimenting you on your sales ability."

"Oh."

"And on your personality. You've changed, Lisha."

"You have complaints about my former personality?"

Bracken retorted, "Come on, Lisha. I said I was sorry for staying away so long. Let's start over, shall we?"

Lisha slowed her pace. "Okay. But, you're right. I have changed."

"I don't know what it is . . . more relaxed . . . more content. Whatever it is, working there must be good for you."

Lisha chuckled. "If I appear to be more relaxed or more content, it's probably because I've found a way to be at peace on the inside."

"Meditation?"

"Bracken! No, at least not the kind you mean. Do you ever read the Volume? I know your mother made you do it when you were young. But, I mean, lately."

"Who's got time for that?" Bracken answered flippantly. A sudden recollection of Trasent asking about Myra's beliefs spurred him on. "Don't tell me you're starting to believe those tales. Not me! When I look for information, I want to consult the most recent data available, and it's even better if I can find the original source."

"Oh, yes! We mustn't forget Bracken's big search."

"You didn't used to think it was something to sneer at."

"I'm not sneering. It's just that where you're looking, you'll never find truth. You'll find lies."

"At least, I'll find out for myself. Not simply believing words in an ancient book."

"It's more than that, Bracken. A lot more."

They walked in silence until they reached Lisha's home. Bracken touched her arm. "Let's don't fight. It's probably my fault. I'm pretty edgy. Got things on my mind."

"Want to come in?"

Bracken followed Lisha inside. He told her of Trasent's death, finishing with, "So, I'm determined to locate the Mingus Mine. It could hold the key to everything I'm wrestling with."

"Or, it could hold the key to everything evil."

Bracken sighed. "Don't be dramatic."

"Besides, how can you find the mine? You tried once before."

"Easy. Find Layozz. I'll get that map of his one way or another."

"You don't realize what you're saying. He guards that with his life."

"Yeah? Know that leather pouch he wears around his neck? I've suspected for a long time that he had something important in there. And, I don't think it would be too hard to get the pouch away from him."

"You're out of your mind. It takes more than the map. It takes explosives. He told me that once. And you have to know how to read the map, or something."

"I don't think I'll have any trouble reading a map."

"I've seen it. And I'm sure there's more to getting inside the mine than that scrap of paper."

Suddenly alert, Bracken demanded, "You've seen the map?

When? What does it look like? Did he leave that leather pouch laying around?"

"I don't want to talk about it."

"What?" Bracken roared, unable to believe that she wouldn't help him. "Lisha, tell me all you know. Otherwise," he threatened, "I'll find some way to get it out of Layozz."

"He'd never tell. And, even if you got that leather pouch, it wouldn't do you any good. He keeps a fake map in there and pretends it's important."

"You've seen the real one? Where is it?"

"I told you, I don't want to talk about it."

Bracken put an arm around Lisha's shoulders and drew her to the couch. "Please, Lisha, help me."

She bowed her head, golden hair hiding her face.

"Lisha, tell me," Bracken pleaded.

Choking back a sob, she yielded. "One night at his house, when we were the only ones there, he used a big stone. I didn't use one that night. Oh, I don't want to talk about it." Her hands flew to her face. "I want you to stay away from that terrible person!"

"You've got to help me, Lisha."

She sat up straight, shaking off Bracken's arm. "We were . . . we were in bed, and . . . you know that wide leather bracelet he wears?"

Anger flamed through Bracken at the picture of Lisha in bed with Layozz. "Yeah?"

"Well, I wondered why he never took it off. Never," she shook her head, "even when we were . . ."

"What about the bracelet?" Bracken hissed.

"I played around with it for a while. Then, you know the silver part in the middle, which has his name on it? It opened up, and I pulled out a piece of paper. Layozz never knew what I was doing, and I put the paper right back."

"What did it look like?"

"Most any hand-drawn map. Only, it had some little squiggles in places you wouldn't expect to find squiggles."

Bracken slapped his knee. "I'll get it. And I'll find the Mingus Mine. And I'll get inside, too."

"No, Bracken. Forget you ever thought of this stupid idea." Her voice broke. "You'll find nothing but evil at that mine."

Bracken cupped Lisha's face in his hands. "Don't you see, Lisha? I have to explore every possibility." He tilted her head and wiped away the tears that spilled down her cheek. He kissed her, gently at first, her forehead, her eyes, her mouth. Then, he drew her closer and began to kiss her in the old way.

Lisha pushed back. "No. Things are different now."

"Not that different."

"I'm different. It's not right for us to . . ."

"Not right? Since when?"

"We're not married."

Bracken released her and strode across the room. "I know we're not married. What difference . . . oh, I get it. You're playing the Miss Virtuous role."

"It's not a role. I've adopted new standards." She lifted her chin defiantly. "And I don't care what you think."

"Or, maybe that talk about Layozz brought back fond memories. Maybe you're saving yourself for him!"

"Bracken!"

"I'm leaving. You can have Layozz—what's left of him when I finish. I'm going after that map."

"Wait! Don't fight with Layozz," Lisha cried. She dashed to a cabinet, opened it, and removed a replica of a quaint dwelling from another era. Bracken recognized it as a cherished remembrance from Lisha's grandmother. She reached her hand inside its hollow walls and pulled out a piece of paper. "Here! Here's a copy of the real map. I drew it the next day. I am an artist, you know." She thrust the paper at Bracken. "Take it. Go find your precious mine. Go blow yourself up!"

CHAPTER 28

Bracken made good time getting to Accad. Lisha was right. The map might lead to the mine, but Layozz probably held the key to getting inside. He would strike a deal with Layozz. He would convince the Mingus dealer that he'd found the mine and would keep the location secret if Layozz cooperated in getting Bracken inside. Bracken must make Layozz believe that he didn't want a cut of the stone trade; he only wanted to get to the heart of the Mingus realm.

Layozz's dwelling in the Community was deserted. A search of the usual haunts turned up no clues. Tired and hungry, Bracken stepped into the Brazen Eagle. At the service window, he ordered bread and tea from an unsmiling man behind the counter and asked, "Where's Zactor?"

The man, older than Bracken, leaned both hands on the counter and sized up the newcomer.

Bracken explained, "Just passing through. Wanted to say hello."

The attendant shuffled to the rear. Soon Zactor waddled to the window, fatter than Bracken remembered.

"Name's Bracken. I'm a friend of Layozz. Went by his place, and couldn't find him."

"Haven't seen him," Zactor said flatly, wiping his hands on his apron.

Bracken motioned to the patrons. "Think anybody here could give me a lead on him?"

"Doubt it."

Bracken wanted results. He cleared his throat and announced loudly, "Well, if you see Layozz, tell him Bracken is doing some prospecting on Mt. Shidow, and he's looking for a partner."

He grabbed the bread, took a swig of tea, and walked out. If that remark didn't pry Layozz into the open, Bracken would have to get inside the Mingus mine without Layozz's cooperation.

* * *

Bracken had no trouble finding the old base camp and its hidden supply of explosives he and Silas had brought to Mt. Shidow on their first search for the Mingus Mine. Following Lisha's sketch of the map, he arrived in the mine's vicinity in a surprisingly short time. Darkness stopped him, and reluctantly he made camp.

By firelight, he perused the map, amazed at Lisha's precise drawing. Had she planned to use this for blackmail? Perhaps sell it? Why hadn't she done so? What did the squiggles, as she'd called them, mean?

Bracken arose with the morning sun, invigorated, pulsing with anticipation. The map guided him over a high outcropping of rock and along a dry stream bed to a singularly tall evergreen. From that landmark, he sighted across two more rocky pillars to another stream bed that led to a jagged rock overhang, which signified the mine's entrance.

There, sweating profusely from his climb, Bracken examined the pile of rubble beneath the overhang. Since there'd been no sign of Layozz, he had no choice but to continue on his own. He set a small explosive charge in a strategic spot. When the dust settled, he saw that the charge had done its work, and he pushed aside the remaining boulders that blocked the coveted entrance.

Inside, the beam from his lamp played over the tunnel's chiselled interior. The cool air contrasted sharply with the temperature outside. His excitement soaring, Bracken followed the shaft's twisting contour deeper into the earth.

The lamp's beam stopped at a metallic wall. Bracken rushed forward, his boots scraping over the uneven ground. Beyond that barrier, he would meet the source of the Mingus stone.

To his dismay, the partition with its closed hatchway appeared impregnable. The wall was fused to the tunnel. Bracken's lamp illuminated the aged clothing and helmet stored nearby. Ignoring them, he tugged uselessly at the hatchway's cover. The urgent probing of his fingers had no effect on the recessed lock console built into the wall. He toyed with the thought of blowing the partition to pieces, but that was an unpredictable undertaking so deep into the mine. What was Layozz's secret?

Once again, Bracken pored over Lisha's drawing. The paper, having lost its crispness in the damp mine, fell limp before the beam of his lamp. It was unbelievably accurate in every detail. Only the squiggles seemed meaningless. Bracken squinted his eyes to gain a new perspective. Suddenly, the squiggles jumped into focus so that a distinct pattern stood out, superimposed over the drawing. Bracken had found the key that would conquer the last barrier to the Mingus Mine!

His hand flew to the lock console. His fingers following the pattern, he punched a corresponding arrangement on the panel. With a loud click, the oval hatch swung open.

Recklessly, Bracken stepped over the threshold into what seemed to be a small chamber. Immediately, his body began to tingle with the most intense Mingus sensation he had ever experienced. Alarmed, he thought of the clothing and helmet stored on the other side of the partition. But before he could retrace his steps, he was catapulted from the chamber.

Helpless, caught in a spiraling swirl of cadmium brilliance, Bracken's body seemed to rise with the lightness of a feather captured in a rushing updraft. Waves of oscillating fluorescence formed an inverted funnel reaching above him into infinity. Liquid streams of crystal carried him aloft, bathing his body in velvety ecstasy. Then, in a moment of metamorphosis, Bracken's soul seemed to spread forth like a gossamer sail. Billowing under the force of an astral wind, his whole being accelerated, through palpitating, unidentifiable surroundings. Time stretched like a silken thread, until it snapped. Only his most vivid memories remained, as if all others had washed into the abyss below.

Bracken's pulsating journey continued, propelling him at last through the mouth of the funnel. His body curved in a gentle arc and came to rest on a glossy, green plain.

Glowing orbs danced and bobbed, ascending and descending in a rhythmic cadence between the shimmering plane on which Bracken stood and the prismatic city that hung suspended in the atmosphere over his head. As if his sudden appearance had disturbed them, the bubbles of light floated near him briefly and then moved away, emitting fluttering purrs of sound.

A large oval wafted its way through the others and stopped in front of Bracken. "I've been expecting you," communicated an embryo-like being from within its pulsating glow, "but only on the lower levels."

Bracken recognized Hiffornak from previous visits to the Mingus realm.

Hiffornak quavered in a short vertical curtsy, tiny arms and legs fluttering from its bloated torso. "What brings you here? Where are those you were to bring with you to our realm?"

This time, Bracken planned to control their encounter. "I will lead others here after my questions are resolved."

Hiffornak moved slightly to Bracken's right, in deference to another larger and brighter orb, which approached silently, apparently to observe, and continued, "With time and care, I'm sure you will soon realize all answers."

Bracken resisted Hiffornak's soothing tones. "I've heard that before. I can't wait any longer." He leaned forward, trying to see through the glow, to uncover the core of the embryo. "You promised me the knowledge to save Ebbern, but you deliver only words. You give me only platitudes and pleasing phrases."

"Accept what destiny offers. Obviously, you mourn not only for one friend, but now for a second one. Do not confuse your feelings of compassion with your quest for truth."

Startled, Bracken seethed with resentment that even his grief lay bare before this being.

"Compassion is a relevant term," Hiffornak intoned. "Your limited perception and human feelings allow only one viewpoint concerning deaths. If you could see death from our position, you would find it easier to accept."

Reckless now, Bracken shouted, "I would expect a great deal of compassion from you, a being that has reached a state of permanent transcendence."

Above, bubbles of light continued their ethereal ballet. Hiffornak turned to its neighboring orb, emitting low hums punctuated with a fluttering buzz.

Then, Hiffornak returned to Bracken employing a persuasive monotone, "There is so much to learn. One should not stagnate himself. The Mingus realm offers unlimited possibilities for you and for the friends you bring here."

Bracken grew silent, once again engulfed in the light creature's increasingly convincing dialogue. It would be so easy and so pleasant to succumb, to cease looking for answers and merely let the power and wisdom of this realm permeate him. Others seemed to find answers without the constant, driving compulsion that Bracken felt—Lisha, his mother, perhaps even his father. What did they find in antiquated writings to give them peace?

Suddenly, a violent need to resist overcame Bracken. He brushed aside Hiffornak's web-like verbiage that threatened to enfold his mind. He begged in despair, "Who are you? Stop giving me your philosophies. Be honest with me. Tell me what I can do to save my planet."

Again, the orb began recycling a previous response.

Determined to discover the secrets of this realm, Bracken's zeal manifested itself in a totally desperate act. Plunging for the creature, he pushed his way into its surrounding cloud of light. Immediately, Hiffornak vanished, absorbed into the second orb hovering in the background. Bracken's momentum carried him against this larger, masterful sphere of light. He encountered it with such a force that his body penetrated it.

Its sheen crackled. Sheets of lightning shivered through Bracken's body. At first, he didn't believe what he saw. He refused to believe, to accept this odious revelation. But the undeniable truth pierced Bracken's mind.

He found himself staring at the horrific majesty of the familiar, but malevolent face of Nebuzarr.

In a frenzy of terror, Bracken fled. Laughter rang from the now-darkened specter. It pursued him across the green plane, bringing with it an army of flying, writhing creatures. They soared amid shimmering, popping bubbles of light, their wings tipped with iridescent green. With a dissonant screeching symphony, they formed a spiraling orbit around Bracken. He reached the edge of the abyss, which was no longer filled with magnificent cadmium brilliance.

Without hesitation, he plunged into the chasm, knowing that it held his only hope of escape.

That hope disappeared as the regiment of pursuing wraiths swooped down with him into the blackness. Falling, he struggled to awaken from the nightmare. But, there was no relief. Below, loomed a bed of blackness. Around him as he tumbled downward, dim shafts of light partially illuminated the swirling mass of ugly creatures. In pairs, they broke formation and came upon him, their long claw-like hands tearing at his flesh. He thrashed back uselessly. As if temporarily satisfied with their pleasure, each pair withdrew in an orderly fashion, allowing two others to take its place. Again and again, this diabolical choreography repeated itself. Bracken's screams of pain and fear were matched by the creatures' screeches of delight at his anguish.

Bracken fell downward in an endless dive of agony until, at last, he was no longer falling. The wraiths were gone. Now, he found himself crawling through a bottomless, slithering coil of snakes. Multiple fangs sank into his flesh, injecting a venom that rushed to his brain, driving him to near-madness. On and on he crawled, twisting and pushing his way through writhing serpentine bodies. He struggled without release until the scaly reptiles began to withdraw. In their place came one monstrous snake, which wrapped itself about him and began to crush his body with the strength of an evil god.

Bracken reached the point where he could bear no more. His life ebbing, he slowly surrendered to the serpent's squeezing brawn.

All light disappeared, replaced by a fiery red glow, which enclosed Bracken in a burning tunnel of red. Mysteriously, the powerful serpent uncoiled itself from Bracken's limp body and vanished. The red glow cooled into pale, innocuous light.

Bracken did not know how long he lay in a state of semiconsciousness. Periodically, he awoke to see distant lights shimmering in darkness before slipping back into oblivion. Gradually, the periods of wakefulness grew longer. He saw that he was lying outside the entrance to the Mingus Mine. A remote morning sun smudged the sky with dull orange.

Bracken tried to move. Bolts of pain discharged in every strand of his nervous system. He looked down at his battered form. His torn clothing gaped open, revealing bruised and cut flesh. He lapsed into unconsciousness.

Again, he roused from his stupor and felt the searing heat of the sun now directly above him. A bitter voice prodded him with angry curses.

"Fool!" Layozz raged. "Trying to rob me after all I've done for you." The Mingus seller's face bulged in livid indignation. "How did you find it? How did you get in?"

"Easy," Bracken muttered through clenched teeth.

"That's the last time you or anybody else will do it!" Layozz underscored his declaration with a sharp kick to Bracken's ribs and pointed to the mine entrance. "Take a final look at the Mingus Mine. Because, soon, you won't recognize it—if you live to do any prospecting."

Bracken tried to sit, but crumpled into a groaning heap. "You're not going to murder me?" The painful effort of asking was wasted. Bracken knew the answer.

"That depends on how fast you can crawl." Layozz calmly flicked off a dried leaf caught on his shirt. "I'm setting a charge—from a safe distance, of course. You may be out of range by the time it explodes." Layozz marched down the dry stream bed. He stopped once to cackle with unrestrained mirth, "Let's say that you have a crawling chance."

Driven by panic, Bracken dragged his body from the mine entrance, the rocky ground shredding the skin on his elbows and grinding his belly into raw meat. Knowing he could never get away in time, he clawed his way behind a large rock.

The ground rumbled. Shards of granite flew by like arrows. Bracken crouched, drawing himself close to the protective rock just as the first boulders rolled down the slope.

Choking on the dust, holding his ribs, Bracken knew something had gone wrong with Layozz's charge, even before he heard a scream from below.

CHAPTER 29

After Trasent's death, Bracken began reporting directly to Arnaman and moved into Trasent's old office. Today he arrived at the Currency Center with the eager steps of a man happy with himself and with his work. He'd nearly recovered from his hideous encounter in the Mingus Mine, and grief for his friends had lessened.

Golens deposited a lengthy report on Bracken's desk. His pink face bore the reserved mask that had marked his demeanor since Bracken's change in status.

"Thanks for getting this to me promptly," Bracken accepted the material. "You must have worked late last night."

"I knew where to lay my hands on most of it."

Bracken tried to break through the new barrier between them. "I admire you, Golens. You're so organized that you can work under pressure without succumbing to the gambit of stress-related health problems. You'll never have ulcers."

Golens tittered nervously, "Guess not."

"Or drop dead of a heart attack."

Golens paled at Bracken's choice of words.

Bracken jerked back from the touch of Trasent's desk. "I . . . I shouldn't have said that . . . about a heart attack." Bracken licked his lips. "I hope you know that I feel privileged to sit at this desk. I intend to earn my place here."

Bracken's one-time supervisor nodded. "The word is, you're right for the job."

"I'll do what I can to get you assigned to projects where your talents can be used and," Bracken added meaningfully, "noticed by the right people."

A look of pleasure cracked Golens' mask. "It's always been my goal to move up the ladder here. I'm a team player, you know." He crouched over the desk. "And, don't feel bad about that heart attack remark," Golens said magnanimously. "A friend of mine knows the medic who answered the call that day. He said Trasent didn't have a heart attack."

"What?"

At Bracken's intense interest, Golens nodded his head rapidly. "Yeah. The other medic didn't think so either."

"But, everybody . . ."

"I know, and ultimately, his heart did fail—for some reason. Even though Trasent passed out and fell off the equipment, the emergency room people found no evidence of heart attack. They doped him up on pain medication and admitted him for observation. Those medics should know a heart attack, shouldn't they? I heard that trauma from the head wound triggered heart failure later."

"That's crazy! I saw that wound. It couldn't . . . ," Bracken's protest died. A picture of Trasent in the sterile medical facility bed, head swathed in a bandage, flashed before Bracken's eyes. Had the small cut been more serious than it first seemed? Serious enough to stop the beating of an apparently healthy man's heart?

A knock at the door cut short Bracken's introspection. Golens straightened up when Aleena entered. She acknowledged him and took a chair close to Bracken's desk. As usual, Golens' envy was obvious as he left the two of them alone.

Aleena's teasing smile told Bracken that she enjoyed the talk generated by her frequent visits to Bracken at the Currency Center. He put away thoughts of Trasent and smiled back at her. He knew her calls often had nothing to do with business. He also knew that her personal attention to him enhanced his new status.

As the door closed, Aleena clasped her hands. "The day we've been waiting for is nearly here! The most important day of our lives—the stellar alignment. Oh, Bracken," she cried, "don't you feel the oneness of our spirits? Our paths were destined to cross. Together, we will participate in the greatest gathering of all time."

Aleena's enthusiasm was part of her charm, and Bracken's words warmed with gratitude. "I don't think I tell you often enough, but I owe you a lot. I realize I've been fortunate in my career. First, I had Trasent's help. Now, Arnaman has taken an interest in me."

"How about credit for my motivational seminar?"

"I'm getting to that. You've helped me here, but beyond that, you're responsible for making me aware of the stellar alignment and including me in its great potential."

"Nonsense! You're appointed to be among those who will call forth a new chapter of history. You saw that in the cards yourself."

"Perhaps, but sometimes I feel as if you're some kind of a beautiful guardian angel, guiding me, taking care of me."

Aleena laughed. "At this moment, chosen ones all over the planet are preparing for the night when Ebbern's moons burgeon into full flower. How can you sit behind that desk looking so calm when we are about to join forces with the stars, the planets, and Ebbern's moons? The energy that we call forth will be beyond comprehension, beyond anything that archaic systems throughout the centuries have envisioned. Our strength will forge a network that will bring new order and new hope to the universe."

Infused with her excitement, Bracken rose and pulled Aleena to her feet. They stood, hands joined. A rush of joy engulfed him. His dream of imprinting the world with his signature was about to come true. Hiffornak had promised that the Mingus stone would give Bracken awareness and knowledge to prevent the destruction of Ebbern. The alien Trionites had led him to their leader with the tantalizing promise that he could be among the survivors in an advanced evolution structure, which would save the race and preserve the planet.

Instead, both the Mingus stone and the space disk had brought an encounter with forces so powerful that Bracken cringed at the memory, forces so pervasive as to blur the distinction between the two, leaving only a boiling cloud of evil gathered in an image of the face he'd come to know as Nebuzarr.

Layozz had vanished, possibly buried in the avalanche he initiated. Frimleter had disappeared, a spent, impotent vessel, perhaps discarded in favor of newer, more vibrant Touch-Points.

But, Bracken had been chosen to join with the enlightened. These elite, favored people would gather on the slopes of the majestic Mt. Shidow where, at the ultimate moment of power, they would bring forth an age of global peace.

Aleena, leaned toward Bracken, her soft lips parted, her eyes alive with expectation. Her strong hands pulled him closer.

A firm knock at the door pushed them apart. Hastily retreating to his desk, Bracken called, "Come in."

Arnaman strode into the office. At the sight of Aleena, concern magnified the usual deep creases across his brow. "I heard that you were in the building," he told her, stroking his silver-colored beard. His tone hinted disapproval that he had merely heard of her visit. "I have things to discuss with you."

Aleena's eyes narrowed at this suggestion of criticism. "As soon as Bracken and I have finished."

Arnaman gave a slight nod. "There's an item of particular urgency."

Aleena inspected her perfectly-shaped red fingernails. "I am handling everything."

In a tone that changed abruptly to the familiar one Bracken had come to expect from his new mentor, Arnaman told Bracken, "I want you to represent me at the status review meeting today."

"Yes, sir." Bracken flushed with pleasure.

"See me after the noon meal, and I'll brief you."

When the door closed on Arnaman, Bracken whistled in surprise. "Hear that? I'm representing the top guy in human relations! That should impress the underlings around here."

Aleena raised her dark eyebrows. "I suppose."

"Aren't you impressed?"

"Bracken, you are special without the benefit of Arnaman's favors."

"We know that," Bracken quipped, "but not everyone is as informed as we are."

* * *

The second time Bracken's home was ransacked, it was done with more finesse. He found the door unlocked and the rooms searched, but this time, there was not the mass destruction that looked as if a host of vengeful supernatural beings had visited. Nothing seemed to be missing, except food. The intruders had helped themselves to a generous meal from the pantry.

Bracken checked Trasent's old room. Most of his things had been packed and sent to storage, upon orders from the authorities. Bracken would have preferred to give them away, but Arnaman, who took an active part in settling Trasent's affairs in the absence of relatives, had advised Bracken to do as he was told.

Bracken had purchased the exercise equipment from the estate. Now, as he satisfied himself that the intruders had no interest in physical fitness, he suddenly recalled the one item that he'd deliberately hidden. Standing on a stool in the gathering room, he reached up to an elaborate chandelier replete with hanging glass spangles that reflected a myriad of beautiful lights in every direction.

Bracken's fingers felt their way into the warmth of the chandelier's heart. Carefully, he lifted out a fragile thread and brought down the ruby-colored jewel, which Trasent had given him.

He sighed with relief at the sight of the glimmering, faceted crystal. Although, the jewel must have little monetary value, Bracken felt unexplainably drawn to it, a nostalgic reminder of a deceased friend.

* * *

These days Bracken did not often feel lonely. Later that evening, he found himself standing outside Lisha's home. He realized that not only was he drawn to the ruby jewel, once again he was drawn to this girl.

"I heard you were back." With that simple remark, she opened the door to Bracken.

He stepped inside and took her into his arms. "I was pretty rotten last time we met."

"Yes, you were," she mumbled into his shirt.

Bracken caressed her flowing, golden hair. "Lisha, I'm truly sorry. I was wrong to ask you to compromise your beliefs." He held her at arms' length. "It won't happen again."

"Promise?"

"Absolutely."

Later, over a cup of tea, Bracken said, "Aren't you going to ask about the mine?"

Lisha averted her eyes. "I'm not sure I want to know."

"I want you to know. I found it, but not what I was looking for. It was a dead end." A shiver crawled up his spine at the thought of how nearly true that statement was. "If I'd been looking for a fortune, it was there."

Lisha spoke thoughtfully, "I hope it's buried forever." Her brown eyes sought Bracken's. "Is it?"

He returned her gaze. "As far as I'm concerned, it is."

Lisha removed the cups. She whirled and swiped a cloth across the table, flicking it playfully at Bracken.

He caught it and threatened to pull her onto his lap. When she escaped, he settled back and said, "However, it does appear that somebody thinks I might be hiding some kind of fortune in my pantry. Let me tell you about today's interesting homecoming."

When he'd finished, Lisha said, "What an awful thing to happen! And for the second time!" She grew indignant. "Just because you work at the Currency Center, do all the thieves in Tizra think you've got money and jewels hidden away for safekeeping?"

"Hey! I'm more important around there than you know. It so happens that I'm sitting in at meetings for the big boss. And," he waited for her full attention, "it so happens that I do have a jewel." Bracken pulled out Trasent's ruby-colored crystal. Suddenly serious, he said, "Lisha, I've been a terrible friend to you. Take this, wear it, and try to forgive me."

Startled, Lisha examined the jewel, rubbing her fingers over its smooth surface. She held it near a lamp, admiring how it caught and reflected the light. "It's simply beautiful, Bracken, but I can't take this. It must be valuable."

"I don't think so. Trasent gave it to me just before he died. I suppose because of that, it's come to mean something to me. I want you to have it." He draped the slender thread around her neck. The ruby crystal nestled on her breast.

"But, what if it's truly valuable?"

Bracken shook his head patiently. "It's not. The model wearing it is the treasure."

"Come on," Lisha grabbed Bracken's hand. "I know how we can find out exactly what this is worth."

Over Bracken's protests, Lisha rushed him several doors down the street. They entered a small shop wedged in a converted dwelling owned by Lisha's friend. "He's a jeweler, and he owes me favors," she explained.

Despite Bracken's certainty that the crystal was simply an eye-catching ornament, he hung over the jeweler's shoulder as the man examined it. Could it be a genuine, even rare, jewel? He caught Lisha's eye. It was difficult to resist her contagious enthusiasm.

"Very unusual," the jeweler muttered, "in size and color."

Lisha gave Bracken a delighted smile.

"Not like any other I've seen."

Bracken returned Lisha's expectant look. Maybe he did have a monetary treasure.

The jeweler handed the crystal back to Lisha. "A spectacular example of a man-made crystal," he said with an air of apology. "But, a valuable jewel? No."

Lisha's lips curved in a short-lived pout. "You're not rich, after all, Bracken."

On the way back to her place, Lisha dangled the crystal from her fingers. "Anyway, it was nice of your friend to give this to you. He may have thought it was worth a lot. I'm glad nobody stole it."

Bracken had concluded that Trasent's mysterious attitude over the ruby crystal was caused by medication. But now, the picture of Trasent's panic-stricken face urging Bracken to search for the jewel returned and stubbornly refused to fade. It had seemed vitally important to Trasent that Bracken take the ruby crystal. What had he said? *You take it. There's no one else.* Why had Trasent wanted him to have it? He'd said something more, too. *Hide it.*

Bracken plucked the jewel from Lisha's hands. What a fool he'd been! Trasent probably wanted it hidden for good reason. Their home had been invaded twice by people who may have been searching for this, people who did consider it valuable.

"What did your friend mean when he said this was manmade?" Bracken asked abruptly.

"It was grown, not mined."

"It's artificial, in other words. Fake."

"Personally, I don't like to think of my jewelry," Lisha pointed to the sparkling amber center of a ring on her right hand, "as fake." She giggled. "Manmade sounds better."

Bracken pursued his own line of thought. "Trasent knew something important. Something that upset him, maybe even frightened him."

"You think that bit of glass, which you gave to me," she scowled to make her point, "and then snatched away, holds a secret?" She cocked her head. "You people at the Currency Center growing your own jewels?"

"Sure," Bracken's tenseness eased. "Laboratories on the subfloors."

They reached Lisha's house, and she opened the door, prattling about Bracken sharing the wealth. Suddenly Bracken stopped midstep, stumbling over the threshold.

"That's it!" he yelled. "Trasent rambled about a secret . . . about a global plan being only the beginning."

"The beginning of what?"

Bracken pulled Lisha back outside. "Come on! Let's find out."

CHAPTER 30

The Currency Center appeared deserted except for the usual security force. The guard showed no reluctance in admitting Lisha with Bracken.

They stopped first in Trasent's old office, which Bracken now occupied. Bracken searched through the drawers. All the key cards had been removed before Bracken had taken over.

Lisha fingered her hair nervously. "What are you looking for?"

"One night I pulled a key card from this office and went downstairs to the dead file storage. The key card worked on a door that it shouldn't have opened. Maybe it works on others. There are unmarked doors down there leading to highly restricted areas. I saw Trasent coming out of one unaccompanied. I found out later that nobody is supposed to go in that area without an escort."

Lisha hugged herself and shot a worried look over her shoulder. "I don't think we should be here."

"Golens! He knows everything and everybody." Bracken whipped to a nearby office and let himself in. "You can bet that he's cultivated a friend in security and probably has a master key card. He'd never have the guts to do anything with it, but it's here somewhere." Bracken's own key card opened Golens' files, and a quick search revealed that Golens did have a master.

Bracken led Lisha to the sub-floor and straight to the unmarked door that Golens had told him no one entered alone. At a touch, the key card opened it. They slipped inside and encountered an array of technology that surpassed anything visible on the upper floors of the Currency Center.

In silence, they wandered through rows of information storage and monitoring equipment. Bracken found what he wanted in a small, secluded viewing room in a far corner. The room was bare except for a single large table and four straight chairs. Bracken was unable to locate a light control, but low-level, indirect lighting had automatically clicked on at their entrance.

On the table was a metal encased processor. Near it was a black console small enough to fit in the palms of Bracken's hands. On top of the console rested a clear glass cube. A rectangular slot on the cube's upper surface extended down into its interior. Several cables ran from the console to the processor and to a nearby auxiliary screen.

"It's a reader," he told Lisha, indicating the black console. "It reads laser-encoded material. We use one upstairs to interpret codes on Currency Center cards. I've never seen one with a cube on top. That slot in the cube wasn't made for cards. It was made for this."

Bracken took a slow breath to steady his hands and inserted Trasent's ruby crystal into the opening on top of the cube. The faceted edges of the flat jewel slipped neatly into place.

Lisha watched anxiously. "Nothing's happening."

Bracken pushed a rocker switch on the processor. Lights flashed. He activated other controls until a panel of lights shone on the processor. The auxiliary screen lit up.

"Try this one." Lisha pointed to a lone button on the front of the console.

At Bracken's touch on the switch, the cube began to revolve. The ruby crystal came alive.

The dimly-lit viewing room where Bracken and Lisha huddled over the reader was transformed as tiny rays of red light erupted from the revolving cube. The beams darted erratically, slashing through the air and flying over walls and ceiling. A discordant pattern of tones rose and fell in an eerie volume. Bracken gripped the furniture for support, feeling that he might begin to follow the red lights in their dizzy whirl. Lisha leaned against him, red spots of light racing over her body, her face, soaring away like fiery stars.

Gradually, the frantic pace of light and sound decelerated until the spots moved effortlessly in a slow rhythmic dance. Now the tones were soft, melodic, and repetitious.

Bracken regained his equilibrium and sat down at the screen, which flickered with activity. Lisha peered over his shoulder.

At first, the words on the screen made no sense. Strange, unidentifiable images swept across it, overshadowing the text. Bracken began to piece together bits of information. "This data must have been microscopically encoded into the lattice structure of the crystal. That's why your jeweler friend had never seen one like it." Bracken tore his attention from the screen long enough to marvel at the ruby crystal shining from the cube's center. "That thing must have almost limitless capacity for information storage." He focused back on the screen. "Look, here is a schedule of some sort."

"About . . . about a global plan?" Lisha asked tremulously.

"I can't decipher it all. Some is in symbols, or code, almost like a foreign language."

"Oh!" Lisha gasped as an extraneous image flashed on the screen. "What was that horrible thing?" She covered her eyes. "It looked like a prehistoric animal."

"Just a quirk in the program." Bracken laughed away an uneasy feeling. "Here's a list of meetings, dating back years. People from all over Ebbern have been attending them." He studied the screen and then exclaimed at the realization that one name headed each roster, "Arnaman! He really is important!"

"I don't like this, Bracken! I don't want to know about it."

"You don't want to know about cooperation between the nations of Ebbern?—a move to bring about global stability?"

Lisha peeked through her fingers. "Read what's on the screen now. Public relations. Persuasion. Look! It's a chart defining the value of individuals. Bracken, let's leave."

"You shouldn't be afraid of a global plan for world peace." He concentrated, absorbing as much as he could. "I think Arnaman's job is to prepare the population to receive the idea of world-wide cooperation. Talk about a top-management challenge in human relations!"

"You're crazy. See that?" Lisha pointed with one hand and hammered Bracken's shoulder with the other. "Privilege level. It's tied to value level. Each person is going to be rated according to his value."

The cube's revolutions quickened. The red rays spit out erratically, the pattern of tones disturbed.

Bracken argued stubbornly, "People have been judged by their intelligence and talents throughout history. It's inevitable." As if in agreement, the cube slowed and the red spots resumed their slow, rhythmic dance. "I know it may not be fair, but . . ."

"It's worse than not being fair. That says privileges are going to be doled out according to a person's value rating."

His argument weakened, "But, if it helps mankind better itself? Besides, this sort of thing is eons in the future. And, on the practical side, a little hard to execute."

"It sounds like the end of the world to me."

"You're over-reacting."

Bracken and Lisha watched the screen quietly for a few minutes until the constant procession of information ceased momentarily. After the break, a new topic spread across the screen: *Permanent Identification Number*. Lisha cringed. Fascinated, Bracken watched plans unfold for reading the genetic code unique to each individual. The code would translate into a permanent identification number.

Bracken pulled up another chair and persuaded Lisha to sit. He put an arm around her. "This doesn't necessarily mean something sinister."

"It does to me!"

"High technology can be a little scary at first, until we get used to it. And we don't have this kind of technology now. Hey, I remember when you used to have such an open mind."

"Maybe you don't know all the technology somebody has. And, if this plan is innocent, why the secrecy?" Lisha jumped as another image burst on the screen.

Over tightly spaced columns of statistics appeared two rows of jagged triangles. They clamped together like ugly teeth and vanished. A harsh, angry instant of sound interrupted the crystal reader's melodic tones.

"Wonder if Arnaman knows somebody's been playing a child's game on this reader." Bracken fingered the controls to cut down the screen's contrast. "Anyway, there has to be a degree of secrecy. Not everyone can accept and evaluate new ideas." How could he expect Lisha to understand this? Her reaction when he'd told her of the coming stellar alignment was negative, to put it mildly. She'd gone into a tearful tirade about misplaced faith. On the other hand, Aleena lived by new ideas. She would willingly make sacrifices, if necessary, to bring about global tranquility. He told Lisha, "The world probably isn't ready for this."

"Was Trasent ready for this?" A sneer twisted Lisha's pretty face.

"He worked closely with Arnaman. He had to know of it." Bracken spoke confidently. But through his mind ran Trasent's last words, *I know the real truth now. . . .*

The display shimmered brightly as they came to another break in the information flow. Following that, two words spread across the screen as if to amplify Trasent's statement. *SECOND PHASE.*

Over the words, flashed a scene that was so bizarre and yet so realistic that fear coursed through Bracken. The scene hung suspended for a moment, almost long enough for Bracken to believe that his eyes did not trick him. It portrayed a swamp-like landscape inhabited by hideous beasts. The swamp water bubbled black, and the vegetation flamed with fire. Into this poured twisting, writhing human bodies, like live dolls being dumped from an overhead bucket.

Immediately, the screen faded to gray, then black. The tones blended into one and died. But the dancing red spots increased in number and flew in a frenzied scramble over every surface in the room.

Lisha clung to Bracken begging, "Shut it off!"

Some of the red lights slowed and began to swell in size. Assuming a third dimension, they grew into grotesquely shaped blobs, so that they looked like bloody, disembodied, pulsating heads arrogantly bouncing around the room.

Lisha screamed, "They have eyes! Ugly, evil eyes!"

Bracken tore himself from Lisha's fierce hold and pulled the ruby crystal from the cube. The glistening red blobs vanished.

Quickly, Bracken reversed the procedure he'd used to activate the reader. "That's enough! Let's go." More alarmed than he wanted Lisha to know, he rushed her out the door.

They backtracked to Golens' office, replaced the key card, and as calmly as possible, left the building.

"Enjoy the holiday tomorrow," called the guard.

"Now, look," Bracken told Lisha when they were a distance from the Currency Center, "don't be upset. So we did a little snooping? The worst that piece of red glass describes is a nebulous plan for some sort of future population census. I admit, those weird images had me going for a while. I suppose a clandestine atmosphere and exotic spinning red lights could play tricks on anybody's imagination."

But, later that night, alone in his room, Bracken lay awake, question after question bombarding his mind. What more was on the ruby crystal? Could knowledge of data encoded in a piece of glass have caused Trasent's personality to change as radically as it did? Ridiculous! And his death? Heart failure. It had to have been that—plain, ordinary heart failure. The head wound from his fall off the exercise equipment was minor. But it could have triggered serious consequences.

Wearily, Bracken got up and paced the floor. *It was that medical facility,* he told himself, *not recognizing a heart problem, no life support equipment, leaving a critically ill man alone. I'll request an investigation. I should have insisted on one at the time.*

Slightly pacified, Bracken sat in a chair, staring out over the sleepy Tizra streets. In his imagination, he saw Trasent alone in the medical facility room. He relived Trasent's feeble attempt to give Bracken the ruby crystal. He saw himself opening the cabinet door and finding the soiled exercise clothes, a tangled heap on the floor. Bracken frowned. The exercise clothing had not been merely dumped at the bottom of the cabinet. He remembered now. The pockets had been turned inside out, as if someone had searched them. Arnaman had been in the room before Bracken.

Refusing to succumb to unwarranted suspicions, Bracken resumed pacing. Of course, Arnaman, or medical personnel, would have gone through the personal effects of an unconscious emergency patient.

Bracken's wandering took him close to the bookcase. The leather-covered ancient Volume stood straight and rigid on the shelf.

Bracken dropped to the floor. Worn pages whispered beneath his fingers and then seemed to fall open to a place of their own choosing near the end of the book. Bracken removed a slip of paper wedged between the pages, recognizing it as Trasent's personal note paper. So, his friend had borrowed the Volume? How much had he read? Enough to arouse his curiosity, and having seen Myra's inscription inside the cover, make him ask Bracken about her beliefs.

Bracken scanned the pages. Certainly, no one could argue that this was not a piece of good literature. Bracken recalled admitting that to his mother many times. Tonight, the nearly forgotten story grabbed his attention as he read of terrible times when men would worship a false god and be ruled by economic control, and the world would suffer unspeakable pain. Apparently, Trasent had read this too, because he'd marked the place. Bracken skimmed over references to dreadful beasts, accounts that did nothing to quiet his troubled nerves.

He thought of his friend's death, of the way Trasent seemed, well, ready to die. Was it possible that Trasent found a way to escape the horror of death?

As Bracken started to close the book, a passage caught his attention.

Those ruled by pride will seek their own way—not mine. In lust for power and adoration, they will lead as if to peace, and they will destroy, and be destroyed. My truth alone will survive. Only my truth can save.

It always comes back to that, Bracken thought, the truth. Where was indisputable truth to be found?

A picture of a stalwart, unending source of wisdom came to mind. Bracken replaced the Volume on the bookshelf and crawled into bed. The next day, he would seek out this fountainhead of wisdom.

CHAPTER 31

In his cabin high in the Forest of Zorek, Dalfang sat before the fireplace, puffing thoughtfully on his pipe. Bracken tossed a log from the wood box at the side of the hearth on the fire and spread his hands toward the warmth.

Outside, subdued sunlight distilled its way through the fog. The sea drizzle lent a misty sheen to the slender needles of high evergreens. Drops of expanding moisture gathered on verdant ferns and spilled to the moss-covered ground.

Feeling rested after his long hike to the cabin, Bracken reiterated the purpose of his visit. "I want to go to Malchag. I want to meet the leader."

Dalfang's weathered fingers caressed his pipe's smooth bowl. "You have travelled many realms and byways since your last visit. Did you find their promises fulfilled?"

Bracken looked into the ancient face. "The Mingus stone transported me to an awesome upper level, where I was told that Ebbern was threatened with destruction, but that the stone would give me knowledge and awareness to prevent it." Pain cracked Bracken's composure. "Instead, I lost Silas. And my awareness was only of evil."

The older man's pale blue eyes shone from their deep sockets. "The pulsating allure of the stone proved false?"

Bracken nodded grimly.

"Yet, you continue to seek something of eternity."

"Then, I was told by powers from another dimension that our race must be restructured, and that I could be among those who would perpetuate the race. But with them, my questioning marked me as unfit."

"Ah, Bracken. You are missing the truth that lies within yourself. Harness the good there and use it to transform your world. The internal power you possess is like a stream whose waters can be directed to build or to destroy."

Bracken said thoughtfully, "I believe I am learning what potential lies within me. New friends are encouraging me to use my abilities, to join with them in creating a force of energy that will usher in an era of global unity."

"Still . . . you have questions, do you not?"

"I'm torn. Being chosen for such a momentous task is the culmination of my lifelong dream. To be awarded leadership in a new era would prove that all my searching has not been in vain. I cannot refuse the honor. I don't want to refuse it. I've earned it." Bracken's voice fell, "Yet . . ."

"Malchag has taught me many things," Dalfang said. "I've grown old learning of its ways. Quiet reflections of its beauty give understanding to those who are willing to see the value of tranquility. In its soil and sky, in the trees and the high mountains rests an enchantment that leaves the soul refreshed, not drained."

"I need the plain and unaffected quality of that parallel universe to quiet the questioning in my heart," Bracken said longingly.

Dalfang drew on his pipe. "It is time for you to go to Malchag," he said. "When you arrive, Dayon will show you the path to Wissim's palace in the mountains. Within you, my son, is a flow of good that waits to be guided by wisdom."

* * *

Bracken breathed deeply of fresh-scented air as he hiked through the rolling foothills below the snow-capped peaks of Malchag. Occasionally, the well-traveled path plunged into the forest. Tall, narrow trunks rose and opened into a massive canopy of dark leaves, dotted with seed cones.

Bits of rock grated under his feet as he mounted a twisting pathway. Above him, a ridge of high crags ripped its way toward a sapphire sky. Squat trees with brittle-looking branches clung to the vertical sides of the canyon walls.

At one point, the path became so steep that Bracken thought he could go no further. However, at the top of a narrow ravine, a stairway appeared, leading up the mountainside. Its steps, worn with travel, had been hewn from rock. Beyond, lay a high meadow with a winding, sparkling stream.

Blue-green grass squeaked beneath his boots as Bracken reached a brook. Tiny white fish darted in its waters. Bracken bent over the icy water and drank, disturbing the reflected oval of the sun bobbing on the flux of the brook's surface.

Behind him, Bracken saw the rolling plain of Malchag. For the moment, he felt at peace, free, like a bird soaring above the confusion of his universe—the other universe. He walked on, following the stream up the grass tableland to its source. A waterfall poured down from a jutting bluff into a round pool.

Here, the path ended. Frustrated, Bracken searched until, at last, he sighted a narrow tunnel secluded behind the splashing water. He waded through the pool, slipped behind the falling stream, and stepped into a passageway. A tiny square of light shone at the other end.

A startling sight greeted him there. A slender tongue of rock reached from the tunnel's end out into space and touched the high cliffs that stretched up to meet it from the other side of a deep gorge. It formed a thin bridge. Far below, a thundering river carved its course through the canyon.

On the other side, he encountered snow. Rivulets of water ran from beneath great cakes of frozen white and washed over lichen-covered rock. Sparkling icicles clung to rocky overhangs, disappearing as the path descended again, leaving the snow behind.

Bracken worked his way down a winding ravine until, coming around the edge of a steep dome, he sighted a fertile land falling away toward a distant forest. Within this forest, nestled a chalk-white palace with a needle-shaped pillar pointing to the sky.

Bracken's emotions leaped. He played out in his imagination the welcome he would receive from Wissim. Bracken was, after all, a future leader of the enlightened era. However, he would hasten to make it clear that, although they shared a common ground as fellow leaders, Bracken came in a humble search for learning.

The sun was low when Bracken stood at the castle's huge gate and called to the sentinel in the tower.

"Who are you, traveller, and where do you come from?" asked the swarthy-skinned keeper of the gate.

"Bracken. I've come from Nerkush, through the western gate of Malchag."

"For what purpose?"

"I've come to sit at the feet of your leader and learn his wisdom."

"In the morning, the door of truth will be opened to you," replied the gatekeeper.

Disappointment at the delay swept over Bracken. But he followed meekly as an old man led him to the castle's guest quarters. Dressed in a hooded cloak, the man carried a flaming torch to guide their way through the labyrinth of hallways and courtyards. Strange languages echoed and melodic music drifted along with them. A resonant bell rang in the tower above.

The torch-bearer stopped at a wooden door ribbed with bands of black metal. "This is your room. After you have refreshed yourself, you may eat."

Later, a younger man appeared and led Bracken to a brightly lit dining hall. Finlanleys welcomed him with nods and laughter as they ate their evening meal and sang songs in honor of their leader, Wissim.

The next morning, yet another attendant roused him with a sing-song greeting and left a bowl of fruit. Despite the comfort of his quarters, Bracken had slept fitfully, the phantoms and specters of dreams stealing his rest. He felt worn and frazzled.

The attendant returned. "Your audience will take place at the second bell." He led Bracken through the palace into a neatly-trimmed garden edged with lacy trees. It was divided in the center by a wide walkway paved with bluish-gray rock. On either side of the promenade, fleshy white blossoms floated on the smooth surface of twin ponds. A raised six-sided dais in the center of the promenade formed the focal point of the garden. "You may wait here until our leader arrives."

At one end of the promenade, Bracken sat alone in the beautiful surroundings. Everything was perfect—the green mosslike plants that edged the walkways, the carved wooden bench where he rested, the castle's white needle spire—all perfect.

The bell rang, an odd, strange sound. It rang a second time. A door at the far end of the garden opened. Bracken straightened expectantly. Two lines of solemn Finlanley musicians entered and proceeded formally down the promenade toward him, playing a plaintive processional. Behind them, an entourage of Finlanleys followed, carrying a great throne, which they gently deposited on the dais.

The musicians merged, flowing like streams of water in front of the throne, swaying, rippling, in a complex hypnotic pattern. Bracken strained to see Wissim, but the throne seemed veiled in a blue cloud. The ceremonial choreography contrasted sharply with the simplicity Bracken associated with Malchag.

Suddenly, the music and the choreography stopped. With a whisper of motion, the attendants dropped to the paving, allowing Bracken to see the throne's occupant. At first, he thought he had lost his mind. That face! The hideous smile! It was the mocking visage that had confronted Bracken on the upper level of the Mingus realm. It was the face that had lurked behind the space disk commander's veil. And, it was the face that called Silas to his death.

Through suffocating terror, Bracken uttered, "Wissim?"

A low, mocking voice answered, "Now you know. You came seeking wisdom, and you have found it." The corners of the ugly mouth lifted in a grim smile.

The knowledge beat at Bracken, hammering into his brain a terrible confirmation. There was a link—a connection—between the awareness of the Mingus stone, the power of the space disk, and the wisdom of Malchag. They were all tools of one unspeakably evil personage. Nebuzarr!

The Finlanleys broke their silence with eerie, shrieking screams. Bracken stared in horror, watching their outer coverings begin to melt, dripping like wax, leaving behind the writhing, tentacled shapes of demons.

"You grew fat on the lies we fed you, Bracken," shouted Nebuzarr over the clamor of his demons. "You could have been of such use to me." The venomous shout rose in unleashed fury. "But, I am weary of waiting for your soul to ripen. Now is the time for its harvest!"

Blue-blackness, like the swirling funnel of a violent storm, churned in Bracken's mind. He had reached this moment only to find a lie waiting behind one more door in his search for truth. Nebuzarr rose. He seemed to grow larger and larger. Bracken could not look at him. Yet he must. He must confront this evil force.

"No one escapes!" The voice boomed from the platform like a great hollow echo, a voice forsaken by its body, a terrible voice that howled and thundered around Bracken.

A thrashing blue-black tide engulfed Bracken. He searched for a single flicker of promise for his life.

Suddenly, the hellish shrieks from the dais ceased. Nebuzarr's terrible tirade quieted, as if something drew his attention away from his quivering victim. Red rays—the kind that flow from the setting sun—bathed the garden, softening the evil scene, unbelievably casting a sort of strange beauty to Nebuzarr's countenance.

Without warning, a lifeline was thrown to Bracken. He heard his name called. The tide sucking him under receded. Replacing it came a delicate red vapor that wrapped him in a feathery softness.

Like the clockwork of a giant timepiece locking in infinite suspension, the parallel universe of Malchag stopped.

The lifeline supported Bracken, drew him away. Farther and farther, he moved from the presence of Nebuzarr. He knew not the source of his strength, but an insistent force pulled at him, making him follow. When he stumbled, the lifeline jerked unmercifully until he responded.

He heard his name again. "Bracken!"

Running from the chalk-white palace, Bracken knew someone was leading him. His vision was clouded, his senses numbed. He scurried through the forest. Billowing red vapor surrounded Bracken. A bluish-green canopy hovered overhead. Was there hope that he might be hidden from the evil personage that demanded his soul?

The lifeline pulled him closer and allowed him to pause. His breath came in huge, surging gasps. His vision cleared. He looked for the source of the lifeline, and saw a slender, white hand. The hand clasped Bracken's with masterful strength. His eyes focused on the white hand, the arm, the countenance of his savior, Aleena.

CHAPTER 32

Aleena's multi-storied home stood like a smooth white fortress above the coastline off the Sea of Aurin. Bracken had been a guest there during the few days since their escape from Malchag. He had somewhat recovered from that shattering experience, but the hours here in close contact with Aleena had added a new vista to his mental torment.

Now, he stood on an outdoor terrace of the uppermost tier. Two more tiers sprawled down the cliff, their white, walled terraces gleaming in the afternoon sun like spacious steps.

Aleena's resources and her capabilities appeared limitless. She explained her feat of dragging him from the grip of death with, *Why, Bracken, you know I go to Malchag often. I'm quite familiar with the terrain.*

He heard his name called softly. Aleena slipped through a sliding door and beckoned Bracken to an outdoor table where a servant had placed a polished tray of refreshments.

Bracken put aside his torment and indulged himself in the luxury of the moment. Sitting across from this beautiful woman of power and status, he sipped his drink, with the heady knowledge that this lifestyle was his to enjoy today and all the tomorrows in the foreseeable future.

Aleena reinforced his thoughts. "Bracken, it's wonderful having you here. I get lonely in this big house."

"Lonely! With guests dropping in from all over the globe?"

"It's not the same. You and I have a closeness." She stretched a slim foot beneath the table and briefly curled it around Bracken's ankle. "It's because we know what is important."

When Bracken didn't respond, she continued, "Tomorrow morning at Mt. Shidow, we will prove that to everyone. Together we will lead the call to usher in the new era."

"It's what we've wanted for a long time." He regretted the note of reserve that crept into his response.

"I'm going to be so proud of you. You're a vital link in our chain of energy. I have promised that you will fulfill your potential."

"Promised? What an odd choice of words."

"There will be no more lies, no more oppression, no more secrets." Aleena sparked with intensity. "No more secrets." She pushed away from the table and pulled Bracken to his feet. "Tell me," she pleaded, "that you have no secrets from me. I couldn't stand it if I thought you were keeping anything from me, anything at all." Her eyes, moist and compelling, searched his. "Nothing must go wrong tomorrow. If you hold back anything, you endanger the stellar alignment."

Bracken leaned on the polished plank that topped the terrace wall and gazed over the coastline to the blue waters beyond. "You know I'd never endanger the most important day in history."

Aleena turned him to face her, her red painted nails tapping a sensual path up his shoulders. "We have a little while before it's time to start for Mt. Shidow."

Bracken captured Aleena's hands and brushed them across his lips. "I think I need a nap—a real nap—if we're going to be up all night."

A deep laugh bubbled from Aleena's throat. "Very well. We do want to be our best for the morning." She stepped smartly toward the interior of the house. "Anyway, I must change into a more suitable outfit. You'll love it. I picked it up long ago in Accad in a specialty shop, just for this occasion."

* * *

In the semi-darkness of evening, Bracken first noticed the big trans-max traveling behind him and Aleena because it kept pace with her hurtling red trans-speed. "The power drive in that thing must be a custom job." He indicated the vehicle following them.

"Let's lose it." She laughed and accelerated.

But just then, they passed through a small community and Aleena was forced to slow her pace. Bracken got a good look at the other vehicle before it dropped back. The sight of two convex bubbles on its roof stirred familiar recollections. Again on the open road, the trailing vehicle increased its speed to match Aleena's.

"Tomorrow morning!" Aleena sang out. "The first day of a new era! Aren't you excited?"

"Of course, I am. It's going to be . . . ," Bracken stopped mid-sentence, startled by a sudden roar to the left. On the driver's side, a dark blur moved dangerously close, traveling at a velocity faster than theirs. The trans-max was passing them. Aleena turned to the right to avoid crashing into it as it veered ever closer to the front of her rig. Struggling for control, Aleena was forced off the road. They slammed to a stop, tilted at an angle on an incline. The trans-max halted ahead of them, blocking the way. To the right, the incline dropped into a ditch.

Aleena, still gripping the wheel, drew a trembling breath. Shaken, Bracken looked for some defense as he saw the trans-max side cargo door slide open and two men jump out.

"Reverse! Get it in reverse!" he shouted.

But the barrel of a hand weapon pointing at Aleena's head overruled Bracken's command. The protruding stomach of a man armed with another hand weapon showed itself on Bracken's side.

Bracken knew now why this trans-max was familiar. It was the same one that had pulled up behind Trasent's trans-rig that night at the

Brighton Inn. Its occupants had attacked him and Trasent. He squinted past the paunch to a face that told him this was also the group that had come after Layozz on the streets of the Community and later in a wild battle at his house. Bracken cursed his luck to have been seen with Layozz.

The man on Bracken's side barked, "You! You've got something we want!"

On Aleena's side, a fellow with arms like tree trunks ordered them out.

Bracken argued, "I've got nothing to do with Layozz. He never gave me anything, and I don't know where he is."

Foul breath puffed into the trans-speed as the portly man bent close and snarled, "That small-time peddler! We lost interest in him." He stopped to yell across Bracken and point with his weapon, "Turn that power drive off, lady!" Aleena fumbled with the controls. The hand weapon swung back to Bracken. "The present from your new friend . . . where are you hiding it?"

"Yeah," growled a voice from Aleena's side. "You've got tasty eats in your pantry," the man with the tree trunk arms cackled, "but, we want something worth real money. We want the ruby jewel!"

A third vehicle appeared on the road behind, approached rapidly, and then slowed and swung its lights to illuminate the scene. The two men by Aleena's vehicle shielded their faces from the glare. Aleena, who had not shut off the power drive, jammed the trans-speed into reverse and, in a flurry of spitting gravel, backed up. Weaving and bouncing over the uneven ground, the trans-speed leaped onto the road. Another shift, and Aleena headed forward at full-throttle.

"War mongers!" she shouted over the roar beneath her feet. "They mean to stop the stellar alignment!"

But Bracken's thoughts tumbled in a frenzy of realization. *They want the jewel! They don't care about the mine anymore. They've wanted the jewel ever since that night at Brighton Inn. I was getting into Trasent's trans-rig and they mistook me for him. They wanted him and his jewel.*

"Look!" Aleena cried. "They're coming after us."

The big trans-max was closing the gap with incredible speed. The road climbed through a hilly pass. Still the trans-max gained.

Then, in a confusion of lights, the third vehicle, a powerful trans-rig, overtook the trans-max. It swerved out even with the trans-max, but it was close—too close. Just then, Aleena rounded a curve in the road, and Bracken lost sight of the neck-in-neck race behind them. The road curved again.

"Slow down," Bracken yelled.

She braked long enough for Bracken to look back and see a single set of lights holding steady on the surface of the road. But the lights from the big trans-max wove erratically, shone briefly on the opposite side of a steep ravine, and then disappeared. He gasped and held on as Aleena accelerated.

"I told you nothing would stop us, Bracken. Not even a bunch of thugs. Imagine the Pirax coming along! I always thought they were never around when you needed them!"

"That wasn't a Pirax vehicle."

"It had to be. Chasing those imbeciles for speeding." She laughed gleefully. "Serves them right."

"No lights or sirens."

"Quit worrying."

"Aleena," Bracken said suddenly, "take the turn-off to Tizra."

"What?"

"A friend of mine there might be in danger. I have to see if she's all right."

"Really, Bracken. You know where we're going tonight. There simply isn't time for a side-trip."

"We have to take the time. I have good reason to think that this friend—you've heard me talk about Lisha—might need help."

"Whatever for?" Aleena continued at full speed.

The turn-off to Tizra sped by in a blur. "We passed it," Bracken shouted angrily. "Look, Aleena. This is important, too. Turn around and go back. I'll just make sure she's okay. Maybe take her over to my parents for the night until I get back."

Their speed held steady. Bracken's anger boiled over. "I said, turn around! If those thugs are still after Trasent's jewel, then it's more important than I thought. I shouldn't have involved Lisha."

The trans-speed's brakes screeched. It skidded into an abrupt U-turn. Pulling off the road, Aleena demanded, "You told her about Trasent's jewel! What did you tell her?"

The trans-speed still rocked with the suddenness of the stop when Aleena's tirade died as suddenly as it has begun.

Bracken reeled under the revelation that Trasent's jewel was no secret from Aleena. He should have guessed. She hadn't asked questions when the thugs demanded it.

Aleena reached a hand over and stroked Bracken's cheek. "You poor man. Of course, you're worried about your friend. We'll rush right over to Tizra."

"How did you know about it?" Bracken asked above the whine of Aleena's headlong acceleration. "How did you know that Trasent gave me that ruby crystal."

"Silly! He and I were friends, and he mentioned it. I just assumed that he gave it to you. That piece of glass isn't really important anyway." Aleena's soothing voice rolled over Bracken, lulling his churning emotions and easing his fear for Lisha. "I can't imagine why those terrible men thought it might be."

Bracken dropped his head in his hands and moaned, "I should never have taken Lisha to the Currency Center."

"What are you talking about?" Aleena's smooth voice rippled through Bracken's confusion.

"She was there when I put the crystal in a reader."

"Well," Aleena's nails drummed on the wheel, "analyzing a crystal isn't so momentous. But, Bracken, I don't think you should have taken an outsider to the secured areas of the Currency Center."

"I know. I don't have clearance for that area myself."

"Well, then," Aleena shrugged, "probably Arnaman's mysterious processing machines didn't mean a thing to either you or your friend. I'm sure all those red lights flying around would only confuse me." She laughed softly. "It's just as well that I'm not one of his employees."

Later, driving at a more normal speed, they neared their destination. Aleena asked, "Care to tell me about what you saw on the screen? Or, do you think it would be all right?"

"Aleena," Bracken asked quietly, "How do you know about the red lights?"

Reflected in the softly-lit control panel, Aleena's white face looked angelic, even under the stress of the evening. "Part of my job. If I'm going to conduct motivational seminars, I have to know the inner workings of an organization."

Bracken was forced to accept that. She and Trasent had been close. Because she already knew how the jewel was read, she might know part or all of what was inscribed in it. If he wanted her help in assuring Lisha's safety, it was only fair to confide in her. And, the basis of their partnership was trust. The basis for the entire stellar alignment was trust.

Briefly, Bracken related what he and Lisha had learned from the screen, including the system for identifying people by genetic code. None of it seemed to surprise the beautiful woman.

Sharing this with Aleena eased Bracken's tenseness considerably. Now, if he could just be sure of Lisha's safety. That had suddenly become extremely important to him. If anything should happen to Lisha . . .

"How do you feel about the information inscribed in the ruby crystal?" Aleena asked casually.

"What we read on the screen didn't upset me. It did Lisha." Bracken decided not to mention the errant images that had really upset Lisha. "But, when the equipment shut down without warning, I admit that did shake me up."

"It shut down?"

"Like a power failure, with no back-up."

As if getting to Tizra had been suddenly upgraded to highest priority, Aleena accelerated. The trans-speed shot forward, and Bracken's head snapped in the opposite direction.

"Where do we go?" Aleena demanded, as they flew into town.

"Past this quarry. First street beyond that high stone wall. Slow down!" A vehicle stood in front of Lisha's home. Mystified, Bracken cried, "That's the trans-rig you thought was the Pirax." Outside its open door, two men wrestled with a third person. "It's Lisha!" Bracken jumped from Aleena's trans-speed.

But Lisha spotted him and yelled, "Go back!"

Bracken stopped not because of Lisha's command, but in utter confusion as he recognized one of the people scuffling with Lisha. That silver hair belonged to Arnaman.

"They know about the crystal!" Lisha yelled. The second man clamped his hand over her mouth and shoved her further into the open door of the trans-rig. But, with a yelp of pain, he jerked his hand back, and she called, "They're going to kill us both!"

A light came on in a neighboring house, then another.

Bracken tackled Lisha's assailants, knocking Arnaman aside. The older man reeled away, slamming into the fender of his own vehicle. He recovered, ordering, "Get her inside!" and skirted around to the driver's door.

But Bracken succeeded in pulling the other man off Lisha. She dodged out of the way, and for the first time, Bracken got a good look at his dark-skinned opponent.

Suddenly, there was an explosive sound, and a volley of heat pellets sprayed overhead. Bracken ducked. The dark-skinned man escaped into the trans-rig. Bracken grabbed Lisha and dove to the ground, his body shielding hers from the next round that spewed above them. Arnaman's trans-rig wheels spun, grabbed for traction, and skimmed over the street, chased by another explosion of heat pellets.

Bracken twisted his head to find their benefactor. He saw a powerful automatic weapon, held in the slender hands of Aleena.

Just then, an ear-shattering screech came from the direction of Arnaman's trans-rig. The low-slung vehicle careened, bounced off a post and crashed into the high stone wall. It crawled along the wall on two wheels, dropping back to the pavement at the wall's end. It traced a wild pattern down the road until, completely out of control, the trans-rig jumped a guard rail and nosed into a water-filled quarry.

As Bracken and Lisha picked themselves up, Aleena's trans-speed pulled alongside. The automatic weapon had vanished. "Don't worry. I didn't hit anybody," she called, "but let's get out of here before we get delayed with a lot of questions."

The three of them drove away at a sedate speed. People, some in nightclothes, poured onto the street. Most ran toward the scene of the accident, apparently unaware of the struggle that had taken place moments before.

Lisha exclaimed from the rear seat, "Those men wanted the ruby jewel!"

"Did they get it?" came Aleena's shrill question.

"She doesn't have it," Bracken said.

Aleena's eyes snapped, registering the information.

Lisha's voice trembled. "They wanted me so they could get it from you, Bracken. How could they even know about me? And that we used the scanner?"

"A security system of some kind," Bracken said over his shoulder. "We must have been discovered that night. That's why the equipment shut down."

"Never mind," cried Aleena. "We have to be at Mt. Shidow before dawn. Where can we take your friend?"

Bracken pointed ahead. "Turn right at the next corner. My parents live on that street. Lisha, you stay with them tonight."

"Who were those men?" Lisha demanded.

"I work for one of them," Bracken said, the full shock of that just hitting him. "Arnaman! I can't believe that he meant harm to either of us."

"Believe it," Aleena said through clenched teeth. "That impatient, pompous fool overstepped his authority once too often. He never did value discretion."

"I don't understand," Lisha said.

Aleena held the red trans-speed at a slow speed, waiting for Bracken's directions. Lost in thought, he suddenly pointed to his family's house.

"Stop here. I'll take Lisha in."

Aleena turned to her extra passenger. "You won't mind going in by yourself, will you? Bracken and I are running late."

Bracken gasped and slammed his fist into his hand. "That fellow with him! Now I remember. I saw him at the Currency Center." He opened the door and helped Lisha from the trans-speed. "I'll take her in and be right back."

Aleena revved the power drive. "There's no time for small talk, Bracken."

"You're going to that stellar alignment, aren't you?" Lisha stood beside him, near tears.

Bracken ignored both women. A chilling realization shook him. The dark-skinned man with Arnaman tonight was the one who had carried a tray of food into Trasent's office just before Trasent's collapse.

Lisha grabbed Bracken's arms. Near hysteria, she pleaded, "Don't go with her. That stuff about global oneness and energy and starting a new era is wrong. It's evil!"

Although Bracken's own nerves were stretched to the breaking point, he tried to calm Lisha, to convince her that he must follow this call. "The stellar alignment is the best—the only—hope of bringing about peace. Try to understand."

"Two men are at the bottom of the quarry, no doubt dead. You and I could have been killed. I don't call that peaceful."

"What happened just now has nothing to do with our efforts to bring about world peace." Bracken's words lashed out with more sting than he intended.

Lisha released her fierce grip on him. She clapped her hands over her mouth, her brown eyes wide with surprise.

"I didn't mean to be so sharp." Bracken wished she'd be more understanding. If only she'd appreciate his responsibility.

"The Volume tells about these things." She sniffed and twisted her hands like a little girl. "I don't want you to be swallowed up in that evil."

"Lisha . . . please. You'll be okay here with my parents."

Tears spilled down her cheeks.

"I'll come for you tomorrow. We'll talk."

"There's nothing more for us to talk about."

Aleena leaned across the passenger seat and hissed, "Bracken!"

He climbed into the trans-speed. "Lisha, try to understand. This is my chance to be what I've always wanted to be. Tonight, answers are waiting that I've searched for all my life."

Lisha stepped backed. "I can't stop you from going. But I know that what you're doing is wrong."

The trans-speed drove away, its lights rendered nearly useless in the increasingly bright glow of Ebbern's full moons.

CHAPTER 33

The early morning air still held the night chill as Bracken waited anxiously with the others, but the inner fire of his hope warmed him. He was a part of this great stellar alignment that would usher in the dawn of a new era, the crystalline dawn.

Mt. Shidow loomed like a silent watchman waiting to witness a new chapter of history to be played out on the meadow below. Three thousand of the enlightened, gathered from all over Ebbern, had assembled within a circle of monoliths, called the rocks of truth. At its heart, reigned a massive keystone. Bracken felt honored to be among the elite, and yet confident that he was chosen because of his talents and because he was a seeker of truth.

Soon, the gatherers would join forces with the stars, the planets, and the moons of Ebbern. Soon, one giant network of strength would bond, focused to scatter the darkness of the passing millennia. Hidden lines of oppression would fall from Ebbern. The bondage of archaic ideas and worn philosophies would shatter, to be replaced by an age of delight and truth that would never end.

Bracken saw why Aleena had called this beginning the crystalline dawn. As the sun's first rays struck the tallest monoliths, the moisture-laden sides of those stone sentinels shimmered back a visual echo of hope. Something great was in the air—something mysterious, almost frightening.

Aleena stood near the keystone with the other leaders, her trim figure alive with energy. As the sun crested over the horizon, brilliant shafts of light swept across the ground between the monoliths. Then, the light seemed to focus on the keystone. A command went forth. The leaders began to move slowly, calling forth a chant to the three thousand at the edge of the circle.

The ring of the enlightened marched solemnly around the center keystone repeating the ancient intonation. Excitement grew within Bracken. He heard voices weaving within the chant—new voices—voices that praised him for his courage, voices that praised all the chosen for their wisdom, for their beauty of soul, and for their uniqueness.

You are the ones, the ones who will build the new and forever world. Sons and daughters of the crystalline dawn, join your hearts. Join your thoughts. Join your wills. You control Ebbern's destiny. You control it all. You are gods.

As the song grew more and more harmonious, so did Bracken's

thoughts. They seemed to fuse with those of the other singers into one throbbing voice.

But then, as Bracken sang the anthem of hope and defiance, a troubled feeling came over him. An insistent refrain from another source shook him from his revelry, like the gentle hands of his mother waking him from a long night's slumber. The refrain was familiar, reaching into his past, growing from seeds planted in his childhood. Despite his rejection of it, he knew that the refrain had always been there, touching him, leading him, and opening his eyes though he refused to see. Even now, Bracken resisted, clutching at the harmony of the song of the crystalline dawn.

But the refrain came again and again, as if the pages of the Volume had been opened and would never close. A question entered the refrain. *Do you not walk the path of blasphemy? In your pride, do you not claim credit due only to one?*

Suddenly, as if a curtain parted, Bracken looked within and saw the root of his search for truth. His conscience bore deeper and deeper until, there, quivering at the bottom of his soul, lay his true self infused with pride. His pride had become an evil that seethed at his very core. Suddenly, Bracken hated that evil. He hated his vanity, his desire for glory.

He fought off the spell of the chant and slipped through the throng. Outside the ring of monoliths, he walked to the base of Mt. Shidow and stood lonely and apart. Words filtered to him from past thoughts. *To lust for power is to destroy.* The words drowned the song of the chosen. Memories paraded by. Each incident of his selfishness mocked and saddened him. The surging chant of the crowd taunted and repelled him.

He stared into the dark corners of his trembling spirit and wept. He wept for his sins, and he wept a pleading, yearning cry for real truth. Falling to his knees, he closed his eyes and searched his heart. The storm within calmed. Torrents from a driving cloudburst gave way to the gentle washing of a warm afternoon rain, and Bracken found peace.

The distant chanting continued, now tentative, almost pleading. Bracken heard the sound of footsteps behind him.

"Why did you leave the circle, Bracken?" Aleena's voice rolled over him. "We're nearly at the moment of release. Why would you leave just when we need you the most?"

This beautiful woman represented what Bracken had sought. He still wanted her approval. He did not wish to lose the intriguing ties of friendship between them. But, now a breach parted the delicate fibers that had woven their lives together.

Bracken scrambled up from the ground and went to sit on a flat boulder, averting his face from Aleena. "I'm troubled. Something is wrong with me."

She followed and forced him to look at her. "It's all right, Bracken.

Nothing is wrong with you." Her own eyes dimmed, as if lurking doubts claimed a toll even on her. In the space of a heartbeat, she recovered. "It's just a shift, a fault in the cosmic structure of the universe. You were caught in a kind of ripple between the ages. Come back to the circle."

Bracken pressed his fingertips to his temples to clear away the tension that stifled his thinking. He had to be honest. "Aleena, I've been reading the Volume. This whole thing is wrong."

The expression on her lovely face soured.

Bracken raised his hand, begging her to listen. "I know you think that its ancient platitudes are for another day, another age."

"It's an archaic relic that reveals but a small part of the truth," Aleena countered. "Oh, Bracken!" she begged. "We have come so close to our goal. Don't turn back now. You can already see the unity, the love, the energy. We are nearly there. Moments from now, the final alignment will take place. The crystalline dawn will be fulfilled."

Bracken examined the boulder beneath him, worn smooth with the years, seeking solace from its solidity. He spoke slowly, each phrase an effort. "I can't help it. I can't seem to shake the words of the Volume. They haunt me. I must listen to them. What else can I do?"

He got to his feet, pleading, struggling to convince his friend. "The Volume tells of a day when Ebbern will be bathed in a false peace." He waved away the denial poised on Aleena's lips. "This bid for global peace is not what it appears to be. I believe you suspect the truth, but your own desire for power forces you to ignore it."

Aleena's once-tender mouth hardened into a grim line. Her eyes narrowed into colorless points of ice. "You're insane, Bracken. You are the one who believes a lie. You have swallowed the same old empty stories that the elders have clung to. Can't you see that it's part of a scheme for them to retain their own corrupt power? The new leaders will show us the way now."

"I know that some people twist the words of the Volume for selfish purposes," Bracken admitted, "but not everyone has done that, and the greed of a few doesn't change what the Volume says. It doesn't change what's coming to Ebbern. The Volume foretells that we on Ebbern will be tempted. The spell of the evil one will be overpowering, and his allurements almost beyond resistance. And, when he has lured his followers into adoration and trust, so that they choose him and turn against the teachings of the Volume, then, at that ultimate point of deception, he will betray them."

Through Aleena's clouded eyes filtered evidence of a fiery rage. "Who is this deceiver of the gullible, this destroyer of good?"

Bracken tried to gather Aleena into his arms. She flung herself away.

"Don't shut me out!" he implored. "Listen to me. The evil one behind all this baits us with every hope we've had, every dream we've pursued. The bait works because of our pride. We want to believe that we are set apart and better than the stumbling masses. We want to believe that our talents and skills will rid the world of bondage. But, we're wrong. The very monster we seek to slay lies waiting, lurking in our own hearts, cloaked in the enchantment of the enlightened age."

In a change of mood, Aleena slipped her arms around Bracken's waist with playful, beckoning sensuality. "Didn't our times together mean anything to you? Don't sacrifice our dreams for the future in a passing flurry of misplaced idealism."

"You've got it wrong, Aleena. The awareness from an upper level, the power from another dimension, the wisdom from a parallel universe that I sought . . . they are all tools of one evil force. I believed in them and I followed them. That was my misplaced idealism. I searched fervently, but I searched outside the Volume. And this gathering," Bracken swept his arm over the meadow, "is a sham used to feed our own egos."

The pitch and rhythm of the droning on the meadow intensified. "Please, Bracken, don't leave me." Aleena's face pulsed with life, intensifying the loveliness of her fine features, her delicate skin. Beguiling eyes invited him. "Won't you join me?"

With an effort, Bracken unclasped Aleena's hands from his waist. The glow on her face dimmed as she asked, "I suppose you'll go find that whimpering Lisha?"

Surprised, Bracken uttered, "Yes," only then realizing that he would do exactly that. Suddenly, it became imperative that he seek Lisha's forgiveness and repair the broken ties with her and with his family. Somehow he must build a new relationship to bridge the breach that parted him and his father. He would find a way to smooth the ugly scars on all their hearts.

Aleena's red lips drew into a pout. "But, Bracken, I promised that you'd be one of us." Her dark brows knitted together. "You're so important. Even more than Trasent."

"Trasent?"

"Yes, the foolish man. He should never have snooped into areas beyond his access level. He wasn't cleared for entry to the *Second Phase*."

Bracken's mouth went dry. His stomach knotted.

"Then Trasent began making noises about genocide. What a terrible word! I almost suspect he was starting to take the Volume seriously." Aleena shook her head sadly. "Really, poison was less painful than an actual heart attack would have been."

The shout in Bracken's heart crept out in a whisper of disbelief. "What are you saying?"

"Of course, you don't know about that second phase. Nevertheless, we need the ruby crystal back. I tried to find it and," she bowed her head in childish remorse, "I'm sorry I tore up your house so badly."

Bracken clasped his hands over his ears. He would not accept the appalling images that assaulted him. Why was Aleena torturing him with thoughts too terrible to have originated from that lovely, vivacious person?

"You see," she said, "it's too early to reveal all the magnificent plans . . . and there are unscrupulous thieves . . . and besides, I want you back."

Aleena's words fell away. Below, the chanting ceased. An oppressive stillness dropped from the upper reaches of Mt. Shidow and hung over the meadow.

"Please, Bracken," Aleena begged. "I've used all the prowess given to me, and I've exhausted all patience. Come with me to the circle before it's too late." She lunged for Bracken, pulling at him with fierce strength that seemed foreign to the delicate-looking body that quivered with urgency. "Please . . . please, come with me!"

Then, like the flickering of a candle in the wind, Aleena's radiance fluttered, and her human warmth was snuffed out. She stood as erect as one of the meadow's monoliths. Slowly, her face hardened into a look of determination, then vengeance. It was as if someone else lived within her and was now in control. Those changeable eyes became black holes, revealing an opening deep inside to the shutters that covered her soul. Horrified, Bracken viewed short flashes of drama behind her countenance as a hidden hand seemed to move the shutters back and forth.

Evil power capable of almost any repulsive act lived in that soul—power that had sought Bracken's own soul, that had snapped Trasent's life because he chose the way of the Volume, and power that had produced a cruel counterfeit of Silas.

And then, the shutters flew open. Nebuzarr's face, with all his powerful and gripping terror, mocked Bracken through the window of Aleena's possessed and wasted life.

"I have waited for you long enough, you senseless dreamer," a deep, raspy voice belched from the shell of Aleena. "Time after time, I have relented and heeded petitions for your life. Now, no one pleads that you be spared. You have rejected your last chance to become a disciple for my cause."

In the meadow, a new chorus of chanting burst from the gathered ones. Aleena turned and ran to join the undulating multitude.

An insidious terror grew within Bracken. Nebuzarr was going to kill him.

There was no escape through the meadow's weaving throng. Bracken turned and began to scramble up the rocky side of Mt. Shidow. He clawed and pulled himself upward, digging footholds where he could. He half-ran, half-crawled across an old rock slide. He jumped a crevice and slipped through a cleft in an overhanging ridge, heading higher at every opportunity.

From below, came a change in the chanting. A new word slipped into the melodious chord and another fell away. It was no longer, *You are gods*. Now, the chant proclaimed, *We are gods. We are the children of the new dawn. We rule. We control.*

Clinging by his fingertips, Bracken inched his way precariously around a slim projection on the mountainside. He reached a small ledge. To his despair, a sheer, insurmountable wall towered before him.

From the ledge, Bracken watched the panorama far below. Aleena had joined the inner circle of leaders in the march around the keystone. The pulsing anthem rose to a climax. At that moment, a loud rumble filled the air, vibrating through Mt. Shidow itself. Bracken clutched his head, warding off the intensely painful sound. Brilliant light exploded in shattering flashes from the center keystone. In response, showers of light shot into the air at the edge of the circle and cascaded down upon the chanters.

Cringing against the wall that blocked his escape, Bracken saw Aleena's body poised in seeming ecstasy, her face tilted to the sun. So at last, she had her crystalline dawn!

The falling sprays of light took on color—green, gray, and blue. The three colors swirled and blended until the cascading showers beamed red. Red sparkles filled the air and poured downward like red dust falling from the sky, only to rise up in a tumbling, boiling cloud.

The red cloud rose high, higher than where Bracken stood on the ledge, petrified by a brief glimpse of an image peering out of the cloud. It was the villainous grin, the hooked nose, the sickly rolls of flesh, and the terrible fiery eyes of Nebuzarr. The red cloud imploded, dissipating into an atmosphere of red particles.

Suddenly, in the meadow below, the ground opened. A void streamed around the inside of the ring of monoliths, parting the earth. Where once there had been velvety grass and dancing feet, a gulf appeared, and the assembly of chanters fell from sight into a growing abyss.

Bracken heard cries of the fallen. A cacophony of wailing and anguish rose from a depth beyond his view and reverberated off the side of Mt. Shidow.

The void circled, splitting the ground as it moved toward the center keystone. It picked up speed, closing in around the leaders caught there.

Amid their panic, an even greater terror revealed itself on this cosmic theater of horror. The rocks of truth were transformed from silent monoliths. They became statues of frozen evil, each one bearing an image of the head of a monster whose body rose from the earth. Then, given life by some subterranean wicked breath, the monsters sprang forth with hide and horns. Their hot breath blasted in gusts of heat that steamed upward. The smell of singed hair assaulted Bracken, and he knew it was his own.

Then, suddenly, the heat receded, and the light from the dawn, which had seemed so bright, dimmed. A darkness that walked on dragon's feet, with sweat oozing from its scaly pores, rose out of the pits surrounding the terror-stricken leaders. It burst into a light-extinguishing evil that filled the meadow and raced up the side of the mountain. It pushed a cloud of blackness at the sky to capture and pull the last remaining glimmer of light from the crystalline dawn.

Once again, a screaming vibration tore through the air. Fire spewed forth from the gruesome mouths of the ring of monsters and lit up the dark sky. Billowing clouds of sparks dripped hot ashes. Then, the monsters spit streams of heat focused toward the leaders cowering against the center keystone.

The monsters' heads vomited up hideous creatures, which slid down the paths of flame to the remnant of ground upon which the leaders huddled. They swept up the new self-acclaimed gods and jumped into the pit, carrying their writhing captives to their doom.

Red flames leaped from the void's depths, surging upward into one black cloud that poured over the meadow and moved to envelop Bracken. Helpless, he flattened his back against the mountain. The blackness deepened. Bracken no longer felt the solid wall of Mt. Shidow. He was suspended in a chasm between life and death. A suffocating, overpowering force seized him—the epitome of evil.

Striking one last tortuous blow, the blackness thinned, and through an aperture of murky fog, loomed the triumphant face of Nebuzarr. Nebuzarr was the Night Ruler!

This single evil personage lay behind the winsome promises of every source of wisdom and power Bracken had sought. Hidden by the beauty of the Night Ruler's star was the dark ugliness of deceit. Those on the meadow below were destroyed when the Night Ruler committed the ultimate act of deceit—the destruction of adoring, enslaved followers.

It was suddenly clear to Bracken. The Night Ruler was finished with them now. They had been his shock troops. The first wave in his final deception of Ebbern. But their usefulness was over. They would be replaced by more powerful agents of deception.

Then, from the depths of Bracken's heart came a name, and he knew it would save him forever from enslavement to the Night Ruler. In that name lay the truth that would never end in death.

With a mighty voice, Bracken called out, "Prince of Wonder! Save me!"

The moment he called, the blackness vanished. Bracken found himself standing serenely, high on the side of Mt. Shidow. Fresh, clean breezes blew from a boundless sky, purging evil's foul stench from Bracken's lungs and giving him new life.

A gentle voice seemed to speak to Bracken's soul. In love, the voice welcomed him.

After a while, Bracken descended the mountain. He knew that what had happened to Aleena and the others was a foretaste of what faced everyone who refused the truth and chose to believe the lie. He crossed the meadow, which was once again peaceful, green, and dotted with trees and harmless-looking rocks.

Bracken reached into his pocket and pulled out the ruby crystal. Man had made this lovely ornament. The Night Ruler had fashioned its promise as the newest jewel in a chain of his alluring promises. There would be other equally beautiful, seemingly authentic jewels, which would prove to be deadly fakes. But, Bracken had found his true gem, the eternal truth etched in the timeless writings of the Volume.

He turned his back on Mt. Shidow and began the long trek home to Tizra, to Lisha, and to his family. The sun shone overhead, bleaching the last memories of the crystalline dawn. It was an old dawn. It had begun the night the stars fell.

More Good Books From Huntington House Publishers

Cover of Darkness (A Novel) by J. Carroll

Jack's time is running out. The network's top investigative reporter has been given the most bizarre and difficult assignment of his life. The powers behind the conspiracy (occult and demonic forces) are finally exposed by Jack. Now comes the real challenge—convincing others. Matching wits with supernatural forces, Jack faces the most hideous conspiracy the world has ever known.

ISBN 0-910311-31-5 $7.95

The Image of the Ages by David Webber

Are the secular humanists' plans for a New World Order about to be realized? How will the establishment of this order affect you and your family? David Webber, author of *The Image of the Ages*, explains how modern technology, artificial intelligence, and other scientific advances will be used in the near future to manipulate and control the masses.

ISBN 0-910311-38-2 $7.95

Psychic Phenomena Unveiled: Confessions of a New Age Warlock

by John Anderson

He walked on hot coals and stopped his heart. As one of Los Angeles' most recognized psychics, John Anderson was on top of the world. His ability to perform psychic phenomena converted the most stubborn unbeliever into a true believer in occult power. But John Anderson sensed his involvement in the occult was destroying him. This book was written to expose the trickery behind the New Age magic and address man's attraction to the occult.

ISBN 0-910311-49-8 $8.95

Who Will Rule the Future? by Paul McGuire

Film Producer turned author, Paul McGuire, says: "There are powerful political and spiritual forces that are attempting to usher in a New Age theocracy, promote a New World Order, and control our nation." Is the Christian community ignoring its responsibility to oppose these forces? Christians have retreated from society and abdicated their responsibility. In the next few years, we will pay a heavy price for our neglect. This book calls Christians to move powerfully into our society and confront the direction of our culture before it's too late!

ISBN 0-910311-94-3 $8.95

Crystalline Connection **(A Novel)**

by Bob Maddux & Mary Carpenter Reid

Enter the enchanting World of Ebbern, a planet in many ways like our own. In the *Crystalline Connection* our hero, Bracken, returns to his homeland after ten years of wandering. Once there he becomes involved in a monumental struggle gallantly confronting the dark forces of evil. This futuristic fantasy is fraught with intrigue, adventure, romance and much more. The *Crystalline Connection* artfully discloses the devastating consequences of involvement in the New Age movement while using the medium of fiction.

ISBN 0-910311-71-4 $8.95

Kinsey, Sex and Fraud: The Indoctrination of a People
by Dr. Judith A. Reisman and Edward Eichel

Kinsey, Sex and Fraud describes the research of Alfred Kinsey which shaped Western society's beliefs and understanding of the nature of human sexuality. His unchallenged conclusions are taught at every level of education—elementary, high school and college—and quoted in textbooks as undisputed truth.

The authors clearly demonstrate that Kinsey's research involved illegal experimentations on several hundred children. The survey was carried out on a non-representative group of Americans, including disproportionately large numbers of sex offenders, prostitutes, prison inmates and exhibitionists.

ISBN 0-910311-20-X $19.95 Hardcover

Seduction of the Innocent Revisited by John Fulce

You honestly can't judge a book by its cover—especially a comic book! Comic books of yesteryear bring to mind cute cartoon characters, super-heroes battling the forces of evil or a sleuth tracking down the bad guy clue-by-clue. But that was a long, long time ago.

Today's comic books aren't innocent at all! Author John Fulce asserts that "super-heroes" are constantly found in the nude engaging in promiscuity, and satanic symbols are abundant throughout the pages. Fulce says most parents aren't aware of the contents of today's comic books—of what their children are absorbing from these seemingly innocent forms of entertainment. As a comic book collector for many years, Fulce opened his own comic book store in 1980, only to sell the business a few short years later due to the steady influx of morally unacceptable material. What's happening in the comic book industry? Fulce outlines the moral, biblical, and legal aspects and proves his assertions with page after page of illustrations. We need to pay attention to what our children are reading, Fulce claims. Comic books are not as innocent as they used to be.

ISBN 0-910311-66-8 $8.95

Dinosaurs and the Bible by David W. Unfred

Every reader, young and old, will be fascinated by this ever-mysterious topic—exactly what happened to the dinosaurs? Author David Unfred draws a very descriptive picture of the history and fate of the dinosaurs, using the Bible as a reference guide.

In this educational and informative book, Unfred answers such questions as: Did dinosaurs really exist? Does the Bible mention dinosaurs? What happened to dinosaurs, or are there some still living awaiting discovery? Unfred uses the Bible to help unlock the ancient mysteries of the lumbering creatures, and teaches how those mysteries can educate us about God the Creator and our God of Love.

ISBN 0-910311-70-6 $12.95 Hardcover

"Soft Porn" Plays Hardball by Dr. Judith A. Reisman

With amazing clarity, the author demonstrates that pornography imposes on society a view of women and children that encourages violence and sexual abuse. As crimes against women and children increase to alarming proportions, it's of paramount importance that we recognize the cause of this violence. Pornography should be held accountable for the havoc it has wreaked in our homes and our country.

ISBN 0-910311-65-X $ 8.95 Trade paper
ISBN 0-910311-92-7 $16.95 Hardcover

God's Rebels by Henry Lee Curry III

From his unique perspective Dr. Henry Lee Curry III offers a fascinating look at the lives of some of our greatest Southern religious leaders during the Civil War. The rampant Evangelical Christianity prominent at the outbreak of the Civil War, asserts Dr. Curry, is directly traceable to the 2nd Great Awakening of the early 1800s. The evangelical tradition, with its emphasis on strict morality, individual salvation, and emotional worship, had influenced most of Southern Protestantism by this time. Southerners unquestionably believed the voice of the ministers to be the "voice of God"; consequently, the church became one of the most powerful forces influencing Confederate life and morale. Inclined toward a Calvinistic emphasis on predestination, the South was confident that God would sustain its way of life.

Dr. Curry is a Virginian. He holds degrees from the University of Virginia, Duke University, and Emory University. While teaching at Mercer University's Atlanta Campus, his course on The Civil War and Reconstruction was always very popular.

ISBN: 0-910311-67-6 $12.95 Trade paper
ISBN: 0-910311-68-4 $21.95 Hardcover

Inside the New Age Nightmare by Randall Baer

Now, for the first time, one of the most powerful and influential leaders of the New Age movement has come out to expose the deceptions of the organization he once led. New Age magazines and articles have for many years hailed Randall Baer as their most "radically original" and "advanced" thinker... "light years ahead of others" says leading New Age magazine *East-West Journal*. His bestselling books on quartz crystals, self-transformation, and planetary ascension have won worldwide acclaim and been extolled by New Agers from all walks of life.

Hear, from a New Age insider, the secret plans they have spawned to take over our public, private, and political institutions. Have these plans already been implemented in your church, business, or organization? Discover the seduction of the demonic forces at work—turned from darkness to light, Randall Baer reveals the methods of the New Age movement as no one else can. Find out what you can do to stop the New Age movement from destroying our way of life.

ISBN 0-910311-58-7 $8.95

The Devil's Web by Pat Pulling with Kathy Cawthon

This explosive exposé presents the first comprehensive guide to childhood and adolescent occult involvement. Written by a nationally recognized occult crime expert, the author explains how the violent occult underworld operates and how they stalk and recruit our children, teenagers and young adults for their evil purposes.The author leaves no stone unturned in her investigation and absolves no one of the responsibility of protecting our children. She dispels myths and raises new questions examining the very real possibility of the existence of major occult networks which may include members of law enforcement, government officials and other powerful individuals.

ISBN 0-910311-59-5 $8.95 Trade paper
ISBN 0-910311-63-3 $16.95 Hardcover

From Rock to Rock by Eric Barger

Over three years in the making, the pages of this book represent thousands of hours of detailed research as well as over twenty-six years of personal experience and study.The author presents a detailed exposé on many current rock entertainers, rock concerts, videos, lyrics and occult symbols used within the industry. He also presents a rating system of over fifteen hundred past and present rock groups and artists.

ISBN 0-910311-61-7 $8.95

The Deadly Deception: Freemasonry Exposed By One of Its Top Leaders by Tom McKenney

Presents a frank look at Freemasonry and its origin. Learn of the "secrets" and "deceptions" that are practiced daily around the world. Find out why Masonry teaches that it is the true religion, that all other religions are but corrupted and perverted forms of Masonry.

ISBN 0-910311-54-4 $7.95

Lord! Why Is My Child a Rebel? by Jacob Aranza

This book offers an analysis of the root causes of teenage rebellion and offers practical solutions for disoriented parents. Aranza focuses on the turbulent teenage years, and how to survive those years—both you and the child! Must reading for parents—especially for those with strong-willed children. This book will help you avoid the traps in which many parents are caught and put you on the road to recovery with your teenager.

ISBN 0-910311-62-5 $6.95

New World Order: The Ancient Plan of Secret Societies by William Still

Secret societies such as Freemasons have been active since before the advent of Christ, yet most of us don't realize what they are or the impact they've had on many historical events. For example, did you know secret societies played a direct role in the French Revolutions of the 18th and 19th centuries and the Russian Revolution of the 20th century? Author William Still brings into focus the actual manipulative work of the societies, and the "Great Plan" they follow, much to the surprise of many of those who are blindly led into the organization. Their ultimate goal is simple: world dictatorship and unification of all mankind into a world confederation.

Most Masons are good, decent men who join for fellowship, but they are deceived—pulled away from their religious heritage. Only those who reach the highest level of the Masons know its true intentions. Masons and Marxists follow the same master. Ultimately it is a struggle between two foes—the forces of religion versus the forces of anti-religion. Still asserts that although the final battle is near-at-hand, the average person has the power to thwart the efforts of secret societies. Startling and daring, this is the first successful attempt by an author to unveil the designs of secret societies from the beginning, up to the present and into the future. The author attempts to educate the community on how to recognize the signals and how to take the necessary steps to impede their progress.

ISBN 0-910311-64-1 $8.95

Hidden Dangers of the Rainbow by Constance Cumbey

The first book to uncover and expose the New Age movement, this national #1 bestseller paved the way for all other books on the subject. It has become a giant in its category. This book provides a vivid exposé of the New Age movement, which the author contends is dedicated to wiping out Christianity and establishing a one world order. This movement, a vast network of occult and pagan organizations, meets the test of prophecy concerning the Antichrist.

ISBN 0-910311-03-X $8.95

To Grow By Storybook Readers by Janet Friend

Today the quality of education is a major concern; consequently, more and more parents have turned to home schooling to teach their children how to read. The *To Grow By Storybook Readers* by Janet Friend can greatly enhance your home schooling reading program. The set of readers consists of 18 storybook readers plus 2 activity books. The *To Grow By Storybook Readers* has been designed to be used in conjunction with Marie LeDoux's PLAY 'N TALK phonics program but will work well with other orderly phonics programs.

These are the first phonics readers that subtly but positively instill scriptural and moral values. They're a joy to use because no prior instructional experience is necessary. The *To Grow By Storybook Readers* allows parents and children to work together learning each sound. Your child progresses through the readers and learns to appreciate his own ability to understand and think logically about word and sentence construction, thereby raising his self-esteem and confidence.

You can lead your child step-by-step into the exciting and fun world of reading and learning, without heavy reliance on memorization. Repetition and rearrangement will leave your child begging to read page after page. Whether it's a home educational program or a phonics based program in school, these readers can substantially improve a child's reading capability and his desire to learn.

ISBN 0-910311-69-2 $44.95 per set

Personalities in Power: The Making of Great Leaders
by Florence Littauer

You'll laugh and cry as Florence Littauer shares with you heart-warming accounts of the personal lives of some of our greatest leaders. Learn of their triumphs and tragedies, and become aware of the different personality patterns that exist and how our leaders have been influenced by them.Discover your own strengths and weaknesses by completing the Personality Chart included in this book. *Personalities in Power* lets you understand yourself and others and helps you live up to your full potential.

ISBN 0-910311-56-0 $8.95

The Last Days Collection by Last Days Ministries

Heart-stirring, faith-challenging messages from Keith Green, David Wilkerson, Melody Green, Leonard Ravenhill, Winkie Pratney, Charles Finney and William Booth are designed to awaken complacent Christians to action.

ISBN 0-961-30020-5 $8.95

The Lucifer Connection by Joseph Carr

Shirley MacLaine and other celebrities are persuading millions that the New Age movement can fill the spiritual emptiness in their lonely lives. Joseph Carr explains why the New Age movement is the most significant and potentially destructive challenge to the church today. But is it new? How should Christians protect themselves and their children from this insidious threat? This book is a prophetic, information-packed examination by one of the most informed authors in America.

ISBN 0-910311-42-0 $7.95

Exposing the AIDS Scandal: What You Don't Know Can Kill You

by Dr. Paul Cameron

Where do you turn when those who control the flow of information in this country withhold the truth? Why is the national media hiding facts from the public? Can AIDS be spread in ways we're not being told? Finally a book that gives you a total account of the AIDS epidemic, and what steps can be taken to protect yourself. What you don't know can kill you!

ISBN 0-910311-52-8 $7.95

America Betrayed by Marlin Maddoux

This hard-hitting book exposes the forces in our country which seek to destroy the family, the schools and our values. This book details exactly how the news media manipulates your mind. Marlin Maddoux is the host of the popular, national radio talk show "Point of View."

ISBN 0-910311-18-8 $6.95

Devil Take the Youngest by Winkie Pratney

A history of Satan's hatred of innocence and his historical treachery against the young. Pratney begins his journey in ancient Babylon and continues through to modern-day America where infants are murdered daily and children are increasingly victimized through pornography, prostitution and humanism.

ISBN 0-910311-29-3 $8.95